LTB FIC HAT

Hatcher, Robin Lee.
Fit to be tied

FIT TO BE TIED

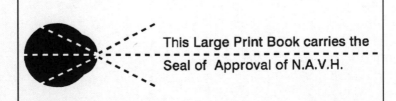

This Large Print Book carries the
Seal of Approval of N.A.V.H.

THE SISTERS OF BETHLEHEM SPRINGS,
BOOK 2

FIT TO BE TIED

ROBIN LEE HATCHER

THORNDIKE PRESS

A part of Gale, Cengage Learning

GALE
CENGAGE Learning™

Detroit • New York • San Francisco • New Haven, Conn • Waterville, Maine • London

GALE
CENGAGE Learning™

LIBRARY OF CONGRESS CATALOGING-IN-PUBLICATION DATA

Hatcher, Robin Lee.
    Fit to be tied : the sisters of Bethlehem Springs / by Robin Lee Hatcher.
        p. cm. — (Thorndike Press large print Christian fiction)
    ISBN-13: 978-1-4104-2438-9 (alk. paper)
    ISBN-10: 1-4104-2438-3 (alk. paper)
    1. Women ranchers—Fiction. 2. English—United States—Fiction. 3. Idaho—Fiction. 4. Nineteen tens—Fiction. 5. Large type books. I. Title.
PS3558.A73574F58 2010
813'.54—dc22   2010001598

Published in 2010 by arrangement with The Zondervan Corporation LLC.

Printed in Mexico
2 3 4 5 6 7 14 13 12 11 10

Once again, to the CdA gals.
You made Cleo's and Sherwood's story
such a fun one to write.
From start to finish, I frequently heard
the sound of your laughter in my mind
and I always remembered
the overflow of your love,
for one another and for writing fiction
for the glory of God.
May He bless each one of you
a hundred times over
for the many ways you have blessed me.

For every beast of the forest is mine, and the cattle upon a thousand hills.

Psalm 50:10

PROLOGUE

Dunacombe Manor, England,
March 1916

"Your father is waiting in the library, my lord."

"Thank you, Chadworth." Head pounding from the previous night's enjoyments, Sherwood Reginald Wakeley Statham, the youngest son of the Duke of Dunacombe, shrugged out of his coat and handed it to the butler, followed by his hat and gloves. "Is Mother with him?"

"No, sir. I believe her grace has taken to her bed."

Sherwood flinched. That didn't bode well for this meeting. His mother had acted as a buffer between him and his father's anger since he was a boy. "Is she ill? Maybe I should go up to see her first."

Chadworth lifted his eyebrows but said nothing. He didn't have to. Sherwood knew he was expected in the library immediately, not fifteen or thirty minutes from now. The duke hated to be kept waiting, especially by Sherwood, the son who disappointed him at every turn.

"I'll go straight in." Might as well receive whatever dressing down his father wanted to mete out.

"Very good, my lord."

Sherwood followed the long hallway to the library, accompanied by the sound of his uneven gait — a sharp click upon the tiled floor followed by a soft slide. He hated it. Hated even more how the walk down this hallway for a meeting with his father never failed to make him feel ten years old again. Not a good feeling for a man of thirty years.

He caught a glimpse of himself as he passed a large, ornate mirror and was immediately sorry. The ragged scar on his face blazed a bright red against his pale skin. Dark circles ringed his eyes, evidence of the many nights he'd gone without sleep, instead drinking and gambling till morning.

When he entered the library, he found the duke standing near the windows that overlooked the extensive gardens of Dunacombe Manor, hands clasped behind his back.

"Good morning, sir," Sherwood announced himself.

His father turned and gave him a dour

look. "So . . . you're here at last."

"I came as soon as I received your message."

"Hmm." The duke walked to a nearby chair and sat, then waited for Sherwood to do the same. "I have come to a decision about this . . . this latest escapade of yours."

This latest escapade. The duke had obviously learned of his involvement with Lady Langley. The scandalous divorcée, twelve years his senior, had a reputation for enticing wealthy young men. Sherwood had been only too willing to become one of her conquests.

"I am sending you to America, Sherwood."

"America?"

"I trust you remember Morgan McKinley. He and his mother stayed with us for a number of months about seven years ago. Yes, well . . . I have arranged with Mr. McKinley to find you employment and a place to live."

So this wasn't a sudden decision that had come about solely because of Lady Langley. This had been in the planning stages long enough for letters to pass back and forth between the duke and Morgan McKinley. Even before he'd made Lady Langley's acquaintance.

"How long am I to stay in America, sir?"

11

"You will remain there a year. You will put your life in order, my boy. You will work for the money you spend and learn the value of it. I am done covering your gambling debts and paying for the liquor you and your wastrel friends consume. If you refuse to go, I will turn you out. Do you understand me, Sherwood? If you do not abide by my terms, you will no longer be welcome at Dunacombe Manor nor will I make good on your debts. You will not see your mother or me again."

Sherwood didn't give his father an argument. He hadn't the energy to protest — not with his head pounding as it was now. At least in America he wouldn't have to see more former school chums leave to fight in the war. Nor be required to attend another funeral when they returned in a box. And perhaps, on the other side of the ocean, the nightmares would stop. Maybe he would be able to sleep again without drinking himself into a stupor first.

"When is it I'm to leave, sir?"

The duke's eyes widened. It was obvious he hadn't expected Sherwood's quick acquiescence. But he hid his surprise a moment later with a brusque response. "You will sail from Liverpool on Monday."

Sherwood stood. "I'll be ready. Now, if

12

you'll excuse me, I shall see Mother. I understand she's unwell."

"See that you don't upset her." And with that, the duke rose and walked to the window, his back once more turned toward his son.

ONE

Bethlehem Springs, Idaho,
April 1916

Cleopatra Arlington studied the horses in the corral. This bunch of mustangs had been captured off the range in the southwest corner of the state. Wild didn't begin to describe the look in their eyes. They were wary, some scared, a few mean, and none of them wanted to be where they were now, walled in by fences.

"But I reckon we'll make saddle horses out of you yet."

Cleo wasn't known as the best wrangler within two hundred miles for nothing. She'd learned a thing or two about wild horses over the years. For that matter, she knew a thing or two about all kinds of wild things, having a tendency to be a bit wild herself. At least according to how society viewed her.

The sound of an approaching automobile

15

drew her around. Was it — it couldn't be. But it was! Coming up the road was her twin sister, Gwen, and her brother-in-law, Morgan McKinley. The couple must have returned to Bethlehem Springs a day ahead of schedule.

Cleo whipped off her battered Stetson as she strode toward the house, grinning her welcome, arriving at the porch steps about a minute before the Ford Touring Car rolled to a stop and the engine went silent.

"Well, look at you!" Cleo said when her sister disembarked from the automobile. "Those are big city duds if ever I've seen any."

That was one thing folks could count on. As sure as Cleo Arlington could be found in trousers and boots seven days a week — saving for two or three hours on Sunday mornings — Gwen McKinley would always look like she'd stepped right off the page of some fashion magazine.

In response, Gwen turned full circle, displaying the dark mauve dress and matching hat to their full advantage.

"I take it that means you did lots of shopping while in New York City." Cleo gave Gwen a warm embrace. "We've missed you around here."

"I've missed you too. Oh, Cleo, I wish

you'd come with us. We had the best time."

"I don't imagine Morgan feels the same, the two of you married only eight months. You didn't need me tagging along. You already had Mother for half of the trip."

A rosy hue flooded Gwen's cheeks as her gaze shifted to Morgan. The love in her eyes both delighted and saddened Cleo. Delighted because she was glad to see her fraternal twin so happy. Saddened because she was beginning to doubt she would ever find the same kind of happiness. Last year she'd fallen hard for a cowboy named Tyler King and had thought he was falling for her, too, but he hadn't turned out to be the man she'd thought him. Did someone exist who could love Cleo as she was and not want her to become a more conventional female? She hoped so. She surely hoped so.

"Is Griff around?" Morgan asked after giving Cleo a hug.

"Yeah." She tipped her head toward the house. "Dad's inside, going through his ledgers. You know how he likes to have the accounts balanced right down to the last penny."

Morgan glanced at his wife. "I'll go in and talk to him while you two catch up."

Gwen nodded as she hooked arms with Cleo. "Let's sit on the porch. It's too beautiful a day to go inside. I've missed the mountains so much. Our trip was fun and seeing Grandfather and Grandmother was wonderful, but it's good to be home at last."

Once they were seated, Cleo asked, "How was Mother when you left her?"

Her sister gave a slight shrug. "Mother's always the same." That was Gwen's polite way of saying their mother thought of herself first and others second.

Cleo set her hat on her knee and traced the brim with her fingertip. "Mother stayed in Bethlehem Springs so long, I started to believe she might stay here for good. I think Dad was hoping she would too."

"But if she'd stayed, Cleo — if she'd come to live with him as his wife after so many years apart — would either of them been happy? I don't think so. Not until she lets God change her heart."

"I reckon you're right there."

Gwen leaned forward on her chair. "But I'm certain she'll come for another visit before the year is out. By November or December, I imagine."

"So soon? I can't think why she would. Look at all the years that went by before she came this time."

"I'm sure of it." Gwen smiled and lowered her voice to a whisper. "She'll want to see her first grandchild."

Cleo opened her mouth to exclaim, but Gwen silenced her with an index finger to the lips and a shake of her head.

"Not a word, Cleo. I'm not sure yet. I haven't told Morgan, and I shouldn't have told you before him."

"Land o' Goshen!" Cleo's voice quivered with excitement. "How am I to keep such a secret, Gwennie? I'll like to burst wide open with the news."

"I don't know how, but please do."

Cleo glanced toward the door, then back at her sister. "What will you do if you're pregnant? About your duties as mayor, I mean. Is there going to be another special election?"

"No. I'll complete my term in office. That will only be for a year after the baby arrives. We shall manage somehow. Then I'll happily retire from public service. At least for a time."

"If that don't beat all."

Griff finished reading the letter, refolded it, and slipped it into the envelope. Then he looked at his son-in-law and waited for further explanation.

Morgan met his gaze. "The Duke of Dunacombe believes it's best that Lord

Sherwood not work at the spa, that he should be kept away from people of wealth and high society who might try to befriend the son of a duke and possibly encourage his . . . less desirable habits."

"Which are?"

"Before Lord Sherwood went off to war, he had the reputation of being quite the lady's man. He showed no inclination to marry or to begin practicing law. From the duke's earlier correspondence, I believe Lord Sherwood has spent most of his time since leaving the hospital on pursuits such as drinking and gambling." He cleared his throat. "And involving himself with a woman of ill repute."

Griff steepled his fingers in front of his chest. "Have you met the young man yourself?"

"Yes."

"And what did you think of him?"

Morgan leaned forward in his chair. "I liked him. A great deal, as a matter of fact. He showed real kindness to my mother and was pleasant and good natured whenever I was with him. I can see why the ladies found him attractive back then. He had a real charm. But I felt sorry for him too. Nothing the fellow did was right as far as the duke was concerned. At least that was my observation."

Griff felt his heart going out to this unknown young man. Injured in the war. Unable to please his father. Using liquor and other disreputable behavior to fill an emptiness inside him. It sounded to him as if Sherwood Statham could use a good dose of hope.

"Griff, I'm hoping you'll let Lord Sherwood live and work on the ranch for the next year."

"Here?" He should have seen that request coming.

Morgan nodded. "I know it's an imposition. I'm not sure how extensive his injuries are, not sure what he'll be able to do. But he'd be isolated on the ranch and away from temptation."

There were plenty of reasons Griff could have used for declining. After all, he'd never met the young man. But that familiar quiet voice in his heart told him he couldn't refuse, that God would have him reach out a hand of friendship to someone in need.

"Yes, Morgan," he said softly. "Lord Sherwood can come to work on the ranch. We'll make a home for him here."

Sherwood stared out the window of the pas-

21

senger car, watching the countryside roll by. After the first thirty-six hours of train travel, he'd begun to wonder if there was an end to America. Its vastness was difficult to comprehend until a person had listened to the *clackity-clack* of wheels on rails for hours on end.

Maybe he should go to the dining car. No, he wasn't hungry. Besides, he'd already discovered that American cuisine left a great deal to be desired. He wouldn't mind a drink, but after suffering through his last hangover aboard ship, he'd decided that it was time to scale back on his alcohol consumption. After all, he wanted those reports going to the duke to be good ones.

He sighed as he looked away from the window. Across the aisle and facing him sat a woman who had boarded the train at a stop called Omaha. She looked to be in her early twenties and was pretty in both face and form. But he'd noticed how her eyes skittered away from the scar on his cheek the first time she looked at him, and she'd been careful not to glance his way again.

Hers was a not uncommon reaction; Sherwood had seen more than his fair share of grimaces and winces since his release from the hospital. But that didn't mean he'd grown used to them. The doctors had told

22

him the scar would eventually look less angry. Time would help it fade, though it would never disappear. There was little else they could do — for the scar or the limp. Perhaps if he hadn't been forced to lie in the trench on the front lines for twelve hours. Perhaps if the stretcher bearers had been able to reach the Regimental Aid Post sooner. Perhaps if the Casualty Clearing Station had sent him back to England without delay. Maybe then . . .

Vain, his father once had called him, and he supposed it was true. He'd been rich, young, handsome, and happy-go-lucky. From the day he attended his first ball, he'd enjoyed the attention of the ladies from sixteen to sixty. As the fourth son of the Duke of Dunacombe, he hadn't had to worry about marrying and producing an heir, the way his oldest brother had. He'd had all the time in the world to enjoy himself before he settled down.

That had been before England declared war on Germany. That had been before he joined the army in early 1915 in a fit of drunken patriotism, certain he and his brothers-in-arms would win the day and be home in England in a fortnight.

But the war hadn't been what he expected, and he and his comrades hadn't beaten the

23

enemy in a matter of weeks. Instead, the war had defeated him. Changed him. Changed the world he knew, once and for all. The conflict had taken the lives of too many of his friends and left him with a bum right leg and a scarred face. And it had helped put him on this train to what had begun to feel like the ends of the earth.

Cleo reached for the empty platter, planning to clear the table as usual, but was stopped by her father.

"Did Gwen tell you why Morgan wanted to talk to me?"

"No. Was it something special?"

He shrugged. "You could call it that. He's been asked to find a place to stay for the son of a friend from England. Morgan doesn't think the resort is the right place for him, so he's asked if we would bring him here for the next year."

Cleo wasn't sure what to say at first. She liked kids, but it seemed a lot to ask. A year was a long time. What if the boy didn't like living on a ranch? "I don't mean to sound unwelcoming, Dad, but do we need some greenhorn kid underfoot? We're coming into the busiest time of year."

"He may be green, Cleo, but he's no kid." Her father gave her a half smile. "His name is Sherwood Statham, he's thirty years old, and he's the son of a British duke. He was severely wounded in the war in Europe and is having a difficult time adjusting again to life in England." Her father cleared his throat. "He'll be coming to the ranch to work, and I'd like you to supervise him when he gets here, show him the ropes."

A dude. A dandy. The son of a duke. This was worse than she thought. He'd be so ignorant he couldn't teach a hen to cluck. And her father wanted her to show him the ropes. What he meant was she was going to have to look after this Statham fellow and make sure he didn't wind up at the wrong end of a branding iron. Was she being punished for something?

"Cleo, men don't soon forget what they see and do in war. We need to show this young man some compassion, patience, and understanding. I imagine his heart and mind need healing even more than his body. That's the way it often is when a soldier returns from war. From what Morgan told me, my guess is that's true of Mr. Statham too."

She felt a sting of guilt. Her father was right, of course. She needed to treat Sherwood Statham with Christian kindness.

But that didn't mean she had to *like* being responsible for him.

Two

Five passengers disembarked at the station in Bethlehem Springs, Sherwood Statham the last among them. His gaze swept the platform for someone who looked familiar. He had a vague memory of Morgan McKinley and hoped he would recognize him.

The family of three — husband, wife, and child in arms — who had disembarked first disappeared through the station's double doors. The other passenger, a cowboy judging by his clothes and hat, carried his satchel to the end of the platform, descended the steps, and strode down the road toward the town while a porter unloaded trunks and suitcases onto a cart and wheeled it toward the station.

Sherwood turned in a slow circle, his gaze taking in the mountains that surrounded the long, narrow valley. Despite the tall, green pine trees, this was an arid land. Very different from the lushness of his native

England. So dry it made his nostrils ache when he inhaled. Why would anyone build a luxury health spa here?

"Mr. Statham?"

The voice was that of a female, but when he turned, he didn't find one. Instead he saw a reed-thin boy dressed in denim trousers, a loose-fitting shirt, dirty boots, and a dusty brown hat pulled low on his forehead. Sherwood looked around for someone else, but there were only the two of them on the platform.

"Are you Sherwood Statham?" the boy asked.

Only he wasn't a boy. He was a girl — although a girl unlike any he'd seen before.

Sherwood swallowed his surprise. "Yes."

She stepped toward him. "I'm Cleo Arlington, Morgan's sister-in-law. Something came up at the last minute, so he sent me to fetch you. He meant to be here himself."

Beneath the shade of her hat brim, he saw eyes of deep blue and a smattering of freckles across the bridge of her nose. She wasn't as young as he'd thought at first. Not a girl but a woman, perhaps close to his own age.

She cocked an eyebrow. "You got a trunk or something?"

He realized then that he was staring at

her. Staring the same way too many people stared at him, with shock in their eyes. "Yes. I saw the porter take my luggage into the station."

"Well, let's get it. The resort's wagon's out front." She turned on her heel and walked away from him, her stride long and sure.

The way he used to walk.

She stopped at the door into the station and glanced over her shoulder. "You coming?"

"Yes." He started forward, concentrating hard, trying to minimize his limp. If she noticed his uneven gait, she didn't let on. Her expression remained unchanged — a cross between impatience and boredom.

Sherwood claimed his portmanteau and smaller suitcase, and the porter set them onto a cart and rolled them outside. Before Sherwood could move to help the man lift the heavy trunk into the wagon that waited near the platform, Cleo grabbed it off the cart and tossed it onto the wagon bed in one easy motion. She wasn't big, but she was obviously strong.

If all women in the American West were like this one, his sojourn here wouldn't be a pleasant one.

"You need help getting up?" She pointed

to the seat of the wagon.

His jaw tightened. "I can manage."

She gave a small shrug of the shoulders, then strode to the opposite side and climbed into place. Reins in hand, she waited for him without a backward glance. He wasn't sure whether to be grateful or perturbed. Thankfully, his assertion that he needed no help proved true.

The moment he was settled, Cleo Arlington clucked to the horses and slapped the reins against their rumps. The team and wagon jerked forward with a jangle of harness. When they reached the road, she headed away from town.

Sherwood looked at her. "Might I ask where we're going, Miss Arlington?"

"To the spa. That's where Morgan is. And call me Cleo. Fancy manners are wasted on me." She glanced his way. "Morgan tells me that your dad's a duke."

Sherwood tried to imagine any of his brothers calling Dagwood Statham, the Duke of Dunacombe, "Dad." It was preposterous in the extreme.

"So what does that mean exactly?" she continued. "What does someone do to become a duke?"

"One inherits the title."

"So you'll be a duke when your father

passes on?"

"No." He shook his head. "I'm the fourth son. The eldest inherits the title and the lands."

"And what do the rest of you do?"

There were several ways he could answer her. He could tell her he'd been trained for the law but had little passion for it. Or that a career — if he'd wanted one — as an officer in the military had been blown up on the battlefields of France. Or he could state his most recent "skills" were gambling, horses, and carousing — none of which were lucrative nor acceptable occupations for a son of the Duke of Dunacombe.

But instead he feigned a laugh. "Isn't it obvious, Miss Arlington? We come to America."

Cleo didn't try to keep the conversation going after that. She sensed this was the last place the dude wanted to be, riding beside her on the wagon seat. Even the way he'd looked at her was rude and overbearing.

Not that she cared what he thought. He was here, and he'd been made her responsibility.

Be kind and compassionate, her dad had reminded her that morning. Easier said than done. Besides, she had a right to feel put out. She had plenty of work of her own to see to without worrying about keeping the likes of him busy. Just look at him. He was every bit the dandy, from the tip of his glossy black shoes to the cut of his suit to the crown of his black felt derby.

Still, it did seem as if he'd had a rough go of it in the war. He'd tried to hide the stiffness in his right leg when he'd climbed onto the wagon, but there was no hiding the scar that ran from below his left eye to below his left ear. Only why did she have to suffer because of what happened to him on the battlefield?

The thought was neither kind nor compassionate.

When the New Hope lodge came into view, she glanced at Sherwood and took vicarious pleasure in his surprise. The lodge was an impressive sight, even for a man who must have seen his share of castles and estates in England and Europe.

By the time Cleo drew the team to a halt, Morgan was striding toward the wagon. "Hello. Welcome." He stuck out a hand toward her passenger. "It's good to see you again, Lord Sherwood. I trust you remember me."

Lord Sherwood? She rolled her eyes. *If he thinks I'll call him that, he has another thing coming.* And yet calling him Mr. Statham once they began working together on the ranch would feel almost as formal as using his title. There had to be a better moniker she could hang on him. But what? He probably wouldn't like to be called *dude* or *greenhorn,* even if that's what he was.

"Of course I remember you." Sherwood shook Morgan's hand. "And your gracious mother as well. How is Mrs. McKinley?"

Morgan shook his head, his smile fading. "She died several years ago."

"Say, I am sorry. I didn't know. No one told me."

"Quite all right." Morgan motioned toward the lodge. "Maybe you'd like to look inside. I'm trying to resolve an issue with our food orders. The opening of the resort is in one week, and we can't afford any mistakes at this late date. Too many guests arriving soon." His gaze shifted to Cleo. "Would you mind being Lord Sherwood's guide? I shouldn't be much longer."

Cleo shrugged. "My time's yours today, Morgan."

"Thanks. I'll join you as soon as I can." Her brother-in-law walked away without a backward glance.

Cleo hopped down from the wagon, and as her boots hit the ground, the perfect name for Lord Sherwood popped into her head. "How about it, Woody? Want a tour of the place?"

"I beg your pardon. What did you call me?"

"Woody. I like the sound of it better than Sherwood."

After a moment's silence, he said, "I'm not sure my mother or father would agree." He descended from the wagon as carefully as he had ascended earlier. "There have been Sherwoods in the Statham family for several generations."

She bit back a smart retort, her father's reminder to be kind tweaking her conscience once again. "Well, Morgan said to show you the lodge so let's go." She started toward the entrance, leaving him to come at his own pace.

Woody? Sherwood's father would have apoplexy were he to hear his son addressed in such a way, especially by someone beneath his station. The Duke of Dunacombe was nothing if not a stickler for protocol.

Sherwood followed Cleo into the lodge, a *U*-shaped, four-storied building made of logs. Rustic, yet magnificent. The lobby was wide and airy with a high ceiling. Elegant throw rugs and runners covered the wood floor, which had been buffed to a high sheen. Original artwork in ornate frames hung on the walls.

Morgan McKinley had cut no corners. One look told Sherwood that everything at this resort would be of the very best quality, including its clientele. Perhaps the coming year wouldn't be as dismal as he'd begun to fear.

"They've got almost a full house for the opening," Cleo said, intruding on his thoughts. "Friends of Morgan's from back East and Europe, most of them. Mighty fancy digs, wouldn't you say?"

"Fine, indeed." He wondered about his duties and where his room would be located. He hoped on the main floor. Climbing stairs was difficult for him.

"Eventually, the railroad will have the spur brought all the way to the resort itself. Until then, guests will be met with automobiles at the station in Bethlehem Springs and come up the road the way we did."

Sherwood moved into the large sitting area off the lobby, looking out the windows at the pine-covered hillsides, running his fingers over the backs of brocade-upholstered chairs and the shiny surface of the grand piano.

Very fine.

He pictured himself seated in this room, dressed in evening attire, listening to someone play the piano while he conversed with a lovely young woman — much as he'd done countless times in similar surroundings before the war. Perhaps he might meet an heiress while working here. If she was someone who could overlook his scarred face —

"Would you like to see some of the guest rooms?"

He turned at the sound of Cleo Arlington's voice, again surprised by her boyish appearance, especially when compared to the buxom and beautiful female he'd been imagining.

She cocked her head to one side. "You're not very talkative, are you?"

He gave her a cool look. "Perhaps I'll have more to say after I've had a chance to get settled."

Cleo's eyes narrowed. But her reply was interrupted by the return of Morgan McKinley.

"Thanks for waiting, Lord Sherwood. I must apologize again for not meeting you at the train station, but as I said, we had a mix-up with our supplies. The last thing I want is to open the lodge with an unhappy chef in the kitchen."

"It's quite all right. I'm sure no matter when I arrived it would be an imposition."

"Not at all." Morgan shook his head. "You and your parents were a great comfort to my mother when we were in England. I'm only too happy to honor your father's request."

Sherwood's jaw tightened. Once again he felt like a boy who'd been sent down from school in disgrace. He and Morgan were of a similar age, and yet Morgan had a life of his own. He wasn't dependent upon his father's whims, as was the case with Sherwood. Maybe he should have let himself be cast out of the family rather than come to America. Maybe he should have —

"I don't suppose we need stand around here any longer." Morgan looked at Cleo. "I've asked one of the men to move the luggage from the wagon to my automobile. Do you want to join us?"

"No, thanks," she answered. "I'll just ride on ahead. Domino doesn't take too well to being tied to a motorcar." She set her hat over her short, soft curls. "I'll see you both at the ranch." She nodded toward Sherwood, tugged the brim of her hat between thumb and forefinger, and left.

Strange girl, that one.

Morgan motioned toward the entrance.

"Unless there's something more you'd like to see in the lodge, we'd best be on our way."

It was only then that Morgan's prior words registered with Sherwood. His luggage had been put into an automobile. He wasn't staying at the New Hope lodge. But if not here, where?

"My wife has a welcome dinner in store for you at her father's ranch."

"You don't live here at your resort?"

Morgan started walking, forcing Sherwood to fall in beside him. "No. Gwen and I have a house in town. My wife is the mayor of Bethlehem Springs."

The mayor? Good heavens! Was his wife anything like her sister?

THREE

As the black and white pinto loped toward the ranch, Cleo's thoughts strayed to the man she'd left with Morgan. Sherwood Statham was everything she'd expected him to be — well dressed, if a bit wrinkled from travel, with an aristocratic look, superior air, and highfalutin accent. The boys at the ranch would make mincemeat of him in no time. He'd be crying uncle before summer arrived, and then she'd be rid of him.

A grin tugged at the corners of her mouth. Perhaps it was wicked of her to think so, but it would be rather amusing to see an English lord mucking out the stalls at Arlington Ranch. In fact, she could think of a number of chores Woody might not take much liking to.

She touched her heels to Domino's sides, encouraging more speed from the gelding. She wanted to reach the ranch before Morgan and Woody caught up with her.

About ten minutes later, she rode into the yard and dismounted at the hitching post. It took only a short while to remove saddle, pad, and bridle, brush Domino down, and turn the horse into the corral. Then she headed toward the house.

The screen door opened, and her father stepped onto the porch. "Did he make it?"

"He made it. Morgan's bringing him here in the motorcar. I rode on ahead."

"And?"

"He's pretty much what I expected." Cleo shrugged as she went up the porch steps. "He's got himself a stiff leg. Moves plenty careful. Not sure how much work he'll be able to do around here."

"We'll start him slow. Let him learn the ropes. I imagine everything will seem strange to him to begin with."

"I still think this is a mistake, Dad."

"Cleo."

"I'm sorry, but I do. Wait until you meet him, and you'll see. He'll be as useless as a milk bucket under a steer. He doesn't belong on a cattle ranch. Morgan's the one who —"

"Enough. Morgan had good reasons for asking us to give the fellow a job instead of taking him on at the resort. Mr. Statham is here and he's going to stay here."

Hard as it was to do, Cleo swallowed the rest of her objections. She'd known it was futile to try. Her father's mind had been made up the moment Morgan asked the favor of him. The only way she'd be rid of the dude was when he left of his own accord.

Mercy, she hoped that would be soon.

The sound of the automobile drew their gazes down the road leading to the ranch complex. At the same moment, Gwen stepped onto the porch, wiping her hands on her apron. "Thank goodness they're here. I was afraid the roast would dry out if they were much longer."

"Morgan's never late for your cooking." Cleo wagged a finger. "If you're not careful, Gwennie, your husband's going to get fat."

Her sister's eyes glimmered with pleasure.

Last summer and fall, the mere thought of Tyler King had made Cleo feel the same way Gwen looked right now — warm and happy and giddy with joy. For a while, she'd believed he meant to ask her to marry him. Maybe he would have . . . if not for Henrietta Hamilton's father and his shotgun.

She drew in a quick breath and shook off the memories. They didn't hurt now the way they had a few months ago. Most of the time, she could think back and be thankful

41

to God for saving her from the biggest mistake of her life. But sometimes, when she saw the happiness on her sister's face, that pain would hit her again — a pain right dab in the center of her heart.

Romantic foolishness.

The Ford Touring Car rolled to a stop in front of the house. In short order, Morgan hopped out of the driver's seat and came up to the porch. Taking hold of Gwen's hand, he led her to the passenger side of the car. Cleo's father followed after them.

As Woody disembarked from the automobile, he grimaced in pain. Morgan must have seen it, too, for he hurried the introductions of his wife and father-in-law, then said, "Let's go inside, shall we? No point standing around when there's a delicious meal awaiting us indoors."

Gwen, ever the solicitous hostess, walked beside Woody on their way into the house, asking him questions about his trip West and, after he'd answered her, telling him that she and Morgan had recently made the same journey across the country. When they reached the dining room, she looked at her husband. "Dear, please bring a footstool for Mr. Statham. I'm sure he'll enjoy his meal more if he can raise his sore leg for a time."

"You're very thoughtful, Mrs. McKinley."

Woody bowed his head in her direction. "Thank you."

Cleo swallowed a sound of derision. When was the last time a new ranch hand had gotten this sort of welcome? Never, that's when. Most new hires were shown to the bunkhouse so they could stow their gear and then put straight to work. Just how was she supposed to make a ranch hand out of him with her entire family treating him like a special guest?

The familial affection around the Arlington dinner table was almost palpable. It made Sherwood more than a little uncomfortable. At Dunacombe Manor, meals with his parents and brothers were formal affairs, their conversations strictly guarded. Sherwood had learned at a young age to watch what he said and how he said it. Usually it was best to say nothing at all.

Griff Arlington said something that elicited laughter from his daughters and son-in-law, and Griff laughed right along with them, the merry sounds echoing about the room. Sherwood tried to envision the same thing happening around the table at the manor, but all he could see was the duke boxing his ears and sending him from the room. No imagination required there. It had happened often enough when he was a boy.

Gwen McKinley, seated on Sherwood's left, leaned toward him and softly said, "I'm afraid we're being rude, Mr. Statham. You cannot possibly understand what we found so amusing."

"It's quite all right, Mrs. McKinley. I'm afraid my thoughts were wandering anyway."

"You've hardly touched your food." Cleo leaned back in her chair. "Not to your liking, Woody?"

If he wasn't mistaken, there was a definite challenge in her tone of voice. She seemed to have taken an instant dislike to him. So be it. "I do not know anyone by the name of Woody, Miss Arlington." He looked at Gwen again. "And your sister is mistaken. This is the best meal I have eaten since arriving in America. It's weariness that has stolen my appetite."

Cleo stood, the legs of her chair scraping against the floor. "I'll have one of the boys help me take your luggage to the bunkhouse. I suppose tomorrow's soon enough for me to begin showing you around."

She had already reached the door before her words made sense in Sherwood's mind. *Luggage. Bunkhouse. Begin showing around.*

He looked at Morgan. "I'm sorry. Am I to understand that I will be staying here on

44

this . . . on this ranch? I'm to work here?"

Morgan looked as surprised as Sherwood felt. "Yes. I thought you knew. Your father didn't tell you?"

"No." Sherwood swallowed. "He didn't tell me."

An uncomfortable silence flooded the room.

Different emotions warred in Sherwood's chest. Shame that he'd been pawned off on this family like an unwanted dog. Anger at his father for setting him up to appear an incompetent fool. Fear that he wouldn't be able to do whatever tasks were assigned to him. Dread that he would fail here just as he'd failed on the battlefield, just as he'd failed in the eyes of the duke.

Griff cleared his throat. "Well, don't let it worry you, Mr. Statham. I promise we'll ease you into things. Cleo and the other cowboys will show you the ropes, make sure you know how things are done."

Sherwood lowered his right leg from the footstool, then stood, feeling awkward and clumsy in front of them. "If one of you might direct me to the —" He searched his memory for what Cleo had called it. "— to the bunkhouse?"

Morgan rose. "I'll take you."

Sherwood nodded to Gwen. "Thank you,

Mrs. McKinley, for the delicious meal." Then he turned toward Griff. "And you, sir. Thank you for your hospitality. I hope you won't regret having me as one of your employees."

"I'm sure that I won't," the older man answered.

Sherwood didn't try to hide his limp or to walk faster than was bearable when he and Morgan left the house. He was too tired to make the effort. And besides, he didn't care what anyone thought of him just now.

They still couldn't think less of him than his own father did. That much was clear.

FOUR

Although invited to accompany the Arlingtons into Bethlehem Springs the next morning to attend church services, Sherwood declined. The last thing he needed was to meet more strangers. Besides, all he wanted to do was sleep. Sleep and hopefully wake up to find the past few weeks were nothing but a bad dream.

None of it was a bad dream, of course. When he opened his eyes late in the morning, he was still lying on an uncomfortable, narrow bed in the bunkhouse. The three cowboys who worked for the Arlingtons — the ones who would be his roommates for the next year — were nowhere to be seen.

He stared up at the ceiling and wondered how he'd allowed his life to reach this low point. When he'd joined the army, he'd thought he would return from France a hero. He'd thought he would make his parents proud of him. But war hadn't been

47

quite the adventure he'd expected. If he hadn't been wounded, perhaps . . .

He closed his eyes, remembering the first time he'd looked in a mirror while in the hospital. His gut had twisted at the sight of the ragged, angry scar, and he'd known in an instant how the young ladies of his acquaintance would react when they saw him. If he'd been the heir to a dukedom and its fortune, perhaps the disfigurement wouldn't matter to a female in want of a husband. But he was not the heir.

His looks hadn't mattered to Lady Langley, nor had his limp. The beautiful divorcée wasn't looking for a husband, only evenings filled with fun, and as long as he was paying for the entertainment, she was content to be with him. But he wasn't fool enough to think she missed him now that he was gone. Nor, truth be told, did he miss her or any of the other hangers-on. Deep down he knew that's why he hadn't fought his father's decision to send him to America. Because he was tired of the kind of life he'd lived since his release from the hospital. Or maybe he was tired of living altogether. Better if he'd died on the battlefield. Perhaps then his father could have been proud of him.

Sherwood's stomach growled as he sat up.

No surprise that he was famished. He hadn't eaten much supper and he'd slept through breakfast. He hoped he would find something in the kitchen to tide him over until the next meal was served.

Without glancing in the mirror above the basin, he washed his face and combed his hair. Then he donned clean clothes and set off for the main house. He'd been informed that the ranch hands took their meals in the kitchen when they weren't out on the range. Not a new experience for him, actually. Many a time during his youth he'd joined Davis Bottomley, the overseer of Dunacombe Manor, for tea in the kitchen. There'd been a wealth of information in that man. It was the overseer, not the duke, who made the Dunacombe lands thrive. Sherwood had understood that even as a schoolboy.

Arriving at the side entrance, Sherwood rapped on the door. "I say, is anyone about?" When no answer came, he stepped inside.

The kitchen wasn't anywhere near as large as the one at Dunacombe, but it was good sized all the same. The room was tidy, and there was no indication that breakfast had been prepared a few hours earlier.

He spied a loaf of bread on the counter

opposite him and headed for it. Taking up a knife, he cut himself a slice, slathered it with butter, and began to eat.

"I see you've made yourself at home," someone said from behind him.

Sherwood turned. The man in the doorway looked to be in his fifties or sixties. Average in height, he had a shiny pate and a generous paunch. The white apron tied around his waist identified him as the cook.

"You must be the fella from England."

He nodded. "Sherwood Statham."

"Everybody calls me Cookie."

"Delighted to meet you."

The older man chuckled as he pointed toward the large table on the opposite side of the room. "Sit yourself down and I'll whip up some grub. That bread won't be enough to hold you until suppertime. Griff and Cleo always have Sunday dinner in town with Morgan and Gwen."

"That's good of you, Cookie. I'm obliged." He walked to the table and sat as he'd been told.

Still chuckling — Sherwood didn't know what the man found so amusing but was certain it had something to do with him — Cookie went to work. It wasn't long before he had a concoction simmering in a skillet. The scent of onions soon filled the air, and

50

Sherwood's stomach growled in complaint. He might not have acquired a taste for American cuisine, but at the moment he'd be glad for whatever Cookie prepared.

Cleo and her father arrived at the McKinley home on Skyview Street before her sister and brother-in-law. Looked like All Saints Presbyterian had run longer than Bethlehem Springs Methodist. That was fine with Cleo. It would give her a chance to get out of her dress and into some comfortable clothes.

But changing into trousers and a shirt wasn't her only reason for wanting a moment alone in one of the upstairs bedrooms. It was the need to quiet her thoughts that drove her up the steps in such a hurry.

Tyler King had attended the Methodist service that morning. Tyler and his very pregnant wife. It was the first time Cleo had known him to darken a church door. Why did it have to be *her* church's door?

Not that she still cared for Tyler. Mostly what she felt was foolish for falling for his charm. But seeing him again was unexpected. It stirred up memories of the hurt she'd felt following his betrayal. Six months had passed since he quit his job at the Arlington ranch, and his path hadn't crossed

Cleo's since. But she knew what had happened to him and to Henrietta. Gossip, like bad news, rode a fast horse.

Lord, I sure wish You'd send me someone to love. Someone who's right for me.

Clothes changed, she took a moment to fold her Sunday dress and place it, along with her best shoes, in the satchel that had held her jeans and boots on the way into town.

Voices drifted to her up the stairs, and she knew Gwen and Morgan were home at last. She finger combed her short hair away from her face, then went downstairs, where she found the family, including Morgan's younger sister, Daphne, in the front parlor.

"Hello, Cleo," Daphne said, a twinkle in her eye. "Morgan tells me you have a new ranch hand working for you."

"Don't remind me."

Daphne laughed. "Well, tell me about him. What's he like? My brother has completely failed to satisfy my curiosity."

"Nothing much to tell."

"But he's an English lord. Don't you find him even a little fascinating?"

Cleo rolled her eyes. "No."

Daphne turned toward Cleo's father. "Mr. Arlington, it seems I must beg for an invitation to visit your ranch. It appears that shall be the only way I can see Lord Sherwood for myself."

"Dear girl, you know you never need an invitation to come out to see us. You're a member of our family now and always welcome."

The conversation turned then, as it did every Sunday, to the sermons that had been preached that morning in the Methodist and Presbyterian churches. Gwen and their father loved to discuss theology.

Most Sundays, Cleo was willing to be drawn into the conversation, but today her thoughts remained stuck on the so-called ranch hand who had piqued Daphne's interest. What was she going to do with him? She understood from her father that he was to be treated like any other cowboy who worked for them. But at the same time, she was supposed to make allowances for his injuries. Even without them, she figured he wasn't cut out for manual labor. Probably hadn't done a lick of work his entire life. And that meant she would end up doing her chores and his too.

She looked at Morgan. *You'll owe me for this, brother-in-law.*

Sherwood entered the barn, pausing inside the doorway. After his eyes adjusted to the dim light of the interior, he saw that the barn held eight stalls, four to the left and four to the right. Only three of them were occupied. Two contained mares with young foals. The third held a horse with its left hind leg wrapped in bandages, its weight shifted to the right. A large room near the entrance held saddles and other tack.

Not all that different from the stables at Dunacombe — except the manor employed eight or ten men to tend the three dozen horses housed within and to keep the tack cleaned and polished at all times.

Sherwood closed his eyes and drew in a slow, deep breath, the smell of horses and leather and hay bringing with it more pleasant memories. He'd been three when he sat astride his first pony, twelve the first time he'd been allowed to ride his horse with the hounds. He'd become an accomplished horseman, and he had an eye for good horseflesh — which had at one time helped him win more often than he lost when gambling at the races.

What he wouldn't give for another chance to take part in a fox hunt. He'd love to ride a powerful steed over tall hedges and wide brooks again. But those days were behind him. He might still manage to mount a horse, but not without great effort and even more pain. Better to keep both feet on the ground.

He walked to the stall that held the injured horse, a tall sorrel mare with a star on her forehead and white stockings on her forelegs. When Sherwood drew near, she sent him a mournful gaze that communicated her pain, then lowered her head toward the floor and huffed out a breath, blowing a hole in the straw.

"I know just how you feel," he said softly.

There must have been a sound from the yard, for all the horses looked toward the barn entrance. Sherwood followed suit in time to see the Arlingtons roll into view in a buggy. Cleo was once again dressed in denim trousers. Had she worn them to church? That would never pass muster in England. For himself, Sherwood avoided religious services as often as he possibly could. Then there was no need to worry about acceptable attire.

Cleo stepped out of the buggy, said something to her father, and then walked into the barn. She didn't notice Sherwood at first. When she did, she stopped short. "Didn't expect to find you in here."

Where had she expected him to be? Still lying on that miserable bed in the bunkhouse?

"Just as well," she continued as she moved closer. "This is where you'll spend a good deal of your time while you're working with me."

"With you?"

"That's right. I've been given the task of turning you into a ranch hand." She gave him a look that said they were both destined to fail.

"Miss Arlington, I am not afraid of hard work."

She opened the gate and entered the stall. "Is that right?" She ran her hand over the horse's back, down its rump, and finally squatted and began to unwrap the bandages on its left leg. "Well, Woody, I guess we'll find out, won't we."

She used that name to irritate him. He was sure of it. And it was starting to work. Perhaps it was time he put her in her place.

But before he could come up with a suitable reply, she spoke again. "How about we get started right now?" She jerked her head toward the barn entrance. "Bring me some bandages, a clean cloth, and the bottle of hydrogen peroxide. You'll find everything on the table in the tack room there."

Sherwood gritted his teeth. He didn't much care for being ordered around by a girl in trousers.

I should have stayed in England.

The duke would have disowned him, but at least Sherwood had friends he could have imposed on for a time. Or did he? Most of the men who could be called true friends, past or present, were either fighting in Europe or moldering in coffins in the ground. His recent companions weren't true friends. They were men — and women — who hoped he would loan them gambling money or who expected him to buy their drinks while idling about in clubs. No, he'd hadn't had a choice but to come here, and now he hadn't a choice but to stay.

In the tack room, he located a stack of clean cloths, a roll of bandages, and the dark bottle of hydrogen peroxide on a tall table. Gathering them up, he returned to the stall. By the time he arrived, Cleo had finished unwrapping the mare's leg, revealing a long row of stitches from thigh to cannon.

"What happened to her?" He held out the supplies.

"She tangled with something on the range. Not sure what. Luckily we found her while the wound was still fresh." She opened the bottle of peroxide and poured the liquid onto the cloth. "She'll be stiff for a while, but she won't have any lasting effects."

"That is lucky."

Cleo glanced up at him, color flooding her cheeks. "I'm sorry. I shouldn't have . . . I didn't mean —" She broke off, pressing her lips together as her gaze dropped to his right leg, then returned to the horse's wound.

It took him a moment to understand what had caused her embarrassment. The mare's leg. His leg. Lucky horse. Not-so-lucky Sherwood.

His spine stiffened. His voice struck like flint. "I don't want or need your pity, Miss Arlington."

Cleo drew in a breath as she stood and faced him. "No, I don't reckon you do. I misspoke and I'm sorry for it."

"Keep your apologies, please."

Huffy, wasn't he?

"I would appreciate it if you would treat me as you would any other employee."

Who was he trying to kid? His manner clearly said he thought himself better than everyone else. But she'd promised her dad she would try her best to be kind to him. Even if it killed her.

"It's obvious you don't need my help here, Miss Arlington. Have you something else for me to do?"

"Call me Cleo. All the boys do."

His shrug said he didn't care what she was called.

If he was trying to get under her skin, he was doing a right good job of it. "It's Sunday. We try not to ask our hands to do much work on Sundays." She glanced toward the other occupied stalls. "But if you'd get clean water for those mares and foals, I'd be obliged. Pump's outside those doors." She jerked her head toward the open door at the opposite end of the barn.

"I'll see to it at once."

Cleo watched Woody walk to the nearest of the two stalls, enter it to retrieve the water bucket, and then carry the pail toward the door. His gait was uneven and pain was written on his face, but there was something proud about the way he carried himself, something that told her he'd meant what he'd said. He didn't want her pity. He didn't want to be given special treatment.

Reluctantly, she allowed her estimation of him to go up a notch.

FIVE

Cleo's charitable feelings toward Sherwood Statham were short lived.

She and her father had finished eating their breakfast the next morning when he said, "You need to take Sherwood into town to buy some work clothes. He needs Levi's and a good pair of boots and some different shirts. Probably a hat too. I saw him in the kitchen earlier, and he's still wearing dress trousers and a white shirt. I think that's all he brought with him."

"I was going to work with more of those mustangs today."

"They can wait until you get back. It won't take long."

A good two or three hours, Cleo would bet.

"Well, if you object, I suppose he could take the buggy into town by himself."

Oh, sure. Send Woody off on his own, then have to go looking for him after he got lost.

That would waste even more time than going to town in the first place. "I'll take him."

"Good." Her father smiled. "It'll be good for the two of you to get better acquainted. He's feeling unsure of himself. It's written all over him, clear as day. Think how you'd feel if I sent you off to England to live with a duke."

Cleo wanted to say that she and Woody would have plenty of time to get acquainted, seeing as how she'd been made his supervisor — the absolute *last* thing she wanted to be — but she'd already lost that argument with her dad. No point bringing it up again. "Any supplies we need, as long as we're headed into town?"

"Nothing I know of, but check with Cookie."

Cleo pushed her chair back from the table, wiped her mouth with the napkin, and stood. She carried her breakfast dishes into the kitchen, half expecting to see Woody still there, lingering over his food, but he was gone. Only Cookie remained.

She set her plate and glass on the counter next to the sink. "I'm going into town, Cookie. Dad said to ask you if you need any supplies while I'm there."

"As a matter of fact, there are a few things we could use."

"Write them down for me, will you? I'll check back as soon as I've got the horses hitched to the buckboard."

"Sure thing."

"Where's the dude?"

"Sherwood? I think he went back to the bunkhouse."

"Thanks."

She headed out the back door and crossed the yard. The bunkhouse door was open to the morning air, and through the screen she saw Woody leaning a shoulder against the wall, shifting his weight off his bad leg while talking to Stitch Calhoon and Randall Thompson.

She rapped once on the doorjamb. "Excuse me, boys. I need a word with Woody."

The narrowing of his eyes told her how much he disliked the nickname.

"Sure, Cleo. Come on in." Stitch stepped to the doorway and pushed open the screen. "Randall and I were just leavin'."

Cleo moved into the bunkhouse and nodded as Stitch and Randall filed out. Then she looked at Woody. "Dad wants me to take you into town to buy yourself some clothes." She pointed at his trousers. "You can't wear those fancy duds while you're working on a ranch."

"I am aware that these are not suitable,"

he answered, sounding as formal as his clothes looked, "but I am afraid they will have to do. My funds have run rather thin at present."

She arched a brow. The son of a duke, broke?

"Miss Arlington, I —"

"Cleo," she interrupted.

"I assure you, it is the truth. My purse is empty. My father sent me to America to earn my way and chose not to provide much beyond the cost of my passage."

The duke sounded like a hard sort. But wasn't it also strange that a grown man like Woody hadn't been earning his own way long before this? It seemed so to her. She'd been working for a wage since she'd finished her schooling. Things must be mighty different in England.

"My dad can advance you something against your first month's wages. No way around it that I can see. You've got to have work clothes." She pushed on the screen door. "I'll go hitch up the buckboard. Be ready to go in about fifteen minutes."

"I'm ready now. Would you like some help?"

She shrugged. "Suit yourself." She strode toward the barn, not waiting to see if he followed.

■ ■ ■ ■

Sherwood set out after Cleo as fast as his right leg would allow. Pain shot from his thigh into his hip, but he clenched his jaw and ignored it. England would fall into the sea before he complained to that female in pants. He wouldn't let her see his discomfort if he could help it. Not ever.

She went into one of the corrals near the barn and led out two horses. After tying them both to a hitching post, she tossed a brush to Sherwood. "You take that one." She pointed to the black gelding. "I'll take this one."

After they'd brushed away the dirt from the horses' coats, Cleo brought out the harness. This time she didn't ask for his help, and he didn't offer. She moved with an easy rhythm, her hands often stroking the horses' necks, backs, hips. She talked to them too — a constant stream of *there you go, good boy, easy fella.* That she was comfortable around horses was apparent. In fact, he suspected she was more comfortable around them than around people. And animals wouldn't mind how fractious she could be.

Before she had both horses in the harness, she paused to glance over her shoulder.

"Cookie's got a list of supplies we're to pick up while in town. Would you mind getting it?"

It sounded like a request, but it wasn't. He set off for the house. When he entered the kitchen, he found Griff and Cookie seated at the table. Their conversation died when they saw him. "Cleo sent me for a list of supplies."

Cookie held out a slip of paper. "Got it right here."

"Thank you." Sherwood took it, then looked at Griff and forced out the words, "I find myself rather short of funds, sir, and your daughter said you would advance what is needed to buy some appropriate work clothes."

"Of course. Tell Cleo to have your purchases put on my account."

Sherwood wondered if he should ask what sort of salary he was to be paid, but pride stopped him. His grasp of dollars to pounds and pounds to dollars was weak as of yet. He would ask later, when he and Griff were alone and he needn't fear appearing the fool before others. It was bad enough that the Arlingtons knew he'd come to America without knowing where he would live and work.

"Thank you, sir."

65

"Young man, you'd best call me 'Griff' the way everybody else around here does. You're going to be with us for the next year. No point being so formal. We're more like family on this ranch."

Since when did being like family preclude formality? Sherwood tried to imagine someone his age calling his father "Dagwood" instead of "your grace." Impossible! It would never happen.

Griff stood and clapped a hand against Sherwood's back. "Give yourself time. You've only been here a couple of days. It'll get easier. I promise."

"Thank you, sir. I mean, Griff." He gave the man a nod. "I had better go. Your daughter does not like to be kept waiting."

Griff muffled a laugh while rubbing his jaw. "No, she sure doesn't."

With another nod, Sherwood turned and left the house. When he rounded the corner and the barn came into view, he saw Cleo already on the wagon seat, looking none too happy.

"Took you long enough," she said when he drew near. "Have you got the list?"

"Yes, I have it." He held up the paper. "Right here." He gave it to her, then grabbed hold of the wagon seat and footboard and climbed up, silently cursing his bad leg for making him awkward.

The moment he settled onto the seat beside her, Cleo slapped the reins against the team's backsides and the wagon jerked into motion. "Pay attention to where we're going so you'll be able to get to town and back on your own when the time comes."

There was no doubt about it: Cleo Arlington was as prickly as a porcupine. She didn't like him, and the feeling, he decided, was mutual. If forced to work under her supervision throughout his entire year of exile, he didn't care to think what he might say to her before it was over. If she were a man . . .

He glanced in her direction.

Cleo sat with her boots on the footboard, her elbows resting on her knees, the reins held loosely between her gloved fingers. From beneath her hat, he saw the soft curls of her short, strawberry-blonde hair, cut about chin length. Her complexion was fair, with a smattering of freckles across the bridge of her nose and cheekbones that told him her hat didn't always protect her from the sun's rays.

She almost *was* a man in her dress, in her manner. And yet he had to confess there was something feminine about the fullness of her mouth and the shape of her eyes. Maybe if she wore a dress and did something with her mop of hair — and kept her mouth shut — she might be halfway attractive. Never the beauty her sister was, of course, but passable.

As those thoughts drifted through Sherwood's mind, Cleo turned her head and found him looking at her. That made her straighten on the wagon seat, as if prodded from behind. "Doesn't look like you're paying attention to the road."

"As this seems to be the only road we've seen since departing the ranch, I find it hard to believe I could get lost."

"Shows what you know. We're still on Arlington land."

"Really? How large is the ranch?"

"Better than thirty-two thousand acres."

"I say. I hadn't imagined." That meant the Arlington ranch was larger than Dunacombe Manor. "How do you manage with so few employees?" The manor had nearly thirty tenant farmers, let alone the vast number of servants it took to keep the house in running order.

"Dad hires on extra hands when it comes time for branding and when we take the cattle to market. But with the land fenced, it doesn't take as many men to run a place like ours. Not the same as it was for ranchers thirty or forty years ago. No long cattle drives, thanks to the railroad."

Sherwood thought she sounded slightly disappointed about the latter.

They fell into a period of silence, a quiet broken only by the rattle of the harness and wagon and the steady *clip-clop* of horses' hooves. But when the road opened onto a bridge that would carry them over the river, Cleo pulled on the reins, stopping the team.

"That way's north." She pointed to the right as she spoke. "The road takes you up to New Hope. The other way's south." She pointed to the left. "The road takes you straight to Bethlehem Springs."

"Leave the ranch, follow the road to the bridge, turn left, and keep going until you arrive in town. You must think me dim witted, Cleo, if you feared I would lose my way."

After a moment's hesitation, she met his gaze, color rising in her cheeks. "I reckon that's what it sounded like."

He thought she might apologize, but instead she slapped the reins against the horses, and the wagon resumed its journey.

Cleo felt small and petty, and she wasn't any too keen on the feelings.

It was true. She had treated Woody as if he hadn't any smarts — or, at the very least, as if he had no sense of direction. She could have let him drive himself to Bethlehem Springs in the buggy if it was so all-fired important for her to be working with those mustangs.

Then again, neither Bert nor Helen Humphrey, owners of the mercantile, would have given a stranger credit against her father's account on just his say so. So it seemed her presence was necessary after all.

She drew in a breath and released it on a silent sigh. Why was she so impatient with Woody? Her brother-in-law was every bit as rich and privileged as this English dude. Morgan wouldn't know the first thing about running a cattle ranch, but she'd always liked him. She'd never given him a hard time. So why did she expect more from this greenhorn sitting beside her?

She liked to think of herself as easygoing, someone who could roll with life's punches and come up smiling. She reckoned others thought of her that way too. But she wasn't easygoing when it came to Woody. He could get her goat without even opening his mouth.

Her father's words of advice echoed in her mind: *Nobody can get your goat unless you've got a goat to get.* The thought brought a smile to her lips. She needed to remember those words next time Woody started to get under her skin.

The wagon rounded a bend in the road, bringing the rooftops and church steeples of Bethlehem Springs into view. A few minutes later, they rolled into town. Once they reached the mercantile at the corner of Wallula and Idaho, Cleo brought the team to a stop.

"Here we are." She set the brake. "You take care of buying your clothes. I'll get the rest of the supplies Cookie wants, and we can be on our way in short order."

She jumped down from the wagon seat and moved onto the sidewalk. From the corner of her eye, she saw Woody's descent. She could tell it wasn't easy for him, and she sensed that he hated he couldn't drop to the ground as easily as she had. It made her wonder what sort of man he'd been before the war. For that matter, she wondered what he'd done after the war to make his father send him to America the way he had, without money or even any notion what he'd be doing when he got there.

Not that it mattered to her. She was merely curious.

The interior of the store made Sherwood feel somewhat claustrophobic. The aisles were narrow, the shelves and tabletops crammed with merchandise of all kinds. A quick look around helped him locate the dry-goods section.

As he glanced through the shirts, a gentleman approached. "Cleo said you might be needin' some help." He stuck out a hand. "I'm Bert Humphrey, the proprietor."

"How do you do." He shook the man's hand. "Sherwood Statham."

"Pleased to meet you. What can I help you find?"

Sherwood told him the clothing items he needed, then lowered his voice. "And if you have any decent liquor — perhaps a fine port or a good brandy — I would be obliged."

"Sorry to disappoint you, Mr. Statham, but you're in a dry state."

"A dry state?"

"We've got Prohibition hereabouts. Can't make, buy, sell, or consume liquor anywhere in Idaho."

Sherwood felt his eyes widen in disbelief. "Not anywhere?"

"No, sir. Not anywhere." Bert Humphrey shrugged. " 'Less, of course, you find yourself a bootlegger who'll sell you a bottle of hooch, and I wouldn't recommend it. Stuff'll make you go blind. Besides, our mayor's a stickler about keeping the law. You wouldn't want to find yourself visiting our local jail."

He couldn't believe his bad luck. He'd decided not to drink as much as had become his custom since his release from the hospital, but he hadn't thought he would have to go without so much as a glass of wine with supper for an entire year.

No liquor *and* putting up with Cleo Arlington. This *was* an uncivilized land.

Sherwood had no reason to change his opinion when, four hours later, he stood in the last of the horse stalls, pitchfork in hand, shoveling manure, hay, and straw into a wheelbarrow. Sweat ringed the armpits of his new shirt and dirt smudged the legs of his new denim trousers. The boots he'd purchased in town already looked a month old.

"When you're done here," Cleo had said after assigning him the task, "come look for me, and we'll see what else you can do."

Sherwood's biceps and the muscles across his shoulders screamed for a rest, and the pain in his leg was reaching the unbearable point. But he wasn't about to stop until he finished. Yesterday he'd told Cleo he wasn't afraid of hard work. He'd meant it. He wasn't afraid. He'd done harder things than this in the army. But that didn't mean he had to like it. Nor did it mean it was easy for him. He hadn't lifted anything much heavier than a deck of cards in recent months, and he was paying for it now.

He paused long enough to wipe his shirt sleeve across his forehead before the sweat could trickle into his eyes.

I won't be beaten. I won't be done in. By heaven, I won't.

That's what his father expected, of course. That he would fail here as he'd failed on the battlefield. As he'd failed at home. For a long time Sherwood hadn't cared. Hadn't cared if he failed. Hadn't cared what his father thought of him. But for some reason he cared now. He would not fail with Cleo Arlington looking on.

Night fell over the ranch, and with it came a blanket of silence. Cookie and Cleo had long since retired to their rooms for the night, but Griff found he couldn't sleep. Not an unusual circumstance. He often found it difficult to shut off his thoughts at the end of the day.

He stepped outside into the crisp night air. Bear, one of the cow dogs that lived on the ranch, came onto the porch. Griff leaned down to pat his head.

74

"How you doin', boy?"

The dog wagged his tail in reply, then lay down with a groan near his master's feet while Griff leaned a shoulder against a post and stared across the yard toward the darkened bunkhouse.

When he'd asked Cleo at supper how Sherwood was getting along, she'd said, "Fine," and hadn't elaborated beyond that. From what Griff had observed earlier in the day, he thought the Englishman was trying his best. After their return from town, Cleo had put Sherwood to work in the barn, mucking out stalls. Not the best job in the world. But if the young man had complained, Griff hadn't heard him.

He tried to imagine either of his daughters doing something that would make him send them away. Impossible. Nothing they could do would make him want to put an ocean between him and his children. Not drinking. Not gambling. Not anything. Whatever Sherwood's misadventures, was the best recourse to send a son halfway around the world? And besides all that, he wasn't a boy, yet it seemed he was being treated like one.

Griff drew a deep breath as he lowered himself to sit on the top porch step. Bear immediately changed positions to press himself against Griff's hip. This earned the

75

dog a few more pats. But Griff's thoughts remained on the new ranch hand. Sherwood Statham was hurt in more ways than just the injury to his leg and the scar on his face. Griff hoped the young man's invisible wounds, as well as the visible, would find healing in the months he was with them.

If there's something I can do, Lord, show me what it is.

Six

Three days later, Sherwood once again stood in the barn, mucking out stalls, when he heard men shouting and the angry squeal of a horse. Curious, he walked toward the doors at the back of the barn. When he stepped through the opening, squinting into the light, he saw Cleo atop a buckskin, its back arched, all four hooves off the ground. When it landed, it hit with such force Sherwood heard grunts from both horse and rider. An instant later the animal was airborne again.

Outside the corral, the three cowboys who shared the bunkhouse with Sherwood — Stitch, Randall, and Allen — shouted encouragement, interspersed with whoops and hollers. Sherwood leaned the pitchfork against the wall of the barn and walked over to join them.

"Ride 'em, Cleo!"

"Yee-haw!"

"Hang on, girl!"

The horse came close to the corral fence, and Sherwood feared it would throw itself and its rider into the wood rails. But one look at Cleo told him she felt no fear. Her expression reminded him of the one worn by riders as they flew over hedges and streams during a fox hunt. Determination was written in the set of her lips, and the thrill of the challenge was written in her eyes.

"You a bettin' man?" Stitch asked Sherwood.

"I've been known to make a wager now and then."

"Then put your money on Cleo. That mustang may throw her a time or two, but she'll beat him in the end."

"Aren't you concerned she'll be injured?"

"Cleo? Nah. She's been ridin' horses since before she could walk." Stitch pointed at the horse in the corral, airborne once again. "I keep tellin' her she oughta turn professional cowgirl and compete in the rodeos. She's good enough to ride most any bronc. Sticks to that saddle like she's got glue on the seat of her britches."

Sherwood could have differed with the cowboy. He'd seen light between Cleo's behind and the saddle every time the horse threw itself into the air. Riding a wild horse was no occupation for a woman.

He wasn't sure how much time passed before the buckskin gave up the fight. It seemed an eternity. The horse's final bucks were halfhearted, its front legs barely leaving the ground. Finally, with a dejected grunt, it stood quivering in the center of the corral.

Cleo began talking to the mustang in a low voice while stroking its neck. The horse moved its ears forward and back.

Stitch leaned close to Sherwood. "It isn't often she has to break one like that. She's got a way with horses, even the wild ones out of the Owyhees like that bad boy. Coaxes them along and next thing you know they're saddle horses."

Sherwood felt his leg begin to throb and knew that when he turned and walked back to the barn there would be no disguising his awkward gait. He couldn't sit a docile horse with assurance, let alone do what Cleo had done just now. He hated that, hated knowing that she knew it too.

"It seems the excitement is over," he said.

"Reckon so."

"Then I had best return to my work."

With a nod, he headed back to the barn, grabbing the pitchfork from the place he'd left it. He didn't waste time once he was inside. He finished mucking out the last stall, then checked to make sure the horses housed inside the barn had clean water in their buckets and hay in their stalls.

The work Cleo had assigned to him his first week on the ranch didn't take a great deal of thought, and after three days Sherwood had found a rhythm. Clean the stalls. Feed and water the horses in the barn and in the corrals. Tidy the tack room and clean the leather tack with saddle soap, checking for needed repairs or replacement. Brush and cool down horses as required.

Although none of his duties would tax a man in top shape, he'd found the muscles in his shoulders, arms, and thighs aching when he got out of bed in the mornings. His right leg complained, the throbbing never letting up, although the pain eased a bit when he propped the leg on a stool or a chair. But he did his best not to let Cleo know of his discomfort. He still had some pride left.

As he exited the tack room, the sound of an automobile engine drifted into the barn. He looked out at the barnyard that separated him from the main house and saw a car roll to a stop. Sherwood recognized the driver and his passenger — Morgan and

Gwen McKinley.

Right then Cleo strode into view from around the corner of the barn, brushing her hands against her Levi's as she walked. "Gwennie, I wasn't sure you two would come today."

"It's Thursday, isn't it?" Gwen stepped from the motorcar.

The two women embraced. "I know it's Thursday, but things must be hopping up at the resort."

"They are."

"But not so busy we couldn't join you for lunch," Morgan said, receiving his sister-in-law's hug in turn. As he stepped back from her, he glanced toward the barn and saw Sherwood standing in the opening. "How are you, Lord Sherwood?" He waved.

Five days on the Arlington ranch made the formal mode of address sound strange in his ears. Even odder than Cleo calling him "Woody."

Morgan walked toward him. "Are you managing well?"

"Well enough."

"Cleo keeping you busy?"

He glanced in the direction of the automobile and saw the two sisters, arm in arm, entering the house. "She is."

"That's good." Morgan nodded. "Would

you care to join us for lunch?"

Sherwood knew the food was the same whether served to the hired help in the kitchen or to the family in the dining room, and he saw no reason to decline Morgan's invitation.

Cleo didn't know what to think when Woody followed Morgan into the house a short while later. He hadn't taken a meal in the dining room since the day he'd arrived in Bethlehem Springs. It bothered her that he thought to do so when none of the other hands did. Not that Cleo was standoffish with the cowboys who worked the ranch; they were her friends and she'd eaten with them in the kitchen plenty of times through the years. But her sister's visits to the ranch — and Morgan's too — were special to her. She didn't want an outsider honing in on their time together.

Looking at her father, Morgan said, "I invited Lord Sherwood to join us."

Why did her brother-in-law insist on calling him that? They weren't in England, and Sherwood Statham had no special status here.

"I hope that is all right, sir," Woody added.

Her dad smiled. "Of course it's all right. The more the merrier."

Good thing Morgan didn't ask for *her* opinion.

Swallowing her irritation, she looked at Gwen. "Excuse me while I wash up. I just got done riding one of the mustangs."

She left the dining room and made her way upstairs to the bathroom. It had been ten years since the house had been remodeled to include this room, complete with running hot and cold water, a porcelain tub, and a toilet. Luxuries, all of them, and ones Cleo was thankful for on a daily basis. She didn't mind getting dirty during the day, but she treasured the ease with which she could bathe every night. No hauling water in buckets from an outdoor pump. No boiling pots on a wood stove. No sitting in a small metal washtub in the middle of the kitchen as they'd had to do when she was little. Oh, the joy of sinking down into a bathtub full of bubbles and rubbing perfumed soap over her skin. And that scented lotion Gwen had brought her from New York City. My, my, if that wasn't something!

She turned on the tap water and splashed her face, then worked soap into a lather and washed away the dirt and grime. After drying her face and neck, she paused long enough to look at herself in the mirror. Her hair was even more disheveled than usual.

No brush could tame it now. Gwen had tried countless times to convince Cleo to let her hair grow longer, but she'd failed to change Cleo's mind. Long hair would be such a bother, working with the horses the way Cleo did.

With a shrug of the shoulders, she left the bathroom and hurried down the stairs. By this time, everyone was seated at the table, including Woody, his right leg propped on another chair, as he'd done the last time he ate with the family.

Woody smiled at Morgan as Cleo took her place at the table. "I'd forgotten you and your mother were staying at Dunacombe at the time of that hunt. I was recently down from university." He chuckled. "We did have a jolly good time that summer, didn't we?"

Cleo looked at him in surprise. Woody, laughing? But Woody appeared a different man from the one she'd worked with this week. When he was with her, just the two of them, he was stiff and abrupt, with nary a smile. Now he seemed in good spirits and at ease, a side of him she didn't recognize. He sure wasn't like that around her.

She pondered that thought. *Maybe the problem's with me.* She hadn't exactly been pleasant to him. Not to mention that she'd intentionally assigned him the most menial and unpleasant tasks to do.

Morgan answered Woody's question. "Indeed we did." He glanced at Gwen. "I've promised my wife a trip to Europe, but it will have to wait a year or two." He reached up and tenderly brushed her cheek. "Once the baby is old enough to travel, we'll go."

An ache curled in Cleo's chest. What she wouldn't give to . . .

She squelched the thought before it could fully form. There was no point entertaining it. Things were what they were. Only one man had tried to court her, and he'd turned out to be a snake in the grass. Just went to show her judgment concerning men wasn't any too good. Better to be content with her life as it was rather than wish for something that might never be.

Her father broke into Cleo's train of thought. "I heard you've already had a large number of guests arrive."

"Yes," Morgan answered. "We're about seventy percent full and expect more to arrive on today's train. We'll be at full capacity by Saturday."

"An auspicious beginning for the spa."

"Gwen and I think so."

Griff turned toward Woody. "I wonder if your leg wouldn't benefit from the use of the waters at New Hope." He looked at

Morgan again. "What do you think?"

"Of course. I believe our therapists *could* help Lord Sherwood. I should have suggested it myself. But it would mean coming up to the resort several times a week."

Her father answered. "That can be arranged."

Cleo couldn't believe her ears. First she was saddled with being responsible for Woody, and now he was supposed to take off from work several days a week to sit in the natural hot waters. What was wrong with her dad? What was wrong with Morgan? Why didn't her brother-in-law just give Woody a job at the spa and be done with it? Or give him a room and let him be a guest for the next year? That would be so much better than leaving him at the ranch where he was in her way.

First chance she got, she would tell Morgan so. Just considering the possibility lightened her spirits.

Sherwood fell into bed that night, exhausted. Lying on his back, he massaged his right thigh. He hoped Morgan was right about the therapists at the spa being able to give him some relief. Months ago, he'd stopped using the pain medication the doctors had given him. Although the drugs helped with the discomfort, he'd never liked the way they made him feel, like his head was stuffed with cotton. Besides, he'd seen what could happen to a man who relied on opiates for too long. The way his leg throbbed now, however, he wouldn't mind a snifter of brandy. But there was no brandy to be had on the Arlington ranch. No liquor of any kind. The devil take Prohibition!

He thought of the men he'd gone drinking with back in England, the ones he'd spent so much time with after his release from the hospital. They would be amused if they saw him in his present circumstances. Uncivilized country.

And what would his father think if he could see him lying on this bed in the bunkhouse, a room shared with three other ranch employees? Probably that Sherwood had received his just reward for being less than the duke expected of him. It had always been thus. Even when he was a small boy, he'd known his father felt no affection for him — that no matter what he did, he would never measure up.

He recalled the Arlington family around the table at lunch today. The conversation had been lively, interspersed with frequent bursts of laughter. And there was no mistaking the affection Griff Arlington felt for his daughters. Although the sisters were polar opposites, Griff treated them the same, loved them the same, took joy in being in their company.

Sherwood wondered what that was like.

SEVEN

Cleo stared at her reflection in the mirror. "I look like a fool in this thing."

"No, you don't," Gwen countered. "You look stunning."

"It's too . . . girly." She plucked at a pink ribbon that decorated the bodice of the gown.

Gwen moved to stand beside her. Their gazes met in the mirror. "You *are* a girl, Cleo. And look how perfect the color is with your hair."

"This is the kind of dress *you* wear. My Sunday dress is bad enough, but at least it's simple and more suited to me." She wriggled, hating the feel of the unfamiliar corset against her skin. "And nowhere near as tight and uncomfortable as this."

"Like it or not, Cleopatra Arlington, you're wearing that dress. I bought it for you in New York to wear to the spa's opening. It's the very latest fashion. Now sit down and let me do something with your hair."

Cleo groaned but obeyed. Arguing was pointless. Besides, this was Gwen's day. Gwen's and Morgan's. Nobody would be looking at Cleo. As soon as she'd said the required hellos, she could fade into the background, maybe even slip outside and hide somewhere. The last place she wanted to be was in a room crowded with glittering members of high society — a label that described most of the New Hope Health Resort's guests.

I should have begged off. I should have said I was sick. She very well might become ill before she was safely back to the ranch again.

On this evening of the spa's grand opening, the sisters were in the bedchamber of the McKinley suite, Cleo now sitting on the small stool before the dressing table while Gwen brushed her hair and frowned into the mirror.

"Oh, how I wish we could do more with your hair."

"We've been over that before, Gwennie."

"I know, but I keep hoping you'll change your mind. It could be so lovely if it were longer and swept up onto your head. What I wouldn't give for these soft, gentle curls."

"The horses at the ranch would be real impressed too." Cleo chuckled. "Just do the best you can with what I've got."

Gwen nodded, then brushed the hair back from Cleo's right cheek and fastened it there with a jewel-studded comb. She repeated the same thing on the left side. Even Cleo had to admit — though silently — that the change was for the better.

She met her sister's gaze in the mirror. "I hope those sparkly things aren't real. What if I lose one of them?"

"You won't lose them."

Which, no doubt, meant the jewels *were* real. Knowing it served as a reminder of the change in her sister's circumstances.

"Come along," Gwen said. "It's time we went downstairs. Morgan and Dad will be wondering what's kept us so long."

"I reckon they'll know it was because of me." She rose from the stool, careful to take small breaths, wondering if she would expire for lack of air before the evening was done.

The main floor of the lodge — lobby, sitting room, dining room — had been transformed by a host of servants last night and earlier in the day. Pine boughs decorated the banister, the fireplace mantels, and windowsills, and the rooms blazed with light from the glittering chandeliers. At the bottom of the stairs, Cleo saw their father and Morgan awaiting them, clad in evening attire. Dashing, the both of them.

Morgan held out his hand toward Gwen as she reached the last step. "You look beautiful, my dear."

"Thank you." Gwen glanced over her shoulder. "And look at Cleo."

"Enchanting."

Cleo contained a snort of disbelief. "Thanks, Morgan."

From a corner in the sitting room, Sherwood watched as Griff Arlington and Morgan McKinley escorted Cleo and Gwen around, introducing them to the growing horde of guests — both people staying at the lodge and those up from Bethlehem Springs for the evening.

He almost hadn't recognized Cleo when she came down the stairs. Was this the same reed-thin woman he saw every day, the one who wore men's trousers and rode wild horses? Hard to believe it was. Not even seeing her with his own eyes kept him from doubting at first.

He sipped the glass of cider in his hand. It was a sorry substitute for champagne, in Sherwood's opinion. Some men of Morgan's wealth and prestige might have ignored the law on a night such as this. Morgan wasn't that kind of man.

Sherwood saw Cleo nod and smile as the introductions continued. But he wasn't fooled. He could tell she was uncomfortable, and he felt a little sorry for her.

"Lord Sherwood. As I live and breathe."

He turned.

The young woman who'd spoken was petite and attractive. Sparkling diamonds ringed her white throat, while more of the same dangled from her earlobes. Her accent was definitely American.

She faltered when she saw the scar on his face, but recovered nicely, her smile back in place, though it looked more forced now. "I can see you've forgotten me, Lord Sherwood, but I've already decided to forgive you." She held out her hand. "Marjorie Lewis. We were introduced during the London season about four years ago. I believe we shared half a dozen waltzes."

He remembered her then. She was an American heiress who'd gone to England to seek a titled husband. He'd met several young women just like her through the years. Four years ago he'd attended a ball or soiree almost every night of the week during the season and met dozens, if not hundreds, of beautiful girls, all of them seeking the perfect match. He'd talked and danced the nights away without any intention of finding himself a bride. He'd thought he had all the time in the world. He didn't know that war would soon break out, changing him forever . . .

But Miss Marjorie Lewis must have failed in her quest for a husband, for there was no ring on the third finger of her left hand.

When Sherwood took her hand and lifted it to his lips, he wished he hadn't removed his gloves. His own hands were calloused from the past week's labors; she was sure to notice. "It's a pleasure to see you again, Miss Lewis."

"You're a long way from England. How is it you're in Idaho, of all places?"

"I'm a friend of the owner." "Friend" might be stretching the truth some, but it was the easiest explanation.

"You know Morgan McKinley?" She glanced over her shoulder at Morgan and Gwen. When she looked back at Sherwood, she said, "News of his marriage surprised everyone. Who is she, after all?"

Sherwood wasn't about to respond to her thinly veiled attempt to garner information. "And what brings you to New Hope, Miss Lewis? You look to be in good health, so I assume it isn't for the therapy."

She laughed, a rather pretty sound. "I am, Lord Sherwood. Superior health. I'm here because my father sits on the board of directors of one of Mr. McKinley's charitable foundations. He thought it beneficial that we attend." She made a sweeping motion with her hand. "You see before you the crème de la crème of Boston and New York society. But perhaps you know some of them."

Before Sherwood could tell her he didn't know a soul beyond Morgan McKinley and his wife and in-laws, a servant drew near, carrying another tray with flutes of cider. He set his empty glass on the tray but waved away a second one, instead keeping his eye on the tray of hors d'oeuvres that wended its way toward his corner of the room.

"Father." Marjorie motioned to a middle-aged man with salt-and-pepper hair and beard, beckoning him to come closer. "You remember Lord Sherwood. We met him when we were in London. He's the son of the Duke of Dunacombe."

"How do you do, Lord Sherwood?" The man bowed at the waist.

"Well enough, Mr. Lewis."

The older man didn't shy away from the scar the way his daughter had. "It appears you've had a bad time of it, young man. Did you get that wound in the war?"

Sherwood felt his jaw tighten. "Yes." His desire for a drink returned.

"Terribly worrisome what's happening over there. Some of our own boys are going off to fight with the Canadians and the British, as if Americans needed to be involved. Young fools. Better we stay out of these European dustups, if you ask me."

Sherwood recalled the trenches — the noise, the bullets, the bombs, the barbed wire, the rain, the mud, the poison gas, the fear — and his stomach twisted as his palms grew moist. The war he'd seen was more than a dustup, and the many deaths of his fellow soldiers deserved better than whatever else the man before him might say.

Even a drink wouldn't have helped. All he needed now was to get away from anyone who didn't understand.

He nodded to Mr. Lewis and his daughter. "Excuse me, will you?" Before they could answer, he walked away, not caring if he appeared rude. He weaved his way through the crowd that filled the large, high-ceilinged sitting room, through the equally crowded lobby, and out the main doors.

It surprised him somewhat, the relief he felt after escaping the congested rooms. In the midst of such parties was where he used to feel the most at home.

He strode along the veranda that fronted the lodge and curved around to one side. Wooden chairs with slatted backs were placed in groups on the covered portico, as if to invite people to lounge and visit with one another. He made his way to the far side and settled onto one of the chairs, pulling another up close and propping both of his feet onto its seat. Then he closed his eyes, thankful for the cool night air against his skin.

Cleo had seen Woody slip outside more than half an hour ago. When he didn't return, she decided to go look for him. She told herself she didn't want him to get lost in these mountains, wandering around in the night. It was as good an excuse as any to escape the hubbub.

Of course, as soon as she was outside, she discovered it wasn't any too dark around the lodge. Light spilled from almost every window of the massive structure, illuminating the surroundings.

She made her way first to where the buggies, wagons, saddle horses, and several motorcars stood waiting for their owners to return. No sign of the dude in the back of the Arlington wagon. Maybe she should look for the boys. Randall or Stitch might know where Woody was.

She sure didn't want to hike very far in this confounded dress her sister had fastened her into. Breathing was enough of a chore just standing and nodding to folks. How did society folk put up with such nonsense? Any woman who did a lick of work sure couldn't mess with them. Why, she could barely sit down in this stupid corset that ran from bust to thigh.

Cleo moved toward the lodge, and that's when she saw a man seated on the side veranda, light from indoors outlining his form. She walked in that direction until she knew for sure who it was.

"I thought we'd lost you, Woody," she said as she approached the steps.

He didn't move. "Sorry. You're out of luck, Miss Arlington. I'm not lost."

A smart quip rose to her lips, but before she could speak, another man's voice — a familiar one — stopped her.

"Cleo?"

She turned around.

"Well, if that don't beat all. It *is* you."

"Hello, Mr. King."

Tyler King whistled softly. "Look at you." His gaze traveled up and down in a way she didn't much care for. "Never knew there was that much woman hiding underneath your usual getup."

She flinched, his words carrying a sting she hadn't expected. "Are you here for the grand opening?"

"Me? No. That's not my kind of shindig. I came up to see a friend who works here. Didn't expect there'd be such a party." He smiled that smile of his, the one that used to make her pulse race. "You need some company? Pity to be out here all by yourself, looking the way you do." He took a step closer. "I'd be glad to sit and talk with you a spell. After all, we're friends, you and me."

How was she supposed to answer that? He was married and his wife was expecting his baby. While supposedly courting Cleo, he'd been taking Henrietta Hamilton, a girl of eighteen, into his bed. And now he thought they were friends? Did he have any idea how many tears she'd shed over him after she learned the truth? Did he know he'd broken her heart? Didn't he —

"I beg to differ with you, sir. Miss Arlington is not out here by herself. She is with me."

Surprised, Cleo glanced over her shoulder toward the veranda where Woody now stood, his hands resting on the railing, his gaze fastened on Tyler. Later she would have to analyze why Woody bothered to help her. But right now she wasn't about to look a gift horse in the mouth. Lifting her chin, she turned back to Tyler. "As you can see, I'm not in need of your company, Mr. King. Now if you'll excuse me . . ."

She climbed the steps, shoulders straight and head high, to where Woody awaited her. When he offered his arm, she took it and the two of them headed for the lodge entrance.

He couldn't possibly know what he'd done for her. Nor could she adequately express her gratitude. "Thank you, Mr. Statham," she whispered after they turned the corner on the veranda.

"Don't mention it, Miss Arlington."

EIGHT

Despite not falling into bed until well after one in the morning, Cleo awakened at the usual time, the remnants of a dream fading away. She remembered nothing except that Woody had been in it. It didn't take much to figure out why he'd been there. He had rescued her from her careening emotions last night. He hadn't known a thing about her and Tyler, and yet somehow he'd understood she was distressed, caught between anger and the danger of tears.

She frowned. Why did Tyler still have the ability to upset her, all these months later? The wound he'd inflicted on her heart hadn't been life threatening. In truth, she'd come to understand that she hadn't loved him after all — not a deep and abiding love, not the kind that Gwen and Morgan felt for each other. Perhaps she'd suspected Tyler's nature wasn't all it appeared to be, even before she'd learned the truth. Perhaps

God's Spirit had warned her to beware.

And yet, when he'd said those things to her last night . . .

Again she recalled Woody's rescue. How had he known she was upset? Her back had been to him and she'd been shadowed by the night. And yet he'd known.

"Miss Arlington is not out here all by herself. She is with me."

Cleo rubbed her eyes with her fingertips as a sigh slipped through parted lips. She would have to thank Woody again when she got back to the ranch later today. She and her father had spent the night as guests of the resort rather than travel home in the dark as so many others had, Woody, Stitch, and Randall included. Good thing he'd been with the boys from the ranch. She didn't have to worry that he'd gotten himself lost.

"You must not think me very bright, Cleo, if you feared I would lose my way."

She winced at the memory. He was right. Sometimes she treated him as if he had no smarts. She needed to stop it. Unhappiness with the task of supervising his work, of trying to turn an English dude into an American cowboy, was no excuse for the way she acted around him most of the time. She ought to give him some credit.

"I'll do better," she whispered as she shoved aside the blankets and sat up on the side of the bed.

Light filtered through the curtains at the windows, falling upon the pink gown she'd worn the previous night. Thank goodness she wouldn't have to wear that wretched thing — or the required corset — again. She would leave them both here when she and her father left this morning. The dress was much more suited to Gwen than to Cleo. Her sister could have it shortened and let out in the bust and wear it herself.

Cleo's stomach growled, and she realized she was famished. She hadn't eaten a thing last night because of the tightness of the dress. She hoped the dining room was open this early. If not, she just might look around the kitchen herself.

Cleo made short shrift of her morning ablutions before donning her Sunday dress — oh, how she wished she could slip into her boots and trousers instead — and heading down the stairs to the dining room. She supposed most of the resort's guests would sleep late and take breakfast in their chambers, and she was right. Only two other people had reached the dining room before her. She wasn't surprised by who they were.

"Morning, Dad. Morning, Daphne. Have

you two been downstairs long?"

Daphne answered, "Not long. We just placed our breakfast order." Morgan's sister looked as lovely and put together as she had last night. "Did you sleep well?"

Cleo kissed her father's cheek before sitting on the chair beside him. "Yes. But I wouldn't have minded sleeping longer."

"Wasn't it a wonderful party?" Daphne lifted a cup of coffee with both hands and took a sip.

Cleo made a noncommittal sound in her throat as she watched a waiter approach the table. She recognized him as one of the servants who had catered to the guests last night. If she was tired, think how worn out he must be. The staff must have worked throughout the night putting the downstairs in order.

"Good morning, miss." He smiled at her, all crisp politeness, as he poured coffee into her cup. "Do you know what you would like?"

"I'll have the same as my father, whatever he ordered."

"Very good, miss." The waiter nodded, gave her another brief smile, and walked away.

Cleo chuckled. "Mighty la-di-da, isn't it?"

Her father raised an eyebrow.

She shook her head. "This may be all well and good for Morgan's wealthy guests, but if he means to bring ordinary folks in who can't afford resort prices, he'd best think of ways to make them feel comfortable. I know I feel like a duck out of water in this dining room, let alone the rest of the place, and I'm family."

Looking thoughtful, Daphne met Cleo's gaze. "I hadn't considered that."

Cleo shrugged. Of course Daphne hadn't considered it. Like her brother, she'd been raised in the lap of luxury. She was used to servants and big fancy houses and the best of everything. If Cleo understood her brother-in-law's intentions, he'd be bringing in the poor and disadvantaged to receive treatment from the spa's physicians and therapists. And this place would make plenty of them feel lost and more than a little lonely.

"You should tell Morgan," Daphne said.

"Maybe I'll do that. After church, I'll have a talk with him."

Sherwood must have been more than half asleep last night when Stitch asked if he would like to accompany him to church in the morning. That's the only reason he could think of for saying yes.

So here he was, riding on this miserable buckboard for the second time in little more than eight hours when he could have been lying on his bed in the bunkhouse, enjoying a leisurely morning without chores.

"You'll like Reverend Barker," Stitch said, breaking the silence that had stretched between them for a number of miles. "He's a fine preacher. I've been attending the Methodist church right along with the Arlingtons since I first came to work at the ranch, and the people there are friendly to everyone. They'll make you feel right at home. I reckon you'll be glad you came."

Stitch was wrong. Sherwood already regretted whatever moment of weakness had put him on this wagon. And no matter how nice the Arlingtons or the McKinleys or anyone else was to him, he wouldn't feel at home. Nothing would feel normal to him until he was back in England where he belonged. Where the air smelled of rain on a morning's breeze. Where the countryside lay a deep verdant green. Where the taste of food was familiar. Where the sound of voices didn't grate on his ears. And where he knew exactly what was expected of him — the youngest son of a duke — whether or not he chose to do it.

The first thing a person saw on the road

that led into Bethlehem Springs was a church, but as Stitch pointed out, it was the Presbyterian church. They were headed for the Methodist church. The cowboy turned the wagon onto Wallula Street and they rolled past the mercantile where Sherwood had bought his new work clothes almost a week ago. Two uneven blocks after that, Stitch guided the team around a sharp turn onto Shenandoah Street.

"That's the boarding house on the right there," the cowboy said. "School's up there on the left. And that there's our church." He pointed with his right hand.

The Bethlehem Springs Methodist Church was small and square, made of white clapboard with a simple steeple above its narthex. Horses and buggies were tied to posts on the side and behind the building, and people could be seen walking toward the front entrance from several directions. Very different from the gray stone chapel on the Dunacombe estate, only rarely attended by any of the Stathams and not a great number of employees and tenants the rest of the time.

Stitch stopped the wagon, and the two men got down from the seat. It wasn't until they were almost to the front door of the church that Sherwood saw Cleo Arlington on the sidewalk, talking to two women in simple shirtwaist dresses, pale tops over dark skirts, very similar to her own. When Cleo glanced up and saw him, there was no mistaking the surprise in her eyes.

It almost made the miserable trip into town worth it.

She said something to her friends and then walked toward him and Stitch. "Morning." Her gaze flicked between them but settled on Sherwood. "I didn't know we would see you in church today."

"I didn't know you would either."

Stitch cleared his throat, excused himself, and went inside.

"You must have gotten to bed mighty late last night. That's a long ride back to the ranch from the resort." She sounded uncertain.

"It was quite late, indeed."

She moistened her lips with the tip of her tongue. "Folks are real excited about the opening of the resort and all the guests who are staying up there. Everyone in town's talking about it. I'm so glad for Morgan and Gwen."

Sherwood nodded.

"We . . . we should go in." She glanced toward the doorway. "The service will begin soon."

"Then I suppose we should."

"Woody . . ." She looked at him once more. "I . . . I'd like to thank you again for what you did last night." Her cheeks grew pink.

"It wasn't anything."

"Yes, it was something. You did me a kindness, and I'm grateful. I won't soon forget it."

He was seeing a new side of Miss Cleo Arlington. No swaggering confidence here. Maybe it was the dress. She'd been uncertain last night as well. Maybe when you took away her boots, trousers, and hat —

"We'd best go in," she repeated, starting for the door with that long stride of hers — a stride unchecked by the hem of the skirt that whispered about her ankles.

Not so different after all.

Cleo was glad when Woody didn't follow her up the aisle to the Arlingtons' usual pew. When she glanced over her shoulder, she saw him settled into the back row next to Stitch. Good. She didn't want anyone thinking they were together. It was bad enough a few people from town had seen her last night reentering the lodge on his arm. She didn't want any busybodies getting the idea that she was sweet on some dandy greenhorn. Which she most certainly wasn't.

Kenneth Barker, the minister at Bethlehem Springs Methodist Church, was in fine form that morning. His sermon was out of the Gospel of John and carried a warning against a person looking over his shoulder and asking Jesus, "What about *him?*"

"Whenever we do that, whenever we compare ourselves with another or wonder why that other person doesn't seem to suffer as we do, Jesus will always answer us in the same way He answered Peter. 'What is that to thee? Follow thou me.' It's important that we keep our eyes focused on what God wants to do in *our* lives. When we follow and trust Him, we can never go astray."

Cleo found herself nodding. Of course it was never good to compare. Wasn't that why she didn't want anyone trying to change her to be like her sister or, for that matter, any other woman? She'd never heard the Lord telling her that she needed to wear a dress in order to follow Him. Naturally she dressed nicer when coming to church, but this wasn't where she lived and worked, day in and day out. Imagine being in this getup while shoeing a horse or breaking a bronc. Ha!

She wondered what Gwen would have to say when they discussed the sermons over

Sunday dinner. Gwen and their father could debate the fine points of theology until the chickens came home to roost and love every minute of it. Cleo didn't mind listening to them for a while, but there had been times in the past when they'd worn her out with it. Now that Morgan and Daphne were part of the family, those discussions had grown much shorter in duration. Thank goodness.

The congregation rose to sing one last hymn while the reverend walked to the front door so he could shake the hands of everyone as they left the church. Even before the final strains of the pump organ faded from the air, Jedidiah Winston, the Crow County sheriff, stepped across the aisle to shake Cleo's father's hand.

"That was quite the event up at the resort last night," he said.

Griff answered, "Yes, it was. A fine evening."

The sheriff looked at Cleo. "And you, my good woman, were a surprise to one and all."

"If you mean the dress, that was Gwen's idea."

"A nice one, I must say."

"You wouldn't think so if *you'd* had to wear it."

The two men broke into laughter. Well,

they *could* laugh. No one would ever try to stuff them into anything like it and think they were doing them a favor.

Cleo slipped from the pew and started down the aisle toward the exit. Up ahead of her, she saw Stitch introducing Woody to a number of other men. She also noticed Rose Winston, the sheriff's unmarried daughter, look at Woody, see the angry scar, and look quickly away, an expression of revulsion on her face as she scurried past him.

As if he has a contagious disease or something.

Was that how most folks reacted when they looked him in the face? She hadn't considered that before. She'd thought mostly about his leg, how the pain and stiffness affected his life. Sure, the scar was red and ragged, but it was just a scar and she'd seen worse ones. How about old man Hampstead, who'd been mauled by a grizzly over in the Tetons country five years back? Or Mooney O'Rourke, who'd been caught in the mine collapse back in aught-three? Seemed to her Woody had plenty to be thankful for. From the look of it, he was lucky he hadn't lost his eye.

The subject of her thoughts glanced away from Stitch and the others, saw her approach, and gave a slight nod.

She hadn't meant to speak to him again. She'd already said all she had to say before the service began. She'd thanked him for his kindness the previous night. She'd made him welcome to her church. That was plenty. But despite her former intentions, she stopped and said, "What did you think? I told you Reverend Barker was a fine preacher."

"Yes. Indeed." He glanced beyond her shoulder. "Good morning, Griff."

Her father extended a hand. "Welcome to our church, Sherwood. Glad to see you here."

Sometimes in life there's that split second when a person knows beyond question what's going to happen next. That's how it was for Cleo.

"Will you join us for Sunday dinner at Morgan and Gwen's?" her father asked. "You'll have a chance to get acquainted with Daphne, Morgan's sister. She told me this morning she never got to meet you last night."

"That's jolly good of you, sir, but I —"

"We'd love to have you. Wouldn't we, Cleo?"

She felt like reminding her father that they weren't in the habit of inviting any of the other ranch hands to Sunday dinner with the family, but she couldn't very well do so right in front of Stitch and Woody.

Stitch grinned as if he'd been given a gift. "Go with Griff, Sherwood. I've got a lady friend here in town, and I just might get my own Sunday dinner invite, if I play my cards right." He winked at Griff.

Woody looked uncertain. "I wouldn't want —"

Stitch placed a hand on Woody's shoulder. "You'd be doin' me a favor. I can't very well go calling with you along, now can I?"

"It's settled, then." Griff grinned. "You'll stay and have dinner with us, then we can all ride back to the ranch together."

Cleo swallowed a sigh. For whatever reason, it seemed that Woody was being admitted into the inner circle of the Arlington family and there was no stopping it. Why was beyond her. He was a stranger to everyone but Morgan, and even Morgan didn't seem to know him all that well. It wasn't like they'd been bosom buddies or anything. Woody only worked at the ranch because her brother-in-law was doing a favor for somebody half a world away.

It took another twenty-five minutes before the Arlingtons and their British ranch hand made it to the buggy. There were always lots of friends to talk to after church, and everyone seemed to have questions about the resort and the previous night's big event.

When at last they reached their buggy, Cleo was about to step into the backseat, knowing it would be more difficult for Woody to do so, but he stopped her.

"I'll sit in back."

She glanced over her shoulder. "I don't mind. It's —"

His voice was firm. "I'll sit in back." He held out his hand, offering his assistance.

She didn't need his help. In fact, she would have liked to tell him not to be stupid. But after a moment's hesitation, she placed her hand on top of his and held on as she stepped into the buggy. Maybe it was being in a dress that did this to her. She couldn't be herself, couldn't seem to think straight when she wore a skirt.

Tarnation, but it was inconvenient.

NINE

This was the third time since his arrival eight days earlier that Sherwood had sat down for a meal with the extended Arlington family. He was growing more used to their lively conversation and teasing banter, their frequent bursts of laughter, even the occasional odd turn of phrase that left him trying to decipher its meaning.

Now, as they awaited the serving of dessert, Griff and his son-in-law and two daughters sat deep in discussion about a state law that was expected to pass and how they thought it would affect the citizens of Bethlehem Springs.

Daphne McKinley, seated on Sherwood's left, leaned closer and said, "I hope we aren't boring you."

"Boring me? No, Miss McKinley. On the contrary, I find I'm never bored when with the Arlingtons."

Her eyes twinkled with mirth. "That's

exactly how I felt when I met them. I came to visit my brother for the summer, but I liked his future in-laws and Bethlehem Springs so much that I decided to stay. And since Gwen no longer needed her cozy little house on Wallula Street, I promptly made it my own and have never been so content."

Settling here seemed an odd choice for a pretty, intelligent, and wealthy young woman, but Sherwood kept that opinion to himself.

Daphne McKinley was a great deal like her brother in both looks and temperament. She shared his coloring — black hair, brown eyes, medium-toned complexion — and there was something about the look in her eyes that said she never missed a thing, that she was always watching, observing, processing, analyzing. As he recalled, she was ten years younger than Morgan; at the time Morgan and their mother, Danielle McKinley, were at Dunacombe Manor, Daphne had been in boarding school.

"I'm told you're a friend of Marjorie Lewis," she said, intruding on his train of thought.

He pictured the young woman he'd seen at last night's celebration. Friend? Hardly. "Miss Lewis and I were introduced four years ago when she was in England."

"How very gentlemanly of you, not to contradict her claim to friendship." Daphne smiled. "Marjorie is prone to exaggeration."

He gave a small shrug.

"I am sorry you and I didn't have a chance to become acquainted before today. Mother spoke fondly of you and your family. She was so grateful for your many kindnesses to her during her stay in England." The sparkle in her eyes faded, and she lowered her gaze to her hands, folded before her.

"I was sorry to learn of your mother's passing."

"Thank you," she said softly. Then she drew a breath, straightened her shoulders, and looked up again. "At least we know she's in heaven, and Morgan and I shall see both her and our father again. That brings us great comfort." A whisper of a smile curved her pretty mouth, as if to prove her point.

Sherwood thought of the men he'd seen die in France, but he found no comfort in picturing them in heaven. Their deaths had been brutal and bloody, painful, and, most of all, senseless. They'd been young men with their lives still before them. What purpose had been served by their deaths? What purpose would be served by the deaths of those still to come on the western

118

and eastern fronts? Didn't God care what was happening? And if He did, why didn't He put an end to it?

"Lord Sherwood, where did you go?"

He met Daphne's gaze. "I'm sorry. I was . . . thinking of something else."

Perhaps his expression revealed more than he wanted it to. Or perhaps his dinner companion merely thought it time to change the subject to something more cheerful. Whatever the reason, she glanced across the table and said, "Wasn't Cleo a vision in that evening gown she wore to the party?"

Cleo must have heard her name, for she turned her attention from her father and sister to Daphne and Sherwood.

Daphne grinned. "I was saying to Lord Sherwood how beautiful you looked last night. That shade of pink becomes you as much as it does Gwen."

Cleo rolled her eyes.

Grimmer thoughts gave way to amusement. "I believe, Miss McKinley, that look she's giving you means Cleo was miserable in the aforementioned gown."

"Why does everyone go on about it so much?" Cleo glared at the two of them. "There were gowns a whole lot fancier in those rooms last night. It was just a dress, for pity's sake. Has anybody made a point of saying that you looked handsome in your tuxedo?"

"You thought I looked handsome?"

Her mouth opened and closed as her eyes registered several emotions by turn. Astonishment. Dismay. Embarrassment.

He hadn't meant to upset her. He'd been teasing, the same way the family around this table always seemed to tease one another. In truth, her comment had given him a moment of pleasure. That anyone should think him handsome for any reason seemed an impossibility. That it should be Cleo —

She shoved her chair back so hard it fell over. "You're as full of wind as a horse with colic if you're thinking I called you handsome." She threw her napkin at him. "I'm going for a walk."

A few moments after Cleo left the dining room, the slam of the front door echoed through the house, amplified by the silence that had gripped those remaining around the table. All eyes turned toward Sherwood.

"I do apologize," he said, looking at Griff. "I didn't mean to upset her."

Daphne touched his shoulder. "It wasn't your fault, Lord Sherwood. It was mine. I was the one who brought up the dress."

"So that's what got under her craw," Griff said softly.

120

Gwen rose from her chair. "I should go after her. It's my fault she's upset. I'm the one who bought the gown for her. You know how much she wants people to like her the way she is."

Griff stayed her with a shake of his head. "Leave her be. Let her walk it off. You can talk to her when she gets back."

Cleo strode along Skyview Street, every so often kicking at a rock with the toe of her boot. She was ashamed of herself for losing her temper and storming out, but she wasn't ready to go back and tell anyone so. Not yet. She needed to calm down first.

"You thought I looked handsome?"

That *wasn't* what she'd said, and it sure wasn't what she'd meant. Handsome? She didn't give two hoots about Woody's appearance, one way or the other. And it wasn't because of that scar either. She just didn't care what he looked like because he didn't matter to her. He was a silly dandy who'd disrupted her life for the next year. That was all.

She felt a twinge of discomfort. He wasn't silly. He'd done her a favor last night, and she'd intended to be nicer to him because of it. She'd meant to stop judging him, to quit treating him with disrespect. But it wasn't like they were friends or even needed to be. He worked for her father, and she was his boss. Should he be asking his boss if she thought him handsome?

When she reached the cross street, she had the option of turning right and going down the hillside into town or turning left and following the road up the hillside into the forest. She turned left.

Soon, the only sounds she heard were her own footsteps, the chatter of chipmunks, and the chirping of birds. The underbrush had come to life with the arrival of spring, green buds shooting up everywhere, and the air was thick with the scent of pine. Here in the forest, the temperature was a few degrees lower, and that seemed to help cool her temper. She stopped walking and looked up through the towering lodgepole pines. "I'm sorry, God. I know I should check with You first thing when I start to get angry. And I don't mean to be thin skinned. But if Woody hadn't said what he —"

She shut her mouth, cutting off the excuse. Was she trying to repent of her behavior or trying to justify it instead?

"I'm full of good intentions." She began walking again, hands now clasped behind her back, and her gaze lowered. "What is it folks say? The road to hell is paved with good intentions? Reckon they're right about that."

With an inhaled breath, she turned around and started back toward the McKinley home. No point putting off what had to be done. If she'd learned anything in her lifetime, it was that obedience really was better than sacrifice, just like the Good Book said. Once she knew what God wanted done, it always made sense to act on it right away. Right now He wanted her to get right with her family — and Woody too.

Somehow she'd known she would find Gwen sitting on the veranda swing, waiting for her return. Cleo gave her a meek smile, and her sister nodded in understanding.

As Cleo went up the steps, she said, "I'm sorry for storming out that way, Gwennie."

"And I'm sorry I coerced you into wearing something you didn't want to wear."

"The dress wasn't all that bad. I shouldn't've made such a fuss about it." Cleo drew a deep breath and let it out. "I reckon I'd best go in and apologize to the rest of them while I'm at it."

"It can wait." Gwen patted the seat beside her. "Come and join me."

Cleo shrugged, then moved toward her sister.

"It's a beautiful day."

"Uh-huh."

"Can you believe that a year ago none of us had met Morgan or thought much about the resort? I certainly never dreamed that I would be doing anything other than teaching piano and writing for the newspaper. So much has happened in such a short space of time."

"True enough."

Gwen placed a hand on her stomach. "And more changes are coming."

"You haven't told anybody but the family, have you? About the baby, I mean."

"No, other than Doc Winston, just the family knows. I'm not too sure how some members of the town council will meet the news of my pregnancy. Not all of them are delighted to be working with a woman mayor in the first place. I don't want to give them another reason to doubt my abilities."

"Land o' Goshen! That just doesn't make sense. They've had the better part of a year to find out what you can do. What's having a baby got to do with you having a brain and the sense to use it? Makes me mad enough to spit to know they still haven't accepted you the way they ought."

Gwen laughed softly. "You expect too much too soon, Cleo. Remember, most women in America cannot even cast a vote.

I've only been in office nine months. Those men have a lifetime of thinking to change."

"I guess." Cleo gave a little push with her foot to set the swing in motion. "All the same . . ." She let the sentence fade into silence, unfinished. Gwen was right. Change took time. But an apology was always best when made sooner rather than later. "I'd better go speak my piece."

Gwen stopped the swing. "I'll go with you."

Inside, the remainder of the party had moved from dining room to parlor. Morgan was playing the piano while his sister looked over his shoulder, humming the melody. Woody and Cleo's father were seated at the far end of the room, deep in discussion, leaning toward each other in their chairs.

Cleo drew in a deep breath and strode across the room. Her father saw her and straightened. A moment later, Woody did the same. She met his gaze and said, "Woody, I'm right sorry for taking out my frustration on you. It wasn't right. I'm ashamed for snapping at you the way I did. I hope you'll accept my apology."

He stood. "I believe it is I who must apologize. I shouldn't have teased you. It isn't my place."

■ ■ ■ ■

Sherwood rather liked watching the play of emotions that crossed Cleo's face. She had such expressive dark-blue eyes. Mediterranean blue, like deep, deep waters. When she was angry, one could see the storm clouds gather in them. And when she was amused, they sparkled like stars in the heavens.

He gave his head a slight shake to clear his thoughts. "I accept your apology, Cleo, as I hope you will accept mine."

"Done." She held out her hand.

He wondered if he would ever get used to her forthright manner. Probably not. But he could cope with it for the next year.

"Done," he said as he took her hand in his and shook it.

TEN

Cleo tossed the saddle onto the gelding's back and reached beneath his belly for the cinch. The horse snorted and sidestepped.

"Easy, Buddy."

The black gelding was young and inexperienced, but he had lots of potential as a cattle horse. He was built for quick turns and had good stamina, the kind a cowboy needed when he was chasing strays up in the hills. Today Cleo planned to give Buddy his first lesson in herding cows.

As she slipped the bit into the horse's mouth, she heard men's laughter coming from the barn. Her father's and Woody's. She was tempted to join them, to find out what they found amusing, but she decided against it. *They* might have time to stand around jawing. She had too much work to do.

She took the reins in her left hand and swung onto the saddle. Buddy tossed his head and sidestepped again, and Cleo nudged his right side with her thigh and heel, moving him back to the left. Only after he was quiet and listening to her did she loosen the reins and allow him to start walking. Buddy was none too happy with the slow pace, but Cleo kept a firm rein. She made sure he understood that she was the boss.

Horse and rider followed the fence line for a good mile before Cleo gave Buddy leave to canter. The air, fresh with the green of spring, tugged at her hat and flowed cool over her cheeks. A grin curved the corners of her mouth. There was nothing in the world more satisfying than a fast ride on a good horse. Absolutely nothing.

The meadowland where the Arlington cattle grazed produced a high amount of forage every year, even without irrigation. The terrain was gently rolling, and the grasses waved in the breeze like the sea. Or at least like Cleo imagined the sea rolled; she'd never made it to the Pacific or Atlantic oceans. Gwen, raised in New Jersey, had told Cleo about her visits to the shore every summer. Maybe someday Cleo would see it for herself. But she had a hard time believing anything in the world could be prettier than what she was looking at right this minute.

Buddy had covered about five miles when Cleo reined in, bringing the gelding to a halt. She patted his neck and talked softly to him. "See those cows over there?"

The horse's ears flicked forward and back.

"Let's see if we can move one of them to the other side of the creek."

She pressed her heels to his sides, and after a few steps, Buddy broke into a jog. The cattle ignored their approach until they were about thirty or forty feet away. After that, heads came up and doleful eyes turned on horse and rider.

Cleo watched for the first cow to break. When it did, she sent Buddy after it, guiding him with the reins, her shifting weight, and the pressure of her legs. As she'd expected, the horse was a quick study. He cut off the heifer's escape, then spun on his back legs and darted in the opposite direction. Repeating the action time and again, they drove the young cow to the bank of the stream and finally across it. Cleo was breathing as hard as Buddy by the time they rode out of the water. The heifer cried her complaint as she trotted a safer distance away from her tormentors.

"Buddy." Cleo patted the horse's neck,

"Next to Domino, you just might turn out to be the best reining horse we've got."

The gelding snorted.

She gave the horse his head, letting him set the direction and pace, and unlike when they'd started out, Buddy seemed to prefer a sedate walk. That suited Cleo just fine. It gave her time to enjoy the scenery.

Although it was early in the season, some wildflowers were in bloom. Anemones, she thought they were called, lavender ones and white ones with bright yellow centers. They spilled across the mountain slopes and grasslands, splashes of vibrant color amidst the green.

Spring was Cleo's favorite season. She loved the promise of new life — calves, colts, puppies, kittens, leaves budding, flowers blooming. She loved the lengthened days and the shortened nights.

Spring was also the busiest part of the year on the Arlington ranch. Calves were branded and the herd culled. In previous years getting the selected cattle to market had meant almost a week on the trail, driving the herd south, out of the mountains and onto the high desert country of southern Idaho. Now that the railroad had brought a spur up to Bethlehem Springs, getting the cattle to market would be a much easier undertaking.

Truth be told, Cleo was going to miss those days-long cattle drives. She'd always liked sleeping under the stars and the camaraderie of the cowboys. And there was something about food on the trail that just seemed to taste better. Maybe she'd been born a generation or two too late. It would have been great to take part in one of those old drives from Texas to Montana, one or two thousand cattle crossing the vast prairies, fording the rivers, ten to twelve hours in the saddle. But those days were long gone, never to be seen again.

She gave her head a slow shake. Chances were if she'd been born a generation or two ago, she never would've been allowed to trail cattle anyway. She reckoned she was better off now, even if some folks around these parts did look at her like she was a two-headed calf.

"Come on, Buddy. We'd best be getting back." She turned the horse toward home and nudged him into a lope.

Sherwood lay on his stomach, his head turned to the right, his eyes closed. Warm, moist air hovered around him while a therapist — Eduardo by name — massaged Sherwood's right leg. More than once, he'd had to swallow a groan of complaint. But he would put up with anything if there was a chance it would make him more mobile. Imagine the satisfaction if he could return to England without a limp, his body healthy once more, no longer a broken man. Perhaps then the duke would find fewer reasons to dislike his youngest son.

His thoughts drifted to the previous Sunday and the family gathered around the table in the McKinley home. What would his father think of these people? Sherwood was sure even Morgan McKinley would fall a notch or two in the duke's estimation. Too informal, especially with those of the lower classes, and married to a woman without suitable family connections and proper breeding.

But Sherwood liked them. All of them. Even, albeit somewhat reluctantly, Cleo. The McKinleys and Arlingtons had been kind to him without showing pity, an emotion he loathed. He didn't want to be pitied. He'd felt enough of it for himself in those first days and weeks back from the trenches. Much of his wild behavior — the antics that had earned him the duke's anger and his banishment to America — had been a desperate attempt to keep self-pity from returning. If he drank enough, gambled enough, womanized enough, caroused enough, then he wouldn't consider how his life had changed. He wouldn't think about his pain or the activities he could no longer do. He wouldn't think about the friends who'd died in France while he'd been sent home to safety . . .

"Mr. Statham," Eduardo said, his voice soft in the dimly lit room, "let's have you roll onto your back, please."

Sherwood groaned as he obeyed.

"Now I'm going to help you with some stretching exercises. The more you move and use your leg, the more range of motion you will regain. When we're finished here, we'll have you relax in the tub." Eduardo waited a moment, then lifted Sherwood's right leg — one hand beneath his ankle, the other beneath his knee — and began to move it up and down.

Sherwood squeezed his eyes shut and gritted his teeth, swallowing another groan. His fingers gripped the sides of the raised bed. If Eduardo noticed his discomfort, he didn't let it stop him.

"I say . . . I do hope you . . . know what . . . you're doing."

Eduardo chuckled. "I assure you, Mr. Statham, I do. It will take time, but there will come a day when you thank me."

"I find that . . . hard to believe." He drew in a deep breath and opened his eyes. "How long . . . have you been . . . torturing the lame and infirm?"

The therapist grinned. "About six years now. After completing my medical training, I worked in a hospital in Boston where I grew up. But Mr. McKinley's offer to work at New Hope was one I couldn't refuse. He's a man of vision, and I believe in what he wants to accomplish here."

Another time, Sherwood might have asked questions about Morgan's vision, but for the moment, it took all his reserves not to complain about the pain that shot through muscle and sinew and bone, from the toes clear into his back. He squeezed his eyes shut and pictured himself striding into the duke's presence, whole and strong once again, and managed to swallow another groan.

Cleo rode Buddy up to the corral and dismounted. She patted the horse's neck once more before wrapping the reins around a rail.

"How did he do?"

She looked over her shoulder and saw her father's approach. "He's a natural." Returning her attention to the saddle, she draped the left stirrup over the seat and began to loosen the cinch. "By the end of summer, he could be the best horse we've got on the ranch. Excepting Domino, of course."

"Of course." Her father moved to stand near the gelding's head. "Sherwood should have a horse to use while he's with us."

She gave him a sharp look. "What for? He can't ride with that bum leg."

"Not yet, but eventually he might be able to, God willing. Morgan said Sherwood was a fine horseman before he was injured in the war."

"Dad, have you seen how hard it is for him to get into the buggy or climb up onto the wagon? He can barely do the chores I've given him. No way could he get onto a saddle horse."

"We have reason to believe his sessions up at New Hope will make him more flexible and build up his strength."

Cleo dragged the saddle from Buddy's back and willed herself not to say anything more about it.

"Before he gets back from the resort," her father continued, "choose two or three horses you think might suit him, and let him have his pick. I believe having a horse will give him something more to work toward."

"I'll do it." She turned on her heel. *But I*

still think it's a waste of time. With a shake of her head, she strode toward the barn.

Inside, she dropped the saddle onto a saddletree and then took a moment to look around. It didn't take long to ascertain that Woody had completed his chores before leaving for the resort. In fact, there hadn't been a day when he'd slacked off. She had to give him that much credit. Even when he was obviously hurting, he hadn't quit or complained. But getting up on a horse and riding with that bad leg? She didn't see how that was possible. Still, if that's what her dad wanted . . .

After giving Buddy a good rub down and turning him out to graze, she made a survey of the horses she thought might be suitable for Woody.

That big roan might be a good choice. The mare was sweet natured and easy going. Nothing startled or frightened her. But her height might be a problem. She was more than sixteen hands. It could be too much for Woody to mount her.

The dun at the far end of the second paddock might be a better choice. Wilson — named in honor of the president because they shared the same December birthday — was closer to fifteen hands and had a lope as easy as a rocking chair. He required a firmer hand than the roan, but he responded well when checked.

Lastly there was the bay gelding she'd bought at auction last fall. He was from thoroughbred stock and had the lines and look of a hunter. As it turned out, the bay wasn't much good around cattle, but he'd be a fine mount for anybody riding for pleasure rather than work.

She grabbed a rope from off a nearby post and went after the selected horses, bringing them one at a time into a corral. She'd just slipped the noose from the last one when she saw their buggy coming up the lane. Woody, back from New Hope. She moved away from the corral and awaited his arrival.

When the buggy came to a halt, she stepped up to the horse, taking hold of the reins. "So how was it? The spa, I mean."

"Delightful," Woody answered, but his eyes and the tone of his voice told a different story. And when he got out of the buggy, so did the way he moved.

"I'll unhitch the horse. Why don't you —"

"Thank you, Cleo, but I can manage. I'm the one who used the buggy. I'll be the one to take care of the horse."

"Suit yourself." She took a step backward, out of his way.

He nodded as he limped past her and began the process of freeing the horse from the traces.

"Dad wants you to pick out a saddle horse for you to use while you're here."

That made him look at her again.

She shrugged. "He figures that when your leg gets better you'll want to ride instead of traveling everywhere in the buggy or wagon." She pointed toward the corral. "I've got three there for you to choose from."

His gaze followed her gesture. After a period of silence, he said, "I'll look at them after I'm finished here."

"Whenever you're ready." It was obvious to Cleo that he didn't want her company. "When you've decided, turn them into that first paddock. Okay?"

"Yes. I'll see to it."

She turned and strode toward the house, leaving him to his work. Once inside, she went upstairs to wash off the dust of the day. Strange, the way she didn't notice the dirt as long as she was outside with the horses, but the instant she entered the house, she couldn't wait to be clean again.

Fifteen minutes later, her face and hands washed, her hair tidied, and wearing clean clothes, she entered her father's ground-floor office. He was seated at his desk as she'd expected him to be, a ledger book open before him.

"Woody's back," she said as she stepped through the doorway. "I told him to look over the horses I put in the corral. He said he would."

Her father leaned back and swiveled his chair toward her. "How did his first treatment go?"

"He didn't say, but he looked like it must've been rough."

"Morgan warned him it wouldn't be easy at first. You might want to give him a lighter workload for a week or two."

"Sure. Whatever you say." She turned her head toward the kitchen and sniffed the air. "Something smells mighty good."

"Cookie's got a ham in the oven."

"Mmm."

"My thoughts exactly." Her father swiveled back to his desk.

"Is there anything I can help you with in here?" Not that she would have been of much help. Cleo and numbers didn't mix well. She was an outdoor kind of gal and hated the idea of sitting down for hours to add, subtract, divide, or multiply. Having a tooth pulled sounded more fun to her.

"Don't think so. I'm trying to make up

my mind about culling more cows than usual."

Now, culling the herd was something she understood, and his suggestion surprised her. "Really? Why?"

"I think it might be a good idea. Don't want to overgraze, you know."

She said nothing more, but instead took the time to study her father. It occurred to her that he looked tired, that he'd looked extra tired for some while now. Maybe it was nothing. All the same, concern took up residence in a corner of her mind.

ELEVEN

Black clouds rolled in from the northwest on Saturday afternoon. The smell of impending rain reminded Sherwood of England, and he felt another twinge of homesickness as he leaned his shoulder against the doorjamb of the bunkhouse and stared across the valley.

What he wouldn't give for a proper English breakfast or a good cup of tea or a glass of port with his dinner. He wouldn't mind an evening at the theater or the opera either. Other than when he was in France and then the hospital, he couldn't recall a period of time when he'd gone so long without attending one or the other. And he missed people. Lots and lots of people. It wasn't uncommon for Dunacombe guests to come and stay for days or even weeks at a time. He wasn't used to the solitude of this place.

The yard was quiet and empty this afternoon. Randall and Allen had ridden into town after their work was done, and Stitch and Cleo hadn't returned from mending fences.

"Sherwood!"

He looked toward the house to see Griff standing on the porch.

"Come and join me."

With a glance toward the darkened sky, he pushed off the doorjamb and walked across the yard. By the time he got to the veranda, Griff was seated in one of the chairs, a mug of coffee in his left hand.

"I asked Cookie to brew some tea for you. It should be ready about now."

"I say. That was kind of you. I'll have a look." He opened the door and went inside, the way to the kitchen familiar to him now. Once there, he saw Cookie setting a small teapot onto a tray. "Griff told me there's tea to be found in here."

Cookie frowned. "Never understood anybody's hankerin' for that beverage. You're welcome to it."

"And I'm thankful." Sherwood took up the tray, complete with cup and a small pitcher of cream, and carried it out to the veranda.

When Griff saw him, he said, "Looks like Cleo and Stitch are going to get wet before

142

they make it back." As if to prove his point, drops of rain began to spatter the ground, raising little clouds of dust wherever they hit. "Hope they took their slickers with them."

Sherwood set the tray on the low, small table between two chairs. Then he sat and poured tea into the cup.

Griff released a sigh. "It's good to see the rain. Been a dry spring. But I wish it wasn't so blasted cold." He shivered, drank some coffee, then looked at Sherwood. "What's the weather like in the spring where you come from?"

"As many rainy days as sunny ones, I'd say."

"Tell me about your home."

"My home." Sherwood pondered the two words. He suspected they meant something different to Griff Arlington than they did to him. Dunacombe Manor had never seemed like home. Even as a boy he'd felt out of place there, despite wanting desperately to fit in.

"You don't need to tell me if you don't want to."

He looked over at Griff. "It isn't that, sir. I was simply wondering how to describe it. Dunacombe Manor has been the seat of the Dukes of Dunacombe since the late sixteen hundreds. It's large and drafty and has been remodeled numerous times over the past two hundred years." He paused, remembering the last time he'd been there. How cold and dark and grim it had seemed. "The war has caused a shortage of coal, and the plants in the great conservatory have died for lack of warmth. In years past, however, they were my mother's pride and joy."

"Gwen has a great appreciation for growing things too. You'll see that for yourself this summer." Griff held the coffee cup to his lips. "Go on. Tell me more. It must have been fun, growing up in such a large home. Lots of places to play hide-and-seek."

"That was probably true for my brothers. They are much closer in age to one another than to me. By the time I might have enjoyed such escapades, they were off to boarding school for much of the year, and when they were home, they didn't want their younger brother tagging along with them." He released a small chuckle. "I guess I did my share of hiding and seeking with different members of the household staff, just to spice things up. The estate maintains a staff of over thirty, and they all live in."

"More than thirty? That's a lot of mouths to feed."

Sherwood nodded. "Indeed. Thankfully,

as the youngest of four sons, I need never be responsible for the property or the people employed there."

"It doesn't bother you that you can't inherit a title and its estate?"

"Not at all."

Griff watched him, as if weighing the truth of his words.

Sherwood could have assured his employer that he meant what he said. At one time, he might have answered differently, but no more. There were benefits that came with being a son of the privileged class, of course, and he'd never been afraid to take advantage of them. But now? Now he'd begun to believe there were more advantages to be found in being one's own man, free from the dictates of the peerage. Griff Arlington was such a man. He worked right alongside the other ranch hands, as did his daughter.

"So tell me, Sherwood. What do you plan to do when you return to England?"

"I suppose I shall have to practice law. It's what I'm trained for and what my father expects of me."

Griff rubbed his chin. "Not much enthusiasm there. A man ought to like the work he does, if at all possible."

"Ah, but things are different here in America, I believe."

145

"Are they?"

Sherwood thought of Cleo in her mannish attire, and he smiled. "You can be sure of it, Griff. Things are very different, indeed."

The rain ran off Cleo's hat brim, a steady sheet of water before her eyes. It hit the back of her neck and slid down her spine. Even the slicker couldn't keep her completely dry — not when the wind drove the rain at an angle. Neither she nor Stitch tried to carry on a conversation. Both were focused on getting back to the ranch as quickly as they could. And it wouldn't be fast enough to suit her.

Half an hour later when they rode into the yard, Cleo saw Woody standing on the veranda. He called to her, but she didn't stop. She wanted to get into the barn and take care of Domino. After that, she was going to soak in a hot bath until the chill left her bones.

As soon as they were in the barn, she hopped down from the saddle, took off her hat, and shook it, then removed the slicker and laid it over a stall rail. "Stitch, why don't you —"

"Cleo." Woody appeared in the barn doorway, even wetter than she after his dash

146

across the yard. "You're needed in the house."

"I've got to take care of Domino first."

"It's your father. He's fallen ill."

She let go of the cinch and whirled around. "Dad?" Not waiting for an answer, she dashed out of the barn and across the yard. Inside the house, she saw Cookie at the top of the stairs. "What is it? What's wrong with Dad?"

"He was sitting on the porch, talking to Sherwood, and started feeling chilled. He thought it was the weather making him cold, but it wasn't. He's running a fever. A mighty high one."

Cleo bolted up the stairs, taking them two at a time. Her father was never sick, certainly never sick enough to take to his bed in the middle of the day. She couldn't remember the last time he'd seen the doctor. Maybe as far back as when he broke a couple ribs after falling off a horse. She'd been about thirteen or fourteen at the time.

When she entered the bedroom, she saw that someone had closed the curtains over the window, covering the room in shadows. Her father lay in his bed, face turned toward her, eyes closed. He shivered beneath several blankets.

"Dad?" She moved to the side of the bed,

leaned over, and placed her hand on his forehead. He was burning up. She looked over her shoulder. Woody stood in the doorway next to Cookie. "Send one of the boys for Doc Winston. And somebody better let Gwen know too."

"I'll go," Woody volunteered.

"No, it'll be faster on horseback, and you're not up to that kind of ride. Send Stitch or Randall."

"I'll take care of it."

Cleo turned back to the bed and knelt on the floor. "Dad? Can I get you anything?"

He opened his eyes for a moment but didn't answer. In truth, she wasn't sure he saw her.

"Cookie, bring me a bowl of water and a cloth to put on his head."

"Right away."

She leaned closer, whispering, "It's okay, Dad. We'll have you right as rain in no time at all."

Silently, she began to pray, asking God's mercy for her father, praying for His healing touch. She told herself she worried for nothing. People caught colds and then were better in a few days. But her dad looked so pale and haggard. She couldn't remember him looking this way before, not even when

148

he'd broken those ribs and been in such pain.

Cookie returned with the bowl of water and several cloths. As he set the items on the stand next to the bed, he said, "I'll warm a brick in the oven to put near his feet. Maybe that will stop the chills."

"Yes, please do that."

The cook's hand alighted on her shoulder. "Don't you go worryin' now. Griff's a tough old bird. He'll shake this thing."

Cleo nodded, but she wasn't comforted. She wouldn't be comforted until the doctor arrived and told her that her father's illness was something minor.

Sherwood remained on the porch, watching the rain make large, muddy puddles in the yard. More than once he started to go into the house. Each time he stopped himself. He would wait here for Stitch's return with the physician. Perhaps then he would have an opportunity to inquire about Griff.

Logically, he knew it wasn't his fault that his employer was sick. Yet it felt as if he were to blame. If he'd noticed Griff's gray pallor a little sooner, if he'd paid attention to the shaking of the older man's hands as he'd lifted the mug to take a sip of coffee, if he'd returned to the bunkhouse as the temperature dropped lower so that Griff had gone inside earlier.

"Sherwood?"

He turned toward the doorway where Cookie stood.

"Cleo wants to see you. She's still up with Griff."

"How much longer before the doctor arrives?"

Cookie shrugged. "Hard to tell, but I don't reckon it'll be much sooner than an hour. Depends if Stitch found him in his office or if he was out on a call. Doc's got a motorcar now, so he might get here faster than I expect."

Sherwood pushed off the railing, went inside, and climbed the stairs as quickly as his right leg allowed. When he reached Griff's bedroom, he stopped at the doorway. Cleo was kneeling beside the bed, holding a cloth on Griff's forehead and speaking softly — too softly for him to make out the words.

He cleared his throat to draw her notice.

She looked over her shoulder. Were there tears in her eyes? He couldn't be sure in the dim light.

She rose and came to him. "Can you tell me what happened? Cookie said you were with him when he started feeling ill."

Granted, he hadn't known Cleo Arlington

for long. Only for a couple of weeks. But he would have given odds that she never showed fear, even if she felt it. He saw it now. Her vulnerability pierced his heart. It made him want to take her in his arms and promise that he would make sure everything was all right. Which would have been a lie. No one could promise her that. Not and be telling the truth. Look at him. Look at the world. There were no promises that life would turn out the way one wanted it to.

He cleared his throat a second time. "We were sitting on the veranda, having a warm drink. He seemed fine at first, asking me questions about my home and my future profession. I'm not sure when I noticed that his hands were shaking and that his color was bad. Then he said he wasn't feeling well. He got up to go inside, and he fainted."

"Fainted? Dad *fainted?*"

"Fortunately, he fell backward into the chair."

She worried her lower lip between her teeth.

"Cookie and I got him up the stairs and into bed. I was on my way to the bunkhouse to send Randall or Allen to look for you when you returned."

She looked toward her father again. "I've never seen him like this. His skin is hot to

151

the touch, like he's on fire, but he keeps shivering like he's about to freeze to death."

"You look cold yourself. You should go change out of those wet things. I can stay with Griff until you get back."

"No," she replied softly. "I don't want to leave him."

"Then at least sit down. You look unsteady on your feet."

He carried a straight-backed chair from beneath the window to the side of the bed. Cleo sat upon it and immediately began tending to her father again, moistening the cloth, wringing it out, and placing it upon Griff's forehead.

Sherwood's presence had already been forgotten. Quietly, he left the room.

TWELVE

Sherwood heard that Gwen McKinley wanted to come to the ranch to help take care of their father as he recovered from the influenza, but Cleo and the doctor forbade her from doing so, lest she put her unborn child in danger. Sherwood also knew without asking that Cleo slept only a little each night. He saw the exhaustion in her face and in the way she moved — the few times he saw her at all.

It was a warm day in early May, ten days after Griff first fell ill, when he sent for Sherwood to come see him. Arriving at the bedroom, Sherwood rapped on the doorjamb. "You wanted to see me, sir?"

The older man sat in a chair by the window, his legs covered by a light blanket, his feet propped on a footstool. It looked as if he'd lost a significant amount of weight over the course of his illness. Since there hadn't been any fat on the man to begin with, the difference in his appearance was startling.

Griff motioned for Sherwood to enter. "Come over here and sit down." He pointed to a chair opposite him.

Sherwood obliged without hesitation.

"I wanted to thank you," Griff said.

"For what, sir?"

Griff smiled, then began to cough, a hacking sound ripped from the lungs, and had to wait a short spell before he could speak again. "Sorry." He drew a careful breath. "I . . . I thought we were through with that 'sir' business."

Sherwood inclined his head in agreement.

"Good. Now, I have a favor to ask of you."

"Of course. Whatever you need, Griff, if it's in my power."

"The doctor has confined me to my room for another ten days or so, and I need someone to take over the bookkeeping and manage my correspondence. I thought, with your education and legal training, you might be able to handle it. I assume you're good with numbers."

"Well . . . yes, sir. I believe I am. But I haven't been in America very long, and I don't know anything about operating a cattle ranch. Are you sure Cleo shouldn't —"

154

"Cleo has too much on her slender shoulders as it is, and I need my ranch hands doing the work they were hired to do. Roundup and branding isn't that far off and Cleo can't spend time pushing paper around when she's needed out there working with the boys. Besides, she detests record keeping and being shut up in an office."

Sherwood was different from Cleo in that regard. Adding numbers in columns sounded much more interesting to him than feeding horses, mucking out stalls, and cleaning tack. As a boy he'd sometimes helped Bottomley, the manor's overseer, with his ledgers. This couldn't be much different, could it?

Griff continued. "I'll be right here in my room if you have questions. And after I'm back on my feet, at least I'd know there was someone who could fill in if something else happened to me. Being sick has reminded me that I'm not as young as I used to be."

It had been a long time since anyone had been as kind to Sherwood as Griff Arlington, and there wasn't any way he could turn down the request, even if he wanted to. And he didn't want to.

"I shall be glad to help you, sir. Whatever you need and for as long as you need."

"Wonderful." Griff leaned forward in his

chair and offered Sherwood his right hand.

He shook it and returned the older man's grin.

"Dad," Cleo said as she stepped into the room, "you're supposed to be resting. What are you doing?"

"I've just hired Sherwood as ranch manager."

Cleo's eyes widened. So did Sherwood's.

Ranch manager? Griff hadn't used that term earlier. If he had, it might have given him pause. Was there more to this than bookkeeping and correspondence? But it was too late to change his mind. He'd already agreed to do whatever Griff needed.

Before either Sherwood or Cleo could say anything, Griff had another coughing spell, so hard this time it brought tears to his eyes and left him gasping for air at the end of it.

"You need to get back in bed, Dad. You've been up long enough." Cleo looked at Sherwood, accusation in her eyes. "And you should go so he can rest."

"Of course. I'll —"

"Wait," Griff interrupted in a hoarse whisper. "I want you to go downstairs to my office and acquaint yourself with my files and ledgers. Go through everything. Spend the day there. Tomorrow morning —" He looked pointedly at his daughter, stopping any objection before it could be spoken, then turned back to Sherwood. "— you and I can go over any questions you might have."

Sherwood nodded, then glanced at Cleo, who stood with her arms crossed over her chest, looking less than pleased with the two men in the room. He decided to make a silent and hasty retreat.

"Ranch manager? Dad, what were you thinking? He doesn't know anything about running a ranch. He's so green we ought to keep him watered so he can sprout."

Her father shook his head as he rose from the chair. "There's a lot more to that young man than you give him credit for. He's suited for the task, Cleo. Give him a chance and you'll see." He waved her away with his hand. "Now that's the end of it. I've made my decision."

She pressed her lips together, swallowing another protest. Her father's voice told her that further argument would be futile. He'd made up his mind. And maybe it was just as well. It meant she wouldn't be Woody's boss any longer. She could go about her daily business without having to think about what the dude should be doing. That would be nice for a change.

Once her dad was in bed again, his back braced with several pillows, Cleo leaned down and kissed his forehead. "I don't want your mind turning to anything about the ranch for the rest of the day."

"Yes, ma'am." He smiled at her, relieving the sting of his earlier brusqueness.

She returned the smile. More than once since he'd taken sick, she'd wondered if he would make it. He still looked much too frail. Griff Arlington had always been a rock, strong and unbeatable. If she were to lose him . . . The prospect didn't bear thinking about.

"Cookie's made chicken soup for lunch. I'll bring you some soon."

"Just a little. I don't have much of an appetite yet."

"And you never will if you don't build up your strength."

Her father gave her another smile.

She swallowed more admonitions and instead gave him good news. "The doctor says it's safe for Gwen to come visit. She'll be here on Thursday as usual. The waiting to see you has just about driven her mad."

"I've missed her." He closed his eyes and slid down a little ways in the bed. "Always miss my girls when they're away."

Cleo waited for him to say something

158

more, but he appeared to have fallen asleep. She turned and silently left the bedroom.

Downstairs, she paused outside her father's office. Ever since she was a little girl, she'd loved to visit her dad in this dark-paneled room with its big oak desk, filing cases, and shelves lined with books on animal husbandry, water management, veterinary practices, and more. The room had a unique smell — woodsy, leathery, dusty, all mixed together. And Dad always kept a sack of lemon drops in the lower right drawer of his desk. She loved those sweet-tart candies. They came with a lifetime of great memories.

She opened the door and looked in. Woody sat at her father's desk, a ledger book open before him.

"Why did he ask you to do this?"

He looked up, but he didn't answer her question.

She took two steps into the room. "Did you tell him you wanted to manage his books? What are you up to, anyway?"

At that, his mouth twisted. "Nothing. Cleo, I did not ask for this task. He offered it."

"Why?"

"I believe he thinks my education and legal training will help me do it right."

He could have asked me. Disappointment sluiced through Cleo. *He* should *have asked me.*

The thought surprised her. If her dad had asked her, she would have given him half a dozen reasons why she didn't want the job and shouldn't be the one to have it. She hated being shut up inside. She wasn't good with figures. And she was much happier working with the horses than doing anything else.

Still, it felt wrong for the position to go to Woody, of all people.

As if reading her mind, he said, "Do you think me incapable of this too?"

"What? No."

"Do you think I would steal from you or your father?"

"Of course not."

"Well, you thought I was — how did you phrase it? Oh, yes, 'Up to something.' You must have meant something bad."

She didn't like the way his words made her feel. Because he was right. That was what she'd meant. She'd accused him of ulterior motives, although she hadn't put it in quite those terms.

"Cleo." Woody rose from the chair, his voice stiff. "Despite what you think of me, I won't fail your father. I owe him for his many kindnesses to me. I know that I am not here because the ranch needed a new employee to clean the stalls in your barn. My father imposed me upon Morgan and Morgan sent me to you."

She saw it then, the pain he tried so hard not to let others see. It was there for only a moment, but long enough for her to recognize it. Not the pain of his war wounds; that would have been bad enough. No, this was the pain brought on by his father's rejection. She recognized it because she, too, had known the rejection of a parent. Her own mother had walked away from her when Cleo was two and hadn't looked back.

Cleo looked at him, wordless. In an instant, her resentment faded, and instead she found herself wanting to offer . . . what? Comfort? Friendship born from a shared experience? It was more than pity, she realized. More than compassion. She felt something she couldn't describe — and wasn't sure she welcomed.

Woody's gaze grew more intense, as if he too realized something was changing between them. The air in the room grew thick.

Cleo took a step backward. "I . . . I shouldn't have questioned Dad's judgment. I'm sure he knows what he's doing." Feeling oddly unsteady, she spun around and left the office as fast as possible.

"Extraordinary." Sherwood settled onto the chair.

He'd actually found himself wanting to kiss Cleo. That was more than extraordinary. It was preposterous. She was the *last* woman he would ever find attractive. He liked voluptuous females, women who *looked* like women — long hair and pretty dresses and dainty shoes and fashionable hats. Not to mention that he didn't need any sort of involvement with his employer's daughter. He was far from England and virtually penniless. Wasn't that enough? Additional complications in his life were most unwelcome.

He raked the fingers of both hands through his hair, hoping at the same time to mentally rake the image of Cleo's rosy, rather full lips, from his memory.

"Extraordinary, indeed."

Thirteen

Gwen arrived at the ranch on Thursday before ten in the morning. After giving Cleo a quick hug, she hurried up the stairs to their father's bedroom. Cleo followed right behind.

Gwen sat on the side of the bed and took their father's left hand between both of hers. "I've been beside myself with worry, Dad, ever since I learned you were ill. It's been dreadful, not being allowed to see you before this."

"You did right not to come," he answered. "You gotta take care of that baby you're carrying."

Cleo leaned her right shoulder against the doorjamb and observed her sister and their father. She took great pleasure in seeing the two of them together. She liked knowing they were so close and loving, despite all the years apart. Too bad the same couldn't be said about the remaining two members of the Arlington family. Cleo and her mother were oil and water — too different to mix well. They'd found that out when Elizabeth Arlington came to Bethlehem Springs for Gwen's wedding, then extended her visit for a number of months. Elizabeth had spent much of that time trying to change Cleo into a mirror image of her twin. Agony. Sheer agony.

Most of the time, Cleo could think about her mother without feeling hurt. But two days ago, when she'd been with Woody in her dad's office, his secret pain had reminded her of the old wound she kept hidden. Not that she was one to dwell on such thoughts. Her mother was what she was, and Cleo was what she was. And hadn't God allowed her to be raised by a dad who loved her and wanted what was best for her?

"Are you eating enough?" Gwen asked, drawing Cleo's attention to the present.

"I'm getting my appetite back."

Gwen glanced toward the doorway, and Cleo gave her the slightest of nods.

"And enough sleep?"

"That's about all I do. And cough. Sleep and cough."

"But Doc Winston says you're getting better?"

"Yes, Gwen. I'm getting better, but staying in this bedroom night and day may drive me mad before too much longer. I'm not used to inactivity."

Cleo said, "Maybe, but if you do too much too soon, Doc says you could have a relapse. So right here's where you're gonna stay."

He gave her a scowl that had little punch to it. "My illness has created a tyrant."

"Better believe it." Cleo pushed off the doorjamb. "I'll leave you two to visit for a spell while I tend to some chores. Gwennie, I reckon you and I will eat lunch downstairs. Don't want to wear Dad out with too long of a visit."

"No, of course not."

When Cleo reached the bottom of the stairs, her gaze moved toward the closed door of her father's office. Woody was in there. She supposed he was working hard, although there was no way she could prove it. It felt strange, knowing he was in the house so much of the time, although she saw less of him now than when he'd helped her out around the barn and paddocks.

She felt a strange sensation down deep in her belly, like the feeling she got riding a bronc — that moment when horse and rider fell toward the earth a split second after hanging suspended in air. She liked that feeling when breaking a wild horse. She

165

didn't much care for it now.

She grabbed her hat from the chair where she'd dropped it a short while ago and slapped it onto her head. Then she went outside and headed for the nearest corral. Star, the sorrel mare whose leg she'd been doctoring for a number of weeks, was alone in the enclosure. When the horse saw Cleo's approach, she gave her head a toss, as if to say, *Go away.*

"Not today, girl. Today you get to work a bit."

She grabbed the lunge line from a fence post before entering the corral. The mare sidled away from her.

"Easy, there."

Star turned first one way, then another, but there was nowhere for her to go, no way to escape Cleo. Soon enough, the rope was attached to the mare's halter, and Cleo began walking her in a counter clockwise circle around the corral. No sign of a limp. Cleo hadn't expected there would be. She let out the line as she stepped into the center of the corral.

"Giddup there." She clucked her tongue and swirled the end of the rope, urging the mare into a jog.

They circled the corral a number of times before Cleo stopped the horse and changed to a clockwise direction. All the while she kept her gaze glued to the mare's left hind leg.

"I say. She's looking topnotch."

At the sound of Woody's voice, Cleo felt that falling sensation again. She didn't allow herself to look his way. Nor did she reply.

"You must be rather pleased with her progress."

How could she ignore that? "Yeah."

"Will you use her when you drive the cattle to market?"

Cleo slowed Star to a walk and shortened the space between them. "No. I don't want to take any chances with her that soon."

"When exactly will the drive take place?"

What was with all his questions? Couldn't he go back to his bookkeeping and leave her in peace?

"It would help me, you see, as I try to budget the expenses and income. Should I ask your father? I didn't wish to interrupt his visit with Mrs. McKinley but —"

"In two weeks." She turned to face him. "We have a roundup twice a year. Normally we sell our mature cattle in the fall after they've had a chance to fatten up. But Dad decided we needed to cull more of the herd this spring, have fewer cows grazing the land this summer. I guess he feels the herd's grown too large."

"There does seem to be somewhat of a cash-flow problem at present."

. "There is?" Cleo shook her head. "You must have figured wrong."

"I don't believe so."

Woody had to be mistaken. If there were financial concerns, her father would have said something to her. Besides, Woody had only been studying the ranch accounts for a few days. He couldn't begin to understand everything this soon.

She slipped the halter from Star's head. "I'll talk to Dad about it later. I don't want him bothered today. Not while Gwen's here."

"As you wish."

She didn't like the way he watched her, couldn't seem to draw a breath while being studied by those bothersome green eyes of his, didn't care for that funny sensation in her belly. Why had being around him begun to make her feel all odd and discombobulated? Just because she'd realized they had one little thing in common was no reason for her to go soft in the head when he was around.

She liked it better when Woody made her madder than a rained-on rooster. She understood that. After all, any greenhorn from England who was underfoot would make a hard-working wrangler feel the same way. But this strange sensation in her belly? She didn't know what to make of it, and she hoped it would go away. Soon.

Sherwood wasn't wrong about the financial condition of the Arlington ranch. Rich in land and livestock Griff might be, but at the moment, he was cash poor. It didn't surprise Sherwood. In England, the landed gentry often had threadbare pockets. The Arlingtons weren't in danger of losing their ranch — the situation wasn't so serious as that — but he had no doubt Griff was culling the herd this spring for the money they would bring at market.

Bottomley, who knew a thing or two about livestock management, had once explained to Sherwood that a man had to balance a need for cash against the future productivity of the livestock in question. Selling off too many cows, sheep, hogs, or chickens that could be used to replenish a farm's livestock could permanently eliminate future income, bringing about even greater hardship at a later time.

Seated at his employer's desk again, Sherwood wished he could talk to Griff now, while his thoughts were fresh. He needed to know what bills to pay and what could wait until after the cattle were sold. But Cleo had made her wishes clear. He would have to wait.

He heard a knock, and as he looked toward the office door, it opened to reveal Gwen McKinley.

"Dad told me you're handling the paperwork for him while he's recovering. I'm glad to know he needn't worry about it."

"I'm doing the best I can." He rose from the chair.

"And how is your leg? Is the therapy helping?"

"Yes, I believe it is. At the very least, I'm not dreading the exercises quite as much as I did two weeks ago."

"I'm glad, Lord Sherwood."

"Gwennie," Cleo called from another room, "come along. Your lunch is getting cold."

Gwen smiled at him. "I imagine that means your lunch is getting cold as well."

"I hadn't realized it was that time." He glanced toward the clock on the desk. Noon already.

"Would you care to join us?"

He shook his head. "That's kind of you, Mrs. McKinley, but I believe I'll eat with the other men in the kitchen."

She gave him a nod before disappearing from the doorway.

Sherwood closed the open file folder on the desk and left the office. When he pushed open the door to the kitchen, he found the other ranch hands already at the table, plates of food in front of them. They welcomed him, and then resumed eating. For a time, the only sounds in the room were those of knives and forks scraping against plates. Sherwood was content to join them in silence while they ate.

His thoughts settled on Cleo. He hoped her sister's visit would cheer her and ease the worry she carried. It had seemed to Sherwood that her slight shoulders would buckle under the weight of it these past twelve days. He'd missed seeing her smile, missed the confident way she usually carried herself, even missed the times she'd treated him as if she thought he couldn't tell the front end of a cow from the rear.

He wished he hadn't mentioned his concern about cash flow to her. The task of managing the financial affairs of the ranch had been given to him by her father. He shouldn't have added to her worries. He should have guessed Griff hadn't told her why he was culling more cows than was normal.

While he couldn't undo the mistake he'd made in telling her, he could make sure he found a way to stretch resources until the sale of the cattle brought in the needed reserves. He could make sure he didn't add any more worries to those Cleo already carried. He would work around the clock if necessary to make certain Griff Arlington found the ranch accounts in a better state than they'd been when he fell ill.

When the meal was done and the cowboys returned to their work outside, Sherwood went to the office at the other end of the house and renewed his efforts to balance cash on hand against expenses.

Griff awakened to a room filled with shadows. How long had he slept? If he judged the light correctly, the dinner hour had come and gone. He scooted up in bed, resting his back against the pillows, making sure to keep his breathing shallow. Deep breaths could send him into a coughing fit in an instant.

It worried him some, this lingering weakness and incessant cough. Not that he was a man unaware of his own mortality. Sickness came to almost everyone at some point, and death came to all without exception. Although he had no fear of dying — his faith was too strong for that — he didn't care much for the idea that he might be less than productive in his waning years.

But his illness had brought about even more concern for Cleo. He'd had plenty of time, lying here in this bed while recuperating, to think upon what would happen to his eldest daughter — the older twin by ten minutes — when the Lord called him home to heaven. Cleo was very much her own woman, something he'd encouraged in her, perhaps more than he should have. She was smart, even without a fancy education. She had horse sense, that one, and seldom in her life had anyone been able to pull the wool over her eyes. She was more than capable, mentally and physically, of running this ranch. All the same, he would feel better about the future if she were married to a good man. If she had the companionship of a husband who loved and cherished her, Griff would rest easier.

Although she'd never said as much, he knew that King fellow had wounded Cleo's heart. In some ways, Griff blamed himself for that. He should have judged the man's character better. He should have sent him packing long before the cowboy got caught in a noose of his own making. Thankfully, Cleo seemed to have moved past her hurt. She might be ready to fall in love were she to have the opportunity, were she to meet the sort of man who could look past her trousers and independent thinking and see the woman inside.

But where was such a man to be found? The men of Crow County were all blind as bats, every last man jack of them. Had to be if they couldn't see the beauty in Cleo for themselves.

Griff reached for the glass of water on the stand next to the bed and took several sips as his thoughts drifted to his other daughter. Gwen hadn't wanted to marry and had expressed her negative feelings about matrimony on many occasions, both to him and to others. So everyone had been surprised — no one more so than Gwen herself — when she fell in love and married a newcomer to Bethlehem Springs. Since no eligible bachelor in the county had the good sense to woo and win Cleo in a similar manner, it seemed another newcomer was needed.

A newcomer . . . hmm . . . Sherwood Statham was a newcomer.

The thought made him laugh out loud. Cleo and Woody? He thought it more likely that pigs would learn to fly before those two could even see eye to eye, let alone fall in love. No, the man for Cleo had yet to be seen. Griff would have to pray God would bring him to Bethlehem Springs, and the sooner the better.

FOURTEEN

Sherwood was surprised when Griff asked him to continue with the ranch bookkeeping even after the older man left his sickbed and became more active. Surprised and pleased. He'd discovered he wasn't merely good at working with figures. He enjoyed it. Enjoyed the challenge it presented. And with Griff's insights and instruction, he was learning more every day about managing a ranch.

He had to admit, however, that he was also glad to resume some of his former chores, especially as the weather warmed and the days lengthened. After a month of therapy at New Hope, his leg had improved far more than he'd thought possible. Far more than the physicians in England had given him reason to think attainable. The pain was tolerable now and the knee's range of motion at least twenty-five percent better than when he'd begun treatment at the spa.

Not as much as he might wish — he would never be completely free of a limp — but some change was better than nothing.

Today he planned to test his recovery.

Cleo and the cowboys, including a number of temporary hands, had ridden out this morning to begin the spring round up. Only Griff, Cookie, and Sherwood remained at the ranch house. This was the perfect time to see if he could mount a horse without help.

He led the bay gelding out of the paddock and into the barn, desiring to be out of view. There, he brushed the horse's coat clean before placing a blanket and saddle onto his back. After cinching the saddle, he checked the stirrups, lengthening the right one more than the left to accommodate the stiffness of his leg.

The gelding tossed his head when Sherwood tried to slide the bit into its mouth, but with persistence, Sherwood prevailed. Now if only he could prevail in his quest to ride the animal.

Gathering the reins in his left hand, he took hold of the left stirrup and placed his foot in it. The bay snorted, and for a moment, Sherwood feared the horse would move too far and cause him to topple. Better to make a quick attempt to mount up.

It felt awkward, getting his right leg over the horse's back, but all in all, it wasn't as difficult as he'd feared. Even getting his right boot into the stirrup went without a hitch, although his leg complained with a couple of jolts of pain. Pain he ignored.

"I say, old boy. It's time you and I became acquainted." He rode out of the barn and turned the gelding down the road toward town.

By heavens! It was wonderful to be astride a horse again. Until this moment, he hadn't known how much he'd missed it. While he'd remembered the thrill of taking a horse over a hedge or galloping across an open field, it had often seemed like the memories belonged to someone else. Now he knew for sure they were his.

The gelding pranced and bobbed his head, anxious to have his rider ease up on the reins, asking to be allowed to run, but Sherwood wasn't ready for that yet. He didn't want his first attempt to sit a horse to end with him lying in the middle of the road.

He glanced at his right leg while shifting slightly in the stock saddle. The seat was broader than the type of saddle he'd used in England and the stirrups felt strange, but he thought he would get used to the differences quickly enough. And if he began to lose his seat, the horn could prove quite useful to him.

He kept a firm grip on the reins, holding the horse to a prancing walk for the better part of two miles. Then he turned back to the ranch. Perhaps tomorrow he would ride farther down the road. And maybe he would surprise everyone by riding his horse into town on Sunday, although it might be a trifle soon for that.

Sweat trickled down the sides of Cleo's face and dust coated her tongue as she trailed the herd toward the ranch house. But while today was hot and tiring, tomorrow would begin the hard work — branding the calves and separating out the cattle that would go to market. Those cows would be corralled in large pens south of the ranch house until it was time to drive them into Bethlehem Springs for shipment by cattle car to the stockyards.

A yearling calf darted away from the herd, and Cleo went after it. Domino was the best reining horse she had trained over the past fifteen years — which was saying something — and it took next to nothing to steer the pinto one way or another. A touch of her heel, a shift in her weight, the reins upon his neck. The most important thing she could do was hang on because when the gelding changed direction, he did it on a dime.

Her pulse raced by the time the renegade calf rejoined the herd, and she loved the feeling. There was nothing like the joy she experienced when riding a well-trained steed. No doubt about it. God had done His best work when He created the horse.

She saw Stitch riding toward her and returned his grin.

"Cleo, that horse of yours is something to behold when he's workin'."

"I know."

"He'd bring a pretty penny if you ever wanted to sell him."

"I'll never sell Domino, Stitch. You know that."

"Yeah. I know." They rode in silence for a short while, then the cowboy asked, "How's Griff doin'? I haven't talked to him in a couple of days."

"He's getting stronger. Doc Winston seemed pleased last time he was out to see him, but he told Dad he must continue to rest for another week or so."

"That can't be sittin' well with him."

Cleo laughed as she shook her head. "No, it isn't."

"I can tell Griff's taken a real liking to Sherwood. I would've sworn he'd be long gone by now. Glad I was wrong. Seems he's been good for Griff. And I reckon you're thankful your dad's got help with his record keepin' so he's not tryin' to do it all himself." He scratched his grizzled chin. "Me and numbers don't get on well together. Guess that's why I never hankered to have a spread of my own. But Sherwood seems to like it."

Cleo had noticed the same thing. In those first days after her father asked him to act as ranch manager, Woody had looked overwhelmed by the prospect. No longer. In fact, whenever she saw him, she couldn't help thinking how well he looked — as if he stood a little straighter, held his head a little higher. And Stitch was right about something else. Her father had taken a real liking to Woody. The two of them were spending more and more time together.

"Listen," Stitch said, breaking into her thoughts. "If you're wantin' to get on back to see how your dad is, why don't you ride on ahead. Me and the boys can bring the herd the rest of the way without any trouble."

He was right. She did want to know how her dad had fared today. This was the first time she'd ventured farther than the barn and corrals since he first came down with the influenza. And without her there, who knew what sort of mischief he might get himself into.

"I'll see you there." She pressed her heels into Domino's sides. The pinto shot forward and galloped around the edge of the herd, headed for home and a bucket of oats.

The May afternoon was warm, the sun casting a buttery yellow hue across the valley, and Sherwood had joined Griff on the veranda — as had become their usual practice once Griff was allowed out of bed — to discuss ranch business.

"I walked that piece of land earlier today," Sherwood said. "It seems to me that with the addition of another two or three acres and the use of irrigation, you could increase your yield of hay per season significantly while at the same time lowering your annual expense."

Griff cocked an eyebrow. "And you base that upon what?"

"I was reading one of the books you have in your office."

"Ah."

"I admit I'm not a farmer, but what the

author had to say made a great deal of sense to me."

"You surprise me, Sherwood."

"Why is that, sir?"

"To be honest, when you first arrived, I didn't hold out a lot of hope for you to settle in the way you have."

"To be honest, I didn't hold out much hope for it either."

They laughed in unison, but Griff's laughter ended in a series of dry coughs. When the spell was under control, he drew a long, slow breath through his nose and released it through his mouth.

"Maybe you should go inside, sir."

Griff waved away the suggestion. "I'm tired of being cooped up."

Sherwood nodded. No one had to explain to him what that was like. His time spent recovering in the hospital had almost made him go insane.

"I informed Cleo this morning that I'll be joining the rest of you for church come Sunday." Griff cleared his throat. "I've been away too many Sundays. I miss hearing Reverend Barker's sermons."

"He does give a man much to think about."

A smile crept into the corners of Griff's mouth. "Tell me what you mean."

183

Sherwood wasn't sure he could explain what he meant. Only that the vicar at Dunacombe wasn't anywhere near the preacher that Reverend Barker was. Each Sunday, Reverend Barker had challenged Sherwood with his words, enough so that he'd returned the following Sunday to hear more.

It was at that moment Cleo loped her horse into the yard, saving Sherwood from having to come up with an answer. When she saw the two men on the veranda, she rode over to the house before dismounting. "How're you feeling, Dad?" She climbed the steps to join them.

"Fine. I'm enjoying the weather."

"You aren't overdoing, are you?"

"No, my girl, I'm not. Do you think sitting on the porch is more strenuous than sitting in my room?"

Cleo smiled as she leaned over to kiss her father's forehead. "No, I guess not."

"Sherwood and I were discussing the possibility of putting a few more acres into hay production and digging some irrigation ditches."

"You were?"

The look she gave Sherwood begged the question: *What do you know about hay production?* He couldn't argue with her. He had no practical experience. All he knew was what was in that book and a feeling inside that said the author was right.

"I think it's a good idea," Griff added with a nod. Then he turned his gaze toward the north. "The cattle far behind you?"

"Not far. They ought to be here in another hour. We'll start branding the winter calves first thing in the morning and begin culling the herd after that's done. Have you decided how many are going to market?"

Griff shook his head. "Let's begin with the ones that aren't pregnant or nursing a calf already. After we see how many there are of those, we can decide the number of productive cows to add to them." He looked at Sherwood. "You and I can go over the finances again in the morning, and then we'll decide."

What was it Sherwood saw in Cleo's expression as her father spoke? It was there and then gone. A look that said . . . what? It bothered him that he didn't know.

But then, why should it bother him? That was even more perplexing.

He stood. "I'll take care of Domino while you two chat."

"Oh, you don't have to —"

"I don't mind, Cleo." He went down the steps, took the pinto by the reins, and led the horse toward the barn.

Cleo removed her Stetson and ran her fingers through her hair as she watched Woody walk away. His gait wasn't as stiff and awkward as it used to be. When had that changed? Those sessions at New Hope must be doing him some good. She was glad of it, for his sake — and felt the shame of ever resenting his visits to the spa.

"He's been a great help to us," her father said.

She looked over her shoulder at him, then moved to sit in the chair Woody had vacated moments before. "He's doing all right."

"I told him I hadn't thought he would do well on a ranch, and he admitted he hadn't thought so either."

"Nobody's more surprised than me."

"Here's another surprise." Her father grinned. "He took his horse out for a ride this morning."

She felt her eyes widen. "You're joking."

"No. I saw him from my bedroom window, plain as day."

"Well, I'll be." She looked toward the barn, but Woody was no longer in sight.

"Don't let on that you know."

"Why not?"

"He didn't mention it so I expect he

doesn't mean for us to know as yet."

Cleo couldn't think of any reason to keep it a secret, unless maybe it was a man's pride. As she rolled that thought over in her mind, she decided pride was reason enough. She remembered the way Rose Winston had looked at him that first Sunday he came to church. No doubt she wasn't the only woman who'd acted that way when she saw him. And over what? A scar. Sakes alive! The things some females chose to be squeamish about.

She rose from the chair. "I'd best make sure Domino gets his oats or he'll be riled at me." She kissed her father's forehead a second time and left him to enjoy the fresh air.

When she entered the barn a short while later, she discovered Domino in one of the stalls, his saddle and bridle removed, his coat brushed, and his nose deep in a bucket while he munched on his favorite grain.

Woody appeared in the doorway to the tack room. "I gave him two scoops. That's his usual, I believe."

"Yeah, it is."

Interesting that Woody knew how much grain she gave her horse. Not once since he'd been at the ranch had she asked him to feed or groom Domino. He must pay close attention to her whenever she was around.

A strange sensation shivered along her spine. Something akin to pleasure.

FIFTEEN

With the spring branding in full swing, Gwen and Morgan didn't come to the ranch for their usual Thursday visit. However, Daphne McKinley arrived in her brother's automobile in the early afternoon. Griff invited her to join him on the veranda, but she demurred, saying she'd come to watch the branding.

"Sherwood," Griff said, "would you mind escorting the young lady out to the pasture?"

"Not at all, sir." He offered his arm, and she took it, giving him a bright smile.

There was something appealing about Daphne McKinley, beyond her pretty face and fine figure. Unless Sherwood was mistaken — and he wasn't — there was a glint of mischief in her dark eyes. He'd already recognized her streak of independence, the same streak he'd observed in Cleo and Gwen. Perhaps all American women were that way. To his surprise, he was starting to like it.

They circumvented the barn, and when they reached the first paddock, Daphne released her hold on his arm so he could open the gate for them. Then the two set out across the paddock, Daphne holding her skirts above the grass to avoid staining the hem. Ahead of them, in the second large paddock, they saw a cowboy wrestle a calf to the ground while another prepared to press a hot branding iron to its hindquarter.

The smell of burning flesh filled Sherwood's nostrils while the bawling complaint filled his ears. In an instant, he was back in France, looking out at a battlefield littered with the dead and dying, the dead lying at odd angles with eyes open, the dying screaming in pain from their burns and open wounds. Terror filled the trenches as men — boys, too many of them — crouched low, clutching their rifles close, wishing they were home with their mothers. Sweat and sickness, chaos and blood and death. *Run, his mind yelled. Run away while you can.*

"Lord Sherwood?"

He heard her voice as if through a tunnel, felt it pulling him back from the edge of a black abyss.

"Lord Sherwood?" Daphne's hand

alighted on his forearm. "Are you all right?"

He blinked several times and gave his head a slow shake as a shudder ran down his spine. "I . . . I suddenly remembered something, something I'd rather not . . ." He pressed his lips together, ending the confession before it could be spoken.

Kindness was written in her brown eyes as she looked up at him. "The war." She said it softly but in a tone that told him she empathized with him. She only thought she understood, of course. No one could understand except those who had been there, those who had lived through hell and come home again. And yet there was something in her gaze that told him she might understand more than he imagined was possible in a pretty young American girl.

"Yes," he answered at last. "The war."

With a nod, she resumed walking, earning his gratitude with her silence. They stopped when they reached the fence separating the two large paddocks.

Daphne peered through the opening between the top rail and the one below. "There's Cleo." She raised her arm and waved.

Cleo rode toward them on her pinto. "I thought Gwen and Morgan weren't coming today."

"They didn't. I came alone. I wanted to see what this was like. I've never seen cows branded before."

Cleo shrugged, as if to say, "Suit yourself."

"It's very noisy, isn't it?" Daphne continued.

"Noisy enough." A calf racing down the fence line drew Cleo's gaze away. "That little guy's mine." She tugged down on her hat brim at the same time she kicked Domino into a gallop. Seconds later, the business end of a lariat flew through the air and dropped around the calf's neck. Domino sat back on his hind legs, sliding to a halt. The calf hit the end of the rope and fell backward, hitting the ground with force.

"Oh, my!" Daphne clapped her hands. "I had no idea Cleo could do anything like that. Isn't she wonderful?" She pulled a small writing tablet from the pocket of her skirt and scribbled something in it with a lead pencil. When she was finished, she glanced at Sherwood, her eyes sparkling with delight. "I like to make notes of my impressions when I see something new so I can remember what it was like later. The sights. The sounds. The smells."

Sherwood smiled back at her, as if in agreement. However, he wouldn't need to take notes about anything he saw Cleo do.

Nothing she did was forgettable. Not the way she rode and roped. Not the way she walked and talked. Not the flash in her eyes when she was angry or the sparkle in them when she laughed.

She was unique. One of a kind. And completely memorable.

It bothered Cleo, knowing Sherwood and Daphne were watching her every move. Made her as jumpy as a bit-up old bull at fly time. Branding wasn't a spectator sport. It was work. Hard, sweaty work. If they didn't want to join in — that'd be the day — they'd just as well head back to the house where they belonged. Look at them. The idle rich, talking and smiling and having a good time while everybody else was busy earning a living. Thank heaven she wasn't one of them. It would make her crazier than a bedbug in no time at all.

After removing Cleo's rope from around the calf's neck, Randall lifted and flopped the young bovine to the ground while Allen drew the iron from the fire. The calf bawled in fear, but the branding took mere seconds. Randall released his hold, and it was up and off in search of its mother. With a cluck of her tongue, Cleo rode Domino after another calf. The next time she thought to glance toward the neighboring paddock, Sherwood and Daphne were gone.

Two hours later, Cleo entered the house. She heard male laughter mixed with Daphne's coming from the direction of her father's office. She thought about joining the merry group and discovering what amused them so, but her desire for a bath was greater than her curiosity. She climbed the stairs and began to unbutton her shirt the moment the door to the bathroom closed behind her.

As soon as the claw-footed tub filled with warm water, she sank down into it until only her nose and knees poked above the surface. In that silent place, it was easy to let the tension ease from her shoulders and neck, easy to forget the complaints of the muscles in her arms and thighs. She wouldn't have minded staying there until the water grew cool, but she couldn't. It was too close to dinnertime. She sat up and began to scrub the remnants of the day's work from her hair and skin. After rinsing away the soap, she stepped from the bathtub and wrapped herself in a large towel.

A knock sounded at the bathroom door. "Cleo," Daphne called. "Are you decent? May I come in?" She didn't wait for a reply but opened the door and stepped inside.

"I'm *not* decent, Daphne. All I'm wearing's a towel."

"Oh, don't be missish. I can't see anything except those wonderful long legs of yours." With a sigh, Daphne turned her back toward Cleo. "Is that better?"

"I reckon it'll have to be." She continued to dry off.

"I found the branding very exciting to watch. I knew you were good with horses, but I had no idea you could ride the way you do. You could be part of Buffalo Bill's Wild West. I can see Annie Oakley doing her trick shooting and you doing all kinds of fancy riding."

"Why on earth would I want to be part of a show like that? Land sakes! Those are for the same folks who like to read dime novels."

Daphne glanced over her shoulder. "And what's wrong with dime novels?"

"I guess nothing unless you'd rather live like a cowboy than dream about it." Cleo glowered at Daphne until the younger woman looked away again. Then she began to get dressed. "I thought you'd learned a thing or two about the real West after living in Idaho for near on a year."

"Oh, I have. But there's so much more I haven't seen. This summer I want to visit

Yellowstone National Park. Maybe you could go with me?"

Cleo buttoned her shirt. "Maybe."

"Perhaps the whole family could go. And wouldn't it be fun to show the American wilderness to Lord Sherwood?"

Cleo felt that funny catch in her stomach. Was Daphne growing fond of Woody?

"I don't imagine he's seen anything like it," Daphne continued. "Europe has its forests and castles, of course, and they're quite glorious, but from what I've heard, Yellowstone is amazing."

"Mmm." Cleo couldn't imagine anywhere more glorious than right where she lived, this valley and these mountains.

"Oh, dear."

"What?"

"I don't suppose Morgan would allow Gwen to undertake such a trip, now that she's with child."

Cleo ran a brush through her damp hair. "No, I don't reckon he will." She set the brush on the edge of the sink. "You can turn around now."

Daphne faced Cleo, her eyes snapping with excitement. "Then you really must go with me. Promise me you'll think about it."

"Okay. I'll think about it."

"Wonderful. Now I suppose I should start

for home."

"You're not staying for dinner?" Cleo stepped past Daphne and opened the bathroom door.

"No. Your father was kind enough to invite me, but I really must get back to Bethlehem Springs."

Cleo didn't try to stop her. As much as she liked Morgan's sister, today she'd just as soon not have her here. Why that was exactly, she couldn't say. Maybe she'd think on it later.

Cleo's father was waiting for the two women when they reached the bottom of the stairs. "Daphne, are you certain you won't stay to eat with us? I've asked Sherwood to make it a foursome."

"I'm sorry." She gave him a hug and a kiss on the check. "I must go home. I have some things I must do before the day is over. I'll come next week with Gwen and Morgan." She turned and gave Cleo a hug. "You think about Yellowstone," she whispered in her ear. "I'm determined to go."

Cleo nodded.

Daphne looked toward the office. "Goodbye, Lord Sherwood."

Woody appeared in the office doorway. "Are you leaving already, Miss McKinley?"

"I must. Thank you for escorting me to

see the branding."

Woody strode forward and took hold of her hand. "It was my pleasure." He lifted her hand and kissed it.

Once again Cleo felt that odd catch.

Strange. Very strange.

Sixteen

Sherwood entered the general store, a bell overhead announcing his presence. The store was empty except for three men standing near the counter at the back of the store, talking in agitated voices.

"I'm telling you, we oughta be fighting right now. I don't care what that Sussex Pledge is about. We oughta be over there."

"But the Germans have agreed to stop sinking liners and merchantmen that aren't resisting them."

"We shouldn't even be talking to 'em. Oughta throw 'em out of the country. Spies. I'm tellin' you. The Germans livin' in America are all spies."

"I'm afraid I don't agree, Mr. Smith. But here's somebody who knows a thing or two about fighting the Germans. Mr. Statham, come over here, if you don't mind. Settle something for us."

Sherwood had caught enough of the

conversation to know he didn't want to become involved, but he saw no way to escape. Reluctantly he walked toward the counter.

"Mr. Statham here's from England, and I learned he fought in France before he was wounded." Bert Humphrey, owner of the mercantile, patted him on the back as if they were long-lost friends. "What do you think, Mr. Statham? Shouldn't America be fighting alongside the Allies? If we'd get in there, we could bring the whole thing to an end in a few weeks."

How many times in the early days of the war had Sherwood heard someone say almost those same exact words? In August of 1914 nearly everyone in England had thought it would be over by Christmas. Almost two years and thousands upon thousands of casualties later, there was no end in sight. The position of the Western Front seemed rarely to change from week to week or month to month, no matter how many brave men fought and died trying to win a battle.

"A little American ingenuity. That's what's called for," said the youngest of the three other men. "We can end what the Germans started."

Oh, the bravado. The self-confidence. The

swaggering, bragging dialogue of the young, of those who knew nothing.

"Well, Mr. Statham," Bert said. "What do you think?"

"I'm sure your government is using every diplomatic means at their disposal to assure the safety of its citizens."

The younger man grunted. "Who needs diplomats? All they do is talk. The Germans have sunk ships and killed Americans. They're the ones who started this war. We shouldn't be wasting time on words. We should give them what they deserve. We should drive them back to Germany with their tails between their legs."

Two years ago Sherwood had probably said something similar. But he had no stomach for it now. Not for war or talk of war. Looking at Bert, he said, "Mr. Arlington asked that I pick up a few supplies." He handed the proprietor the list on a slip of paper. "If it's all right, I will come back for them in half an hour."

"Sure. That's fine."

Sherwood nodded toward the other two men. "Good day to you, sirs."

When he was outside again, he paused on the sidewalk long enough to draw a deep breath. He hated the sudden racing of his heart, the cowardly dampness in the palms of his hands. For several weeks after arriving in America, he'd been able to keep memories of the war at bay. Even when the therapist at the spa was working with him, he hadn't thought about what had caused his injuries. But yesterday, standing in the paddock with the sounds and the smells of the branding assaulting his senses, the details of the battlefield had returned with a vengeance. And now these ignorant men with their brave talk had done it again. He wanted to be free of it. He wanted to forget.

With a shake of his head, he turned on his heel and followed the sidewalk down Idaho Street until it met with Washington Street. Somewhere to the left of him must be the Methodist church. Yes, there it was. He could see the steeple beyond the rooftop of the Gold Mountain Restaurant. That gave him a little better idea of where he was.

He turned right on Washington, passing the hotel and the post office on the opposite side of the street and a bank, a shoe store, and a millinery shop on his right side. He stopped at the latter to look at the hats in the window facing Main Street. Stylish bonnets with feathers and ribbons were artfully displayed against a white cloth. He thought that brown hat would look rather nice on Daphne McKinley, and that dark rose one would flatter Gwen McKinley's coloring. But the one he liked the best, that simple straw boater with its narrow brim and a blue ribbon that matched her eyes, would be perfect for Cleo in her — what had he heard her call it? — her Sunday-go-to-meetin' dress.

The tension eased from his shoulders as Cleo's image filled his thoughts. Picturing her in that straw hat — smiling, laughing, rolling her eyes at something he'd said or done — made it easier to forget other, less pleasant, things.

Raised voices carried to him from across the street. Near the entrance of the High Horse Men's Club stood a man and woman, arguing. The woman was young and large with pregnancy. The man looked vaguely familiar to Sherwood. Where had he seen him before? And then it came to him. He'd seen him at New Hope the night of the grand opening. He was the fellow who'd upset Cleo.

Why? Sherwood wondered, just as he'd wondered that night but hadn't asked. What was he to Cleo?

The woman turned her back to the man and held a handkerchief to her eyes.

"Criminy, Henrietta!" His words carried across the street. "Can't you let me have a bit of peace? Just a little time alone. I come home to you, don't I?"

A spat between husband and wife, it would seem.

Sherwood was about to turn away when the man looked in his direction, saw they'd been observed, and then seemed to recognize Sherwood. The fellow released a string of curses before spinning around and walking into the club without another word to his crying wife. Although Sherwood felt for the young woman, he decided it would be better if she didn't catch him watching as her husband had. He moved on down the sidewalk.

Delicious odors wafted through the doorway of another restaurant, the South Fork, according to the lettering on the window. "World-Famous Pies" was the claim made below the name. Sherwood decided to go inside and see if the assertion was true.

Cleo waited at the station until the train pulled out. God willing, the cattle in those cars would bring top price at market. They'd better or else she would keep wondering at the wisdom of selling off cows that produced good calves year after year. She hoped her father had made the right decision, and she sure hoped he hadn't made his decision based on Woody's urgings. What did Woody know about cattle ranching, after all? Next to nothing.

Wanting something cold to drink to wash away the dust of the cattle drive, she rode Domino into Bethlehem Springs and stopped the gelding in front of the South Fork. After dismounting, she tied him to the hitching post, and then stepped onto the sidewalk. That was when she saw Henrietta King walking toward her. She was close enough for Cleo to see she'd been crying. Her eyes were watery, her cheeks damp, and her nose red.

When Henrietta saw Cleo, she stopped and lifted her chin, as if daring her to speak.

Cleo spoke anyway. "Good day, Mrs. King."

"Miss Arlington." Henrietta's chin tilted upward another notch. She knew, apparently, that Tyler had courted Cleo at the same time he was seeing her. She knew and resented Cleo for it.

Cleo felt something unexpected: sympathy. She felt sorry for the girl. Sorry in more ways than she could enumerate. "How are you feeling? Well, I hope."

"Okay, I reckon." Henrietta looked down at her enlarged abdomen. "I'll just be glad when this is over. It's no fun."

Cleo thought of her sister, of the perpetual joy she saw in Gwen's eyes whenever the subject of her pregnancy arose. But then, Gwen and Morgan had married first and started their family second, quite the opposite of Tyler and Henrietta King.

"You'd better keep away from him, if'n you know what's good for you."

Cleo felt her eyes widen. "I don't know what you mean."

"He's my husband. *I'm* Mrs. King, and I don't want you or Tyler forgettin' it." Henrietta, her face now red with anger, clenched her hands into fists at her sides. "You keep away from him."

"I'm not sure what you mean —" That was untrue. She understood what Henrietta was suggesting. "But you've got my word, I'm not interested in seeing or talking to your husband. Any interest I had in Tyler King ended when the two of you got married."

"Then why's he always bringin' you up to me? Throwin' you in my face all the time. As if he was sweet on you."

Cleo was stunned into silence. What could she say to that?

The door to the restaurant opened, drawing her gaze. She hoped Henrietta had the good sense not to repeat her insinuations in

206

front of others. It was bad enough the two of them had had this discussion on the main street of town. All she could hope for now was that no one inside the South Fork or any other business had overheard what was said. She didn't think their voices had been raised, but she couldn't be sure.

To her surprise, Woody appeared in the restaurant doorway. "My dear Cleo, are you coming in or not?"

"I . . . Y-yes. I . . . I'm coming." She looked at Henrietta. "Excuse me, Mrs. King. I . . . I hope things go well for you." She turned on her heel and entered the restaurant.

Woody's hand alighted on the small of her back. "Our table is over here." He motioned to the one beside the window.

So that was how he'd seen her.

He pulled out a chair for her, then sat on the opposite side.

Cleo felt heat rise in her cheeks as she asked, "Did you hear what she said to me?"

"No."

She breathed a sigh of relief.

"But I could see you were upset. This seemed the best way to be of service to you."

She was silent for a while before saying, "That's the second time you've come to my rescue."

"Is it?"

"Remember the night of the party up at the resort?"

"Oh, that. It was nothing. I could tell the bloke was bothering you."

"You're wrong, Woody. It wasn't nothing. It was a help to me. That time and this one too."

Was that understanding she saw in his green eyes or just curiosity? She wished she knew.

The waitress arrived with a slice of pie and a glass of milk and set them in front of Woody. He looked at Cleo. "Would you like something? This is supposed to be world-famous." He pointed at the pie while giving her a smile.

For some reason, the way he looked at her made the disagreeable minutes outside seem not quite as horrid. "I'd like a slice of that good lemon-crème pie, please," she said to the waitress, "and a large glass of lemonade."

Tart. Cleo preferred tart over sweet. Sherwood found it an interesting discovery. Right up there with learning that she wasn't always sure of herself and that sometimes she appreciated the help of another. Even help from him.

Cleo and the other cowboys had driven

the cattle from the ranch to the holding pens near the railroad station early this morning, and by now the livestock had been loaded into the cattle cars and were on their way to market. But while Cleo's clothes still bore evidence of the drive, her face and hands were dirt free. She must have taken the time to clean up in the railroad station's washroom. The cowboys she rode with most likely wouldn't have done the same. It was just one way she was different from those with whom she worked.

"What brought you to town?" she asked, breaking into his musings. "Didn't you go to the spa today?"

"Yes. I told Griff I would pick up supplies before I returned to the ranch. The wagon is over at the mercantile now."

Cleo turned her gaze out the window. "I suppose we might as well ride back together when we're done here."

He grinned, pleased that she seemed to want to spend more time with him. Although why it should please him was a mystery.

That evening, Sherwood sat on a chair in the bunkhouse, spinning a coin on top of the table. "Stitch?"

"Yeah?"

"Do you know anyone named King?" The two men were alone, a good time for Sherwood to ask some questions of the older man.

"Yeah, I know him. Why do you ask?"

"I observed something in town this afternoon. Cleo met a Mrs. King, and the encounter seemed to upset her."

Stitch joined Sherwood at the table. The expression on his wizened face was difficult to read.

"You needn't tell me if you'd rather not."

"No. I reckon there's no reason you shouldn't know the story."

Sherwood placed his fingers over the spinning coin, dropping it to the table's surface, his full attention now focused on Stitch.

"Tyler King came to work here at the ranch about a year ago. He wasn't from around these parts. He was a good-lookin', smooth-talkin' cowboy, I'll say that for him. Cleo took a shine to him, and he let her think he returned the feeling." Stitch's eyes narrowed and his voice hardened. "Only she wasn't the only gal in these parts he set his sights on. He spread himself a little thin with the women, if you get my meaning."

Of course. Why hadn't he guessed the problem was romantic in nature? It was as plain as the nose on his face. The rascal had

210

broken her heart.

"Got a young gal pregnant and was forced to marry her at the end of her father's shotgun. He tried to say he wasn't the baby's father, but he'd been seen with her once too often for anybody to believe him. He was caught in a trap of his own makin'."

"And Cleo?"

"Well, she tried not to let on, but she was hurtin' for a time."

Sherwood leaned forward. "Do you think she still cares for Tyler King?"

"Nope." Stitch shook his head slowly. "Cleo's too smart for that. She got a glimpse of his real character, and I reckon she's right thankful she discovered what a scoundrel he was before things went any further between them."

It surprised him, the relief he felt, knowing Cleo's heart no longer yearned for a man who'd betrayed her trust. But had enough time passed that she might learn to care for someone else?

It was a question that would trouble him throughout the night.

SEVENTEEN

Cleo removed her Stetson and brushed her hair back from her face. Then she entered the municipal building and followed the hallway to the mayor's office. Gwen's secretary, a young fellow by the name of Adams, showed her in without delay.

"Cleo. This is a surprise." Gwen came around her desk and hugged her sister. "What brings you to town today?"

"I'm training another horse and decided it was time for her to get a taste of town life. Then I decided, as long as I was here, I'd drop in and say howdy."

"I'm glad you did." She motioned to a couple of chairs and they both sat. "How's Dad?"

"He's doing lots better. He felt bad about not staying to eat with you and Morgan on Sunday, but he was done in."

"You aren't letting him do too much, are you?"

Cleo chuckled. "As if I could stop him if there was something he really wanted to do?"

"True, but I hope you try."

Cleo tried plenty. Some days she felt like all she did was nag him to take it easy. It worried her that he hadn't regained his full strength yet, but she wouldn't let on as much to Gwen. One of them worrying about their father was enough. "Woody's still keeping the accounts. I think Dad plans to leave it that way until Woody goes back to England."

"That's surprising. I thought Dad liked all that paperwork."

"Me too. Guess he found out it was kind of nice to let someone else do it for a change."

"Imagine if he'd asked you to do it."

Cleo remembered her initial hurt after learning of their dad's decision to put Woody in charge of the ranch accounts. How silly it had been of her to feel slighted, overlooked. She would have been a disaster. Her father's choice had been the best for everyone concerned. "Good thing he didn't, that's all I can say." She gave a slight shrug of her shoulders. "He likes Woody. He trusts him." She did, too, she knew. As frustrating as he could be at times, there was no doubt

Woody was honest. And, truth be told, not quite as arrogant or pretentious as she'd first thought. He might be a bit of a dandy, but he was a hard-working one. His desire to help her father was obvious and sincere.

It was Gwen's turn to laugh. "I can never get used to you calling him that. With his British accent and the dignified way he carries himself, even with a limp, he seems much more like a Lord Sherwood than a Woody."

"I reckon there's some truth in that," Cleo conceded, "but I'm hoping he'll seem more like Woody to everybody else by the time we send him back to England. That was the job I was given. Turn the dude into a cowboy." She grinned as she pictured Woody in her mind, wearing Levi's and a plaid shirt with the sleeves rolled to his elbows and a good pair of boots. So different from the way he'd looked when he arrived. "I'm having some success, if I do say so myself."

"Cleopatra Arlington, I believe you've taken a liking to him."

She felt her cheeks grow warm. "Don't be silly."

Gwen's teasing smile vanished. "Oh, my. You *do* like him, don't you?"

" 'Course I like him. I like all the boys that work the ranch."

"No. I think it's more than that." Her sister leaned forward on her chair, her gaze locked on Cleo's face.

"You can think what you want, Gwennie. Doesn't make it so." She got to her feet. "I'd best get back to my horse. Don't want her getting spooked by one of the motorcars going down Main Street. Confounded things."

"Don't be angry with me." Gwen rose. "I didn't mean to upset you."

"You didn't upset me." That was a bald-faced lie. "I've just got to get back to my work and leave you to yours." She leaned forward and kissed her sister's cheek. "See you on Thursday for lunch?"

"Of course. Morgan and I will be there at the usual time."

Cleo hurried out of the office and the municipal building as fast as her legs would carry her and still not break into a run.

"Oh, my. You do like him, don't you?"

Of course she liked Woody. The same way she liked Stitch and Allen and Randall, like she'd said. It wasn't as if she fancied him in any sort of romantic way. Why, that was plain preposterous, her falling for a dude, and her sister ought to know it.

She found the filly standing at the hitching post, flicking her tail but undisturbed by anything happening in town. Not that Cleo had expected the even-tempered horse to get overexcited. That had been an excuse so she could leave before Gwen said anything more about Woody.

She swung into the saddle and rode down Main Street to the post office, where she dismounted and tied up the horse for a second time. Inside, she found the postmaster slipping envelopes into individual mail slots.

"Afternoon, Mr. Finster."

He turned around. "*Guten Tag, Fräulein.* How is your papa?"

"He's much better. Thanks for asking. I told him I'd stop by the post office while I was in town and see if there's any mail for us."

"*Ja.* I have it." He set aside the other mail in his hand and pulled several envelopes from the slot marked with the Arlington name. "There is from England a letter for Mr. Statham. He works for you, *ja?*" He handed the mail to her.

"Yes, he works for us."

She glanced at the top envelope and wondered whom the letter was from. *Lord Sherwood Statham.* The writing looked feminine, especially those little curls at the end of each word. She turned the envelope

over. The seal on the back said *Dunacombe.*
A letter from home. She wondered why it
had taken so long for someone to write to
him.

Sherwood mounted the bay in the barn.
However, he had no intention of keeping
his riding a secret from this point forward.
He wanted the others to see him. He wanted
to be more mobile, and a saddle horse gave
him that ability. It had been six days since
his successful first attempt. He'd waited,
hoping for another opportunity when no
one else was around, but one hadn't come.
Now he was tired of waiting.

He rode the gelding out of the barn and
turned him down the road toward town.
Not that Sherwood intended to go that far.
He knew his leg would punish him if he
took such a long ride just yet. He was learning to apply patience in his recovery, thanks
partly to Griff Arlington, thanks partly to
the therapist at New Hope, and last but not
least, thanks to something Reverend Barker
had said during one of his sermons —
something about not running ahead of
God's will. Sherwood hadn't given much
thought to God's will before. Or, for that
matter, to God Himself. More than six
weeks with the Arlingtons had changed that.

He'd found himself hungry to know more about Christ, about the kind of faith he witnessed daily in Griff and his daughters, in Morgan and his sister, and in the good reverend.

Up the road a ways, he saw Cleo cantering a light-colored horse toward him. He drew in on the reins and waited for her arrival.

"Well, look at you." Smiling, she brought her horse to a stop. "When'd you decide to give that a try?"

"Last week." He had to admit, her reaction made him feel good.

She circled him, her gaze taking in the longer right stirrup. "How does he respond to you kicking with only one heel?"

"Not bad. But then, I've kept a short rein on him. No faster than a jog."

"If you want, I can work with the two of you, help your horse learn to respond to other signals."

Sherwood wasn't ignorant of horse training methods and had no need of her instructions, but he didn't tell her so. "That would be most helpful, Cleo. Thank you."

In unison they turned their horses toward the ranch.

"I picked up the mail while I was in town. There's a letter for you."

"For me?"

"From England."

It wasn't hard to surmise whom the letter was from. His father hadn't written Sherwood when he was in the army or while he was in the hospital. There was no reason to believe he would write to him in America. No, the letter would be from his mother. She was the only faithful correspondent at Dunacombe Manor. Although it was possible Bottomley might write.

"Do you miss them?" Cleo asked, breaking into his thoughts. "Your family."

It was a simple question, but the answer was complicated. Too complicated to try to explain to someone who didn't know the duke, someone who didn't understand the hierarchy of British society, someone who didn't know what it was like to fall short in her father's estimation. "England is very far away," he answered at last.

"I know what you mean. Gwen was raised by our mother in the East. Mother moved back to New Jersey when we — Gwen and I — were only two."

Sherwood nodded, not wanting to interrupt her.

"Even though I couldn't remember them, I missed them all the time, especially my sister. It was hard, growing up apart from

219

the other half of my family. Having Gwennie with us these last eight years means the world to me. I don't know how Dad and I would manage if she were to go away again. Your absence must be real hard on your folks."

"All families are not like yours, Cleo."

She gave him a long look, one that said he was a mystery to her. Perhaps it would be better if they left it that way. Better if he didn't let her know more than she did already.

Dunacombe Manor
My dearest Sherwood,

I was pleased to learn that you arrived in Bethlehem Springs without any difficulties on your journey. I had hoped to hear from you again with details of your trip, of where you are living and what you are doing. If you have written such a letter, it hasn't reached us. Please do not delay in writing again.

My dearest son, I know that you did not part with your father on the best of terms, and it grieves me, knowing you felt his treatment harsh. Your father does the best he can. Believe me when I tell you this. He cares for you more than he realizes and certainly more than he shows.

Life goes on at Dunacombe as it has since this dreadful war began. It is quiet and there are few engagements to occupy us. But even if it would not be bad form to have a ball or a hunt, given the current circumstances, it would be a dreadful failure, for there would be almost no young men in attendance.

I have news of your brothers to share.

Marshall has asked Margaret Hathaway to marry him and she has accepted. Your father is quite pleased that his eldest son has made such a match. Lady Margaret will make a fine mistress of Dunacombe when the time comes that Marshall inherits the title and estates. After the wedding, which will take place this summer, it has been decided that they will live at Chilton House. Naturally, some renovations must be made, but I believe the house will suit them nicely.

Haywood, Beth, and the children are all healthy. Their parish has been hit rather hard this spring; many families have lost husbands and sons, and the burden weighs on Haywood's shoulders as he tries to minister to the people of

Brentshire.

Langford writes that he is doing well. He has lost many officers and soldiers under his command in recent months. However, his spirits remain high. He has not lost confidence that right will triumph in the end. However long that may be.

Bottomley asked that I remember him to you.

As for me, my health is somewhat improved, and I look forward to the coming of summer.

Do write and give me your impressions of America. Your father, as you will recall, has been to New York City, but he told me almost nothing other than to say he is not inclined to go again. I am sure you can tell me more than he has ever done.

Your loving,
Mother

Sherwood folded the letter and returned it to its envelope. His mother's words stirred warm thoughts of England and his brothers and mother. As for his father . . . Well, he found it hard to believe the duke cared much about him, beyond whether or not he proved an embarrassment to the Statham name.

Tomorrow he would write a more detailed letter to his mother. He would describe the journey by ship across the Atlantic and then the journey across this vast country by rail. He would even tell her that he'd been employed to shovel horse manure from the stables. However, that would be for his father's benefit. The duke would not take pleasure in a Statham performing such a lowly task, not even when the Statham in question was his youngest son.

EIGHTEEN

Cleo stood in front of the mirror, inspecting her reflection with a critical eye. She'd never cared much about her appearance, one way or the other. She knew she wasn't a beauty, unlike her sister. Gwen was feminine perfection, like a Thoroughbred racing down the track. Cleo was more the gawky filly, all knobby knees and sharp angles.

She smoothed her hair back from her face and turned her head from side to side. She didn't care much for her nose. Too stubby, she thought. Plus her lips were too full and her eyebrows set too far apart. And no amount of lemon juice, as her mother had repeatedly urged her to try last year, could remove the freckles splashed across her nose and cheekbones.

What did Woody see when he looked at her?

With a groan, she squeezed her eyes shut. It didn't matter to her what he saw or what he thought. His opinion was irrelevant. It wasn't as if she liked him. Not in the way her sister had implied yesterday. While she would admit he wasn't as intolerable as she'd first believed him to be, neither was he of particular interest to her. They had next to nothing in common. They might become friends, but that was all. In ten months, more or less, he would return to his homeland, where he could go back to doing whatever it was British lords did. England was where he belonged, just like this ranch was where she belonged.

She opened her eyes, ran a brush through her hair, and hurried out of the bedroom. She'd best start breaking the last of those mustangs. A wild ride might be the trick to shake loose all the thoughts that had plagued her lately. Thoughts of Woody and the times he'd been good to her even when she hadn't been so kind to him. Thoughts about the loneliness she sometimes saw written in his eyes. She'd even caught herself recalling the times they'd bickered, enjoying the way she could get under his skin with just a comment or two. And his laugh. She liked remembering his laugh, something he didn't do often enough to suit her.

She pushed open the kitchen door and

Woody was the first person she saw. He stood at the stove, spooning scrambled eggs from a big skillet onto his plate.

"Mornin', Cleo," came a chorus of male voices from the table.

"Morning, boys," she answered the three ranch hands. "Morning, Cookie." She drew a slow breath. "Morning, Woody."

"Good morning, Cleo."

She felt the strangest hiccup in her chest when he smiled at her.

Cookie said, "Are you joining us today? Your dad's already eaten and gone."

"Gone where?"

Stitch answered, "Up to the resort. Said he had something important he wanted to talk over with Morgan."

That set off a few alarm bells in Cleo's head. What could be so urgent that her father — not all that long out of his sickbed — would ride out this early in the morning? Morgan would come to the ranch tomorrow with Gwen. Couldn't whatever it was have waited until then?

She looked toward the stove again. Woody and her dad talked over the ranch business every day. If something was troubling her dad, he might know what it was. But Woody's back was to her as he carried his breakfast plate to the table and so her questions went unasked.

"Here you go, Cleo." Cookie held out a plate of scrambled eggs, toast, and bacon.

She hadn't much of an appetite now, but she took the plate from his hand and went to the table, where she slid onto a chair next to Stitch and across from Woody.

Stitch said, "Say, Cleo. Did you know Sherwood's started riding that gelding you picked out for him?"

"Yes, I met him on the road yesterday."

"Maybe he can ride fence with me one of these days."

She shrugged. "No harm if he thinks he can manage it."

"I believe I'd rather like that." Woody spread butter on his toast. "Perhaps I'll be ready in a week or two."

"Sure. Whenever you're up to it." Stitch stood, breakfast dishes in hand, and carried them to the sink. He was followed an instant later by Randall and Allen.

Cleo moved the eggs around on her plate with a fork, waiting until the other men were gone. Then she looked across the table at Woody. "Do you know why Dad went to see Morgan?"

"I'm afraid I don't."

"He hasn't been worrying, has he? You know, about the price the cattle will bring or anything like that?"

Not all that long ago, she wouldn't have needed to ask someone else such a question. There'd never been anything unspoken between Cleo and her father. But after Griff made Woody the ranch manager, things had changed. Even though she was okay with the arrangement — she had no desire to handle the books — sometimes she felt left out, excluded, and it wasn't a feeling she cared for.

"I don't believe your father is unduly concerned about the sale of the cattle." There was a tender look in Woody's eyes. "And you should not worry about him, Cleo. He is well."

For one awful moment, she thought she might burst into tears. And the worst part of it was, she wasn't at all sure why she wanted to cry.

Griff sat on the brocade sofa in the McKinley suite at New Hope, a cup of black coffee in his hand. Morgan sat nearby in a matching chair. For the past fifteen minutes or so, the two had exchanged the expected questions and answers: *How's your health? Much improved. How's everyone at the ranch? Fine. Are you enjoying the weather? It's been warmer than usual for June.*

But finally Griff was ready to broach the subject that brought him to see Morgan. "I'd like to talk to you about Sherwood."

"Is there a problem?"

"No. There's no problem, Morgan. He's a hard worker and has been an enormous help to me, especially after I fell ill. We've become friends. Good friends, I believe. But I would like to understand him better. I sense a hurt in his soul. Perhaps unrelated to what happened to him in the war. Do you know what else there might be?"

Morgan steepled his hands in front of his lips, saying nothing.

"He rarely talks about his home or family," Griff added.

"No. I don't imagine he would."

"Why is that?"

Morgan cleared his throat as he lowered his hands. "It's difficult for me to speak ill of the man who was of assistance to my mother during her illness. However, since you've asked, I'll answer as honestly as I can. His grace, the Duke of Dunacombe, is a harsh man, without any natural warmth for his family. I would say that his single desire for children was to produce an heir for the dukedom. Each subsequent son was of lesser importance than the one before. Five years separate Lord Sherwood from

229

his next oldest brother. By the time Sherwood was born, he mattered not at all in his father's eyes."

Griff's chest tightened in empathy. How that must have hurt Sherwood as a young boy. How it must have confused him.

"The duchess is a meek woman, warm hearted when she's with others, but when faced with the duke's cold demeanor, she retreats into herself. There were many times during our stay at Dunacombe when she remained in her bedroom for days at a time."

Griff was tempted to say he'd heard enough, and yet he needed to know all he could.

Morgan refilled his coffee cup from the silver pitcher. After taking a swallow, he continued. "When I said that Lord Sherwood didn't matter in his father's eyes, that wasn't entirely true. It does matter to the duke that none of his sons bring dishonor upon the Statham name. That seemed to be the one thing at which Lord Sherwood excelled, as far as his father was concerned. Lord Sherwood had a lively spirit that often led to mischief, despite how diligently the duke tried to squash it, but he wasn't wicked." Morgan set down the cup and leaned forward on his chair. "Let me be clear, Griff. I never heard or saw him do anything that made me believe it warranted his father's anger or harsh treatment. Not ever in the months I was at Dunacombe. I know that he drank some and gambled some, but not to excess. His greatest sin back then was his flirtatious nature. The young women adored him, but he had no desire to make a good match and settle down."

"I see."

"To be honest, I rather miss seeing that playful side of him. After what his father told me of his more recent . . . escapades . . . I rather expected —" He stopped abruptly, ending with a small shrug.

"Yes, I know what you expected."

"Griff, I think you'd better tell me what this is about. Why the questions now after all these weeks?"

"It's about . . . Cleo."

"Cleo?"

Griff rose and walked across the sitting room to the window with its view of the mountainside and, a good distance away, the prayer chapel. "While I was ill, I began to worry about her, about what will happen to her when I die. I don't want her to be alone when that day comes. Then I considered how difficult it could be for her to meet

231

the right man. It took someone like you to win Gwen's love. What sort of man will it take to win Cleo's heart?"

"It's hard to say. A cowboy, I suppose."

"That's what I would have said too." He turned around. "But I believe she has a growing fondness for Sherwood."

"Good heavens," Morgan said softly.

"A few weeks ago, I would have thought it impossible."

"Does Lord Sherwood return her affection?"

"I don't know." Griff rubbed his eyes with his fingers. "But even if he does, it can't end well. Can you imagine how Sherwood's friends would receive Cleo? Not that I expect it to come to that. Even if he were to propose marriage, she wouldn't accept. She knows enough about high society to want to avoid it."

"I hope so."

"But that doesn't mean she won't be nursing a broken heart after he leaves."

Morgan came to stand near him. "You don't know that it's gone that far. It could be her attachment is nothing more than friendship."

"Maybe," Griff said, unconvinced.

"Maybe he should live and work here, after all. His father didn't think it wise, but now that he's been here awhile, I can't see any good reason he shouldn't."

Griff considered the offer for a few moments. It might help Cleo if Sherwood was no longer at the ranch. If her affection for him hadn't fully blossomed, maybe his absence would keep it from happening. And yet, sending the young man away felt wrong now that Griff completely understood the family dynamics. Never accepted. Never measuring up. Cast off by the man he called father. It seemed to Griff that Sherwood had been rejected enough for one lifetime.

"No," he answered at last. "I believe he should stay on at the ranch. Cleo is a grown woman. I can't protect her from the hard things in life, as much as I might like to. She'll have to make her own choices." He sighed. "I'll pray for her. I'll pray for them both."

31 May, 1916

Dearest Mother,

How good it was to receive your letter with news of the family.

Extend my heartiest congratulations to Marshall. Lady Margaret has exactly the right temperament to be his wife and mistress of his home. It's a fine match.

They should be quite happy at Chilton House.

Tell Haywood that I am attending church services regularly now, along with my employer and his daughter and one of the cowboys who works at the ranch. I like to think that I'm changed for the better because of it.

Langford is much on my mind. Even though the Americans are not fighting with the Allies, news of the war fills their newspapers, and it is hard for me to know that my brother continues to be in danger on the battlefields of France.

You requested more details of my journey to Bethlehem Springs, and I will try to oblige. The ocean voyage was tense with passengers and crew always watching for signs of a German ship. Thankfully, we never encountered the enemy, and our ship arrived in New York City without misadventure. Once in America, I traveled by rail from New York City across what seemed to be a never-ending, constantly changing, land. We stopped frequently, a few times in large cities, but most often at stations in small towns in the middle of nowhere. The center of this nation is flat and sparsely populated. Then there are the

Rocky Mountains, some mountain peaks remaining snow covered year round. Wildlife is abundant.

The Arlington ranch, where I am employed, is quite different from any sort of enterprise I have seen in England, and the cowboys who work the ranch are a colorful lot. It was difficult for me at first to understand them, but it is not so hard for me now. Recently, the cowboys brought in the herd, where they separated out the young calves for branding and then sent some cattle to market to be sold. It was quite the thing to watch, I assure you.

My health has improved, thanks in good part to Morgan McKinley. I have received care and therapy at his health spa. My leg has improved enough that I can now ride a horse. Not fast nor for long periods, but I do believe that time will come.

My work has varied, and at present I am helping Mr. Arlington with his accounts and record keeping. I have also been reading books on animal husbandry and proper land management. Quite fascinating, actually.

Tell Father that I have learned more in America than he, perhaps, might have expected. Do not worry about me, for I have found that I like this land and these people. In the end, it will be a year well spent.

Your loving son,
Sherwood

Sherwood folded the letter and slipped it into the envelope. He was thankful he'd overcome the temptation to write about mucking out stalls. While it might have upset the duke, it wouldn't bring Sherwood any satisfaction in the end — one more thing he'd learned since coming here.

He placed the envelope in a wooden tray with two other items to be posted, then left the office and went outside. It was late morning, already warm and promising to grow more so before day was done. A couple of dogs lounged in the dirt in the shade of the barn. One of them — a large brown canine of questionable breed, with the name of Bear — rose and trotted across the yard and up the steps. Sherwood hadn't been at the ranch very long before he learned that Bear would befriend anyone who gave him a pat on the head. He obliged by bending down and stroking the dog's coat.

A horse's squeal of anger caused Sherwood to straighten and look toward the barn. He moved off the porch and headed in that direction. As he drew closer, he heard more sounds — snorting, stomping, grunting, another squeal of complaint — followed by Cleo's voice.

"Easy. Easy."

He circumvented the barn, and the third corral came into view. In it, as he'd expected, was Cleo and one of the mustangs. This one, a big black stallion with a rope around its neck, was determined not to cooperate. The horse bucked and reared and fought to get away from the slight woman on the opposite end of the rope. But Cleo had a firm grip, and her heels dug into the dirt in the center of the corral.

How did she do it? How was she strong enough to fight that wild horse and win? And he had no doubt that she would win in the end. The determined set of her mouth told him she wouldn't be the one to give up.

Sherwood kept his distance. He didn't want to distract Cleo or startle the horse. Instead he leaned his back against the side of the barn and continued to watch. He wasn't sure how much time passed before the stallion began to show signs of tiring. Finally he stopped, body quivering, an untrusting gaze turned upon Cleo.

"Easy there. Easy, boy." She moved slowly but steadily toward the horse, and Sherwood could tell she was watchful for any sign the fight might begin again. Watchful and ready for it. But for now the stallion was done. He might fight again tomorrow, but not today.

Cleo was finished as well. She seemed satisfied to stroke the horse two or three times on the neck before slipping the noose from over his head and setting him free in the nearest paddock.

Sherwood moved forward. "You have a way with horses."

She looked over her shoulder, apparently unsurprised to find him standing there. "I should. I've been working with them since I was a kid."

"I've known others who have worked with horses since childhood, and none of the men of my acquaintance are like you. You have a gift."

She smiled as she wiped her forehead on her shirtsleeve. "Maybe so. I reckon God knew what He was doing when He formed me."

It was a sudden shift in conversation, going from horses to God, but not unforeseen. They were all like that — Cleo, Griff, Gwen, and Morgan. They spoke of the Almighty naturally, as if they knew Him. How could one *know* God? Knowing *about* Him, Sherwood understood. But this was different. This family was different.

His eyes narrowed as a question repeated itself in his head. At last, he asked it. "Have you always believed in God in such a personal way?"

"Yes." She opened the gate and stepped out of the corral. "Don't know any other way *to* believe in Him."

Sherwood envied her. He envied the assurance of her faith. He envied the unconditional love she shared with each member of her family. And for the first time he realized how difficult it would be to leave Cleo and the others when his year of exile was completed.

NINETEEN

Sherwood paused at the entrance to the men's private bathing rooms and looked toward one of the two pools. In it, two young boys paddled through the water with the aid of attendants. The lads had polio, Sherwood knew, and both walked with greater difficulty than he did. The older of the two was from San Francisco, the younger from some place in the South. Boys from poor families, the both of them, guests of the resort as beneficiaries of the Danielle McKinley Foundation.

Over his last few visits to the resort, Sherwood had learned these bits of information from his therapist and from the boys themselves. Because of it, his estimation of Morgan McKinley had climbed even higher than it had been before. And it made him ashamed. He, too, was a beneficiary of Morgan's generosity; the difference was the Stathams weren't poor. They could easily afford to pay for the treatment he'd received. But the duke had made it clear that Sherwood would have to work for everything while in America.

He ran the fingers of one hand through his damp hair as he left the pools and walked toward the Arlington buggy. Another week and the therapist said he should be ready to ride his horse to New Hope. He would be glad for that day. His leg would never be perfect. The knee would never again bend as it should. He would always have an uneven gait. But it wasn't as pronounced as it used to be, and for that he was grateful.

"Lord Sherwood."

He turned at the sound of his name.

Morgan strode toward him from the direction of the lodge. "How was your session?"

"Rather good. It won't be long before Eduardo is shed of me."

"I'm told you've made a lot of progress."

"Indeed. I'm deeply indebted to you, Morgan. More than I can express."

"Nonsense."

Sherwood shook his head. "It isn't nonsense, and after I return to England I'll make certain your foundation receives appropriate reimbursement."

Morgan merely smiled, then motioned

toward the lodge. "Would you join me for a cool beverage before you start back to the ranch?"

Something cool to drink sounded good to Sherwood, so he nodded.

A number of guests sat in the chairs on the veranda that wrapped around the lodge, enjoying the shade and the pleasant breeze that blew through the compound. Morgan spoke to a few of them by name. "Afternoon, Henry." "Enjoying your stay, Miss Margaret?" "Samuel, you look like you're feeling better." Then he and Sherwood went inside.

Unlike the night of the grand opening, the entry and sitting room weren't jammed with people. This afternoon, two women sat near the windows reading. Another sat on one of the sofas, needlework in her hands. Two gentlemen stood nearby, debating something to do with taxation. Morgan led the way into the dining room and motioned for Sherwood to sit at a table.

A waiter appeared almost as soon as they sat down. "What may I bring you, sir?" he asked Morgan.

"Lord Sherwood?"

"I'm growing rather fond of that drink you Americans call root beer."

"Yes, sir."

Morgan said, "I'll have the same."

"I'll bring your beverages right out." The waiter turned on his heel and headed for the kitchen.

"When is the restaurant the busiest?" Sherwood asked, looking around at the many empty tables.

"Our guests with children usually dine early. Those without tend to dine later. The restaurant stays fairly busy from about six o'clock until after ten." Morgan's eyes revealed his satisfaction. "We're at about seventy percent capacity at present. Rather good, considering the short while we've been open. Word is spreading, thanks to those who came to stay during our opening weekend."

It occurred to Sherwood that another way he could repay Morgan's kindness was by telling others about New Hope. There were wealthy people in England who felt inconvenienced by the war and an inability to travel to the Continent. They might like to see America and stay at a spa such as this one. Yes, when he returned to the ranch, he would write a few letters.

Morgan broke into his thoughts. "Do you enjoy managing the business end of the ranch? Griff seems to think you're well suited to it."

Sherwood chuckled. "I believe I've surprised us both."

"And Cleo? How are things between the two of you?"

"Cleo?" The question came out of the blue. "We get along well." He pictured her working with that black mustang, dusty from head to toe, that determined glint in her eye. "She's unlike any woman I've known before." A smile crept into the corners of his mouth. By comparison, the ladies of his previous acquaintance seemed staid and dull.

"Cleo's one of a kind." Morgan leaned his forearms on the table. "And no one who loves her wants to see her get hurt."

Sherwood heard a warning in the gently spoken words. Was it for him or someone else?

Cleo elbowed the gelding in his ribs. "Get off me, you lazy brute." He nickered but didn't budge.

This horse did the same thing every time she trimmed his hooves. As she balanced his leg and hoof between her knees, he would lean into her, forcing her to support some of his weight.

She jabbed his side with a little more force. This time he shifted away from her.

"That's better."

With her pocketknife she trimmed old flakes from the sole. Then she took the nippers from her hind pocket and snipped the wall of the hoof, doing as much of the shaping as she could with the tool. She'd learned through the years that using the rasp was the hardest part of horseshoeing. That task came next.

She had just finished preparing the hoof for the new shoe when the buggy rolled into the yard. She lowered the gelding's leg to the ground, and as she straightened, she pressed her fingers against the small of her spine and arched backward. She'd be glad when this last horse was done. So would her back.

Woody got out of the buggy, and she noticed that he did so with a new confidence, a new gracefulness of motion. She was glad for him, glad for all the folks who were being helped up at New Hope. A year ago, she never would have guessed how much good Morgan's resort would do.

Woody saw her looking his way and left the horse standing in its traces while he walked toward her. "I say. You were at that when I left. You must be weary."

Perspiration beaded her forehead and upper lip, and she felt the dampness of her shirt under her arms and along her spine. What a sight she must be. "This is the last one."

"Is there anything I can do to help?" He seemed to ask that a lot lately.

"I reckon not. But thanks anyway."

"Well, let me know if you think of something." He smiled.

Something strange was going on inside her as she looked at him. It felt like a couple of tomcats fighting in a gunnysack. Not the best feeling in the world. Kind of made it hard to breathe.

She turned and reached for the horseshoe. When she turned back again, he was walking away, returning to the horse and buggy. The fighting tomcats went away, too, replaced by an empty feeling that was almost worse.

Must be coming down with something.

She placed her hand on the gelding's hip, then slid it down the leg to the fetlock. Without warning, the gelding jerked his leg forward and kicked out hard, knocking Cleo off balance and pitching her headlong into the side of the barn. Stars exploded in front of her eyes, and then the light faded into a blackness that wrapped itself around her. It was quiet and peaceful and —

"Cleo." The voice came from far away, as

if through a tunnel or a cave. "Cleo."

She groaned.

"Open your eyes."

She tried to obey, but her head had begun to hurt and the light made it worse. She closed them again.

"Come on, Cleo. Look at me."

Releasing another groan, she forced her eyes open a second time. Woody's image wavered above her.

"That's better."

What was better?

"I'm afraid you'll have a nasty knot."

What was he talking about?

Woody leaned close, and she realized then that he cradled the back of her head in the palm of his hand. "Be still. You're bleeding." He took a handkerchief from his pocket and pressed it to the crown of her head.

My word. His eyes were quite amazing up close like this. And his mouth —

"We'd best get you into the house. That cut needs cleaning and may need stitches." He took hold of her hand and placed it over the kerchief on her head. "Hold that there." Then he slipped one arm beneath her neck and the other beneath her knees.

How he managed to lift her with that bad leg of his, she couldn't say, but it was evidence of strength she hadn't known he possessed.

"You don't have to carry me," she said softly.

He ignored her.

She was glad of it.

"Griff! Cookie!" He carried her toward the kitchen. "Cleo's hurt."

"Don't bother them. Really, Woody. I'm okay. Put me down."

He still ignored her.

This time, gladness was replaced by embarrassment. It wasn't as if she hadn't hit her head before. She'd taken more spills in her lifetime than she could remember. A little bump on the head was no cause for anyone to fuss. But apparently that wasn't up to her. By the time Woody carried her into the kitchen, both her father and Cookie had come running.

"What happened?" her father demanded.

Woody answered, "I heard her cry out and when I turned around, she was lying on the ground unconscious."

"I'm all right, Dad. A horse just knocked me against the barn is all."

Woody set her down on a kitchen chair. "That wound on her head may need stitches."

Cookie brought disinfectant to the table,

along with some soft cloths.

"Ow!" She jerked away as her father began cleaning the wound.

"Sit still, Cleo."

"Let me take care of it myself."

"Not until I have a look."

At least she could be thankful none of the boys were around to witness her humiliation. Bad enough to get knocked unconscious by a horse. Worse yet to be carried into the house like some swooning female in a dime novel. Her dad, Woody, and Cookie better not breathe a word of this or she would have their hides.

"It's not that bad," her father said. "No stitches needed."

"I could have told you that," she replied.

Her dad leaned forward and looked her in the eyes. "No, you couldn't have. You've got a lump the size of an egg up there. You should take it easy the rest of the day."

"I've got to finish shoeing that horse."

Shoe him or shoot him.

"I'll see that it gets done." Her father's tone brooked no argument.

Cleo acquiesced with a nod. "Has the bleeding stopped?"

"Yes."

"Then I'm going to wash up."

She drew in a breath as she stood. A wave

of dizziness washed over her, but she willed it away. If she let on to her father that she felt lightheaded, he would hover over her the rest of the day. Not unlike the way she'd hovered over him when he had the influenza.

But that was different.

She turned slowly and gave each of the men — even Woody — a determined smile. "You can all go about your business. I'm perfectly fine." With back ramrod straight, she left the kitchen and went upstairs to bathe.

Sherwood wouldn't soon forget the sound of Cleo's head striking the side of the barn or the cry of pain torn from her throat. For one horrid moment as he'd stood over her — her eyes closed, her face deathly pale — he'd feared the worst. Even he didn't know how he'd managed to kneel beside her or lift and carry her to the house. He supposed his leg must have complained, that pain must have been present from the start, but he hadn't noticed it until now as he walked toward the horse and buggy, his limp more pronounced than it had been in some time.

"Sorry about that, boy."

He laid a hand on the horse's rump. His gaze rose to the second story of the house, and his imagination was teased with the idea of Cleo reclining in a bathtub, steam rising from the water, her short curls growing more unruly in the humid air. By Jove, what a pretty sight she would make!

He gave his head a shake. What was worse? Imagining his employer's daughter in the bathtub or thinking she was a pretty sight. Didn't much matter. Either one would get him killed if Cleo learned to read his mind.

TWENTY

By the twenty-fifth of June, there wasn't a soul in Crow County over the age of sixteen who didn't mention the hot, dry weather at least once a day. There hadn't been a drop of rain since the end of April, and that storm had been preceded by a winter without the usual snowpack. Drought was on everyone's mind, whether they were a farmer, a rancher, or a waitress in a local restaurant.

Cleo saw the worry in her father's face, especially after the three creeks that ribboned through the Arlington land began to run noticeably lower. The men dug irrigation ditches to water the hay fields, but those ditches would do little good if the streams ran dry.

And so it was, when Cleo, her father, Stitch, and Woody came out of church on that warm Sunday morning, the dark clouds rolling across the heavens brought smiles to their faces. The smell of rain was in the air, although it hadn't begun to fall as yet.

"Thank the good Lord," her dad said, looking skyward.

"Amen," Cleo added.

As had happened a number of times in recent weeks, Stitch bid them a good day and went off to visit his lady friend, and Cleo's father invited Woody to join them for Sunday dinner at the McKinley home. Cleo had stopped being surprised or irritated when Woody was included. In truth, she'd begun to feel he was an extended member of the family. She didn't allow herself to wonder if that was a good thing.

After bidding farewell to a few more of their friends, all of them commenting on the promise of rain, Cleo and her father climbed into the buggy while Woody mounted his saddle horse, and the three of them rode up the hillside to Morgan and Gwen's house.

Gwen — four months pregnant with the rounding of her stomach now visible — met them at the door. "Isn't it wonderful? It's going to rain at last."

"An answer to prayer." Their father kissed Gwen on the cheek.

Cleo kissed her sister's other cheek. "With any luck, we'll get such a downpour you'll have to put us up for the night."

"I'd love to. We have plenty of room." Gwen turned toward Woody. "Lord Sherwood, I trust you're doing well?"

"Yes, and I have your husband to thank for it."

The men entered the house, but Gwen turned once more toward Cleo. "I trust you haven't let another horse knock you unconscious since the last time we were together?"

"That happened three weeks ago. I don't even have a bump on my head left to show for it. I wish you and Dad would quit bringing it up."

"We love you. We worry about you."

"You and Dad worry too much. Now let's go in. I'm getting hungrier by the minute."

Laughing softly, Gwen went into the front parlor where their dad and Woody had joined Morgan, while Cleo made her usual dash up the stairs to change out of her Sunday dress. As she changed into her shirt, Levi's and boots, piano music drifted into the bathroom, and she paused. Was it Gwen who played or Morgan? Gwen, she decided. Morgan's expertise hadn't caught up with his wife's as yet.

She was descending the stairs a short while later when she heard thunder rolling in the distance. Rain was welcome, but not lightning. Lightning was the last thing they needed. Underbrush and trees were too dry from the drought. *Please, Lord. Stop the lightning. Make it go away.*

In the parlor, she found her family and Woody standing at the bank of windows that overlooked the town, no doubt repeating similar prayers to her own. She joined them there, hoping to see raindrops already wetting the parched earth.

But there was no rain as of yet, only a rising wind that caused the trees to bend and whistled beneath the eaves of the house. As they watched, the clouds darkened, a perfect contrast for the flashes of lightning that grew in frequency as the storm rolled closer to Bethlehem Springs.

Cleo glanced to her left and saw Gwen standing close to Morgan's side, his arm around her back. It was in this room, her sister had told her last year, that Morgan first kissed her. There'd been a lightning storm that day too. Cleo wondered if they were remembering it now.

What would it feel like to have someone to reassure her with a tender embrace? Her gaze shifted to Woody. What would it feel like to have *him* stand at her side with an arm around her back? Nice, she decided. It would feel nice.

As if drawn by her thoughts, Woody looked

toward her, and their gazes locked at the same moment another peal of thunder rolled across the heavens. Her heart tripped and then raced, but she knew it had nothing to do with the loud noise and everything to do with Woody. It had been like that a lot lately.

She swallowed, her mouth dry.

"Look!" Gwen cried. "Is that smoke?"

Cleo turned her gaze out the window. "Where?" And then she saw it — way in the distance on the south end of the valley, smoke and an unmistakable flicker of orange licking the tops of the trees.

"I'll alert the fire department," Morgan said.

"I'll spread the word for volunteers." Her father headed for the door.

Morgan stepped closer to Cleo, saying softly, "Look after Gwen and Daphne for me."

She didn't have to ask what he meant. As dry as things were and if the winds were right, a fire could sweep through Bethlehem Springs in a flash. Cleo would have to be alert to the danger and take the other women away if the fire spread toward town.

Morgan and Woody followed her father out the door.

"Take care," she called after them.

Daphne turned from the windows. "I'm sure they'll have it out in no time."

"I hope you're right." Cleo drew a deep breath, trying to calm her jangled nerves. "But I've seen what a firestorm can do. Not that many years ago it burned Glen Hollow, a little town to the east, clean to the ground. We'd better all be praying it doesn't do the same thing here."

"Mrs. McKinley?" The housekeeper appeared in the doorway to the front parlor. "Dinner is ready. Will you be sitting down soon?"

"The men had to leave, Mrs. Cheevers," Gwen answered. "The lightning has started a fire."

Alarm widened the woman's eyes. "In town?"

Cleo answered, "No. I'd say it's a couple or three miles to the south." She glanced at her sister. "We probably should eat without them, Gwen. No telling when they'll be back." Silently, she added, *Who knows when we'll get to eat again, if worst comes to worst.*

"I don't think I could eat a bite."

Above the noise of the wind, they heard the alarm bell ringing from the firehouse.

"Let's give it a try anyway. You've got a baby there who needs nourishing. Besides, there's no point in the food going to waste."

257

Cleo motioned for Gwen and Daphne to precede her out of the room. Her plan was to get them both seated in the dining room, eat a few bites, then slip away to observe the fire from an upstairs window.

Following Morgan's instructions, Sherwood galloped his horse along the road that led into the mountains to the southwest of Bethlehem Springs, looking for the occasional cabin and calling out warnings to any inhabitants. The wind blew hard into his face. Not a good sign. It meant the fire would continue to push north. When he reached the end of the road, he turned and rode hard back the way he'd come.

As he neared the town, he saw something falling from the sky that resembled dirty snow. Ash from the fire. There had been times it had fallen just like this on the battlefields of France, often for days at a time.

He kicked the gelding hard with his left heel. Minutes later, he rounded a bend in the road and the Baptist church came into view. Then he saw the billows of black smoke rolling into Bethlehem Springs and heard men shouting instructions. He rode on, looking for somewhere he could be of help.

He turned the bay onto Shenandoah Street and rode past the Methodist church and the schoolhouse. He was at the corner of Shenandoah and Wallula when he saw the fire truck. Firemen and volunteers were wetting down the roofs of the houses on this southernmost end of town, hoping to defeat any hot embers the wind carried there. Others were leading away horses and carrying possessions out of houses, in case the efforts of those fighting the fire failed.

Sherwood dismounted and tied his horse to a picket fence. Then he hurried as fast as his leg allowed toward the fire truck. He slapped a hand onto the shoulder of the nearest fireman.

"How can I help?"

"We've got men over the hill there, clearing brush and trees, trying to make a fire break. They could use you."

He started off without a word.

"Better cover your nose and mouth with a kerchief," the fireman shouted. "The air's even worse yonder."

Sherwood didn't have a large enough kerchief to tie around his head, but he didn't bother to say so. He would have to get by the best he could. He had a feeling that every able-bodied man was needed as quickly as possible.

Pain shot up his right leg as he climbed the hillside. Twice he stumbled and fell to his knee. Ash continued to rain down upon his head, and it felt to Sherwood like a blanket of doom. He hadn't endured this kind of fear since the day he'd charged out of the trench, shouting some sort of battle cry along with his comrades, and believed his life was about to end.

"If You're really up there, God, if You listen to prayers like the priests and reverends say You do, then I hope You will heed all the prayers that are going up to You now."

At the top of the hill, he got a perfect view of the forest fire as it raced toward Bethlehem Springs, moving in a *V*, widening its path as it came closer. God help them if it jumped the fire break that was being carved out of the earth below where he stood. Without rain, it almost certainly would.

"I can't stay here another minute," Daphne said. "I must go home. There are things I must save, things that can't be replaced."

Gwen placed a hand on her sister-in-law's shoulder. "Your house is too near the fire line."

"I don't care. I must save what I can."

Cleo saw the worry in Gwen's face, heard it in her voice. "I'll go with Daphne. We'll get as many of her things out as we can. And in the meantime, you put together whatever you might want to take with you up to the resort, just in case we have to evacuate." She motioned toward the door. "Let's go, Daphne."

They ran to the buggy. The horse shied and tried to bolt, no doubt frightened by the wind and the noise and the smell of fire in the air. Cleo grabbed the reins close to the bit and quieted the animal while Daphne hopped into the buggy. Then she joined her, slapping the reins against the horse's rump. "Giddup there!" The horse would have broken into a run if not for Cleo's tight grip.

Most Sundays, Bethlehem Springs was a quiet place. Not so now. Today people — mostly women, children, and the elderly — were loading up wagons, preparing to leave if the fire reached the edge of town. Cleo had to slow the horse as she weaved the buggy from one side of the street to another to miss wagons and buggies and wheelbarrows.

Straight ahead, beyond that last block of houses, there was a hill. And beyond that hill, a growing inferno threatened to devour Bethlehem Springs. It roared and huffed like a dragon in ancient legends, spewing out thick smoke that stung her eyes and her throat. *God Almighty, save us.*

"Turn here!" Daphne cried, fear sharpening her voice.

Cleo knew this town like the back of her hand, but things looked different in the odd, smoky light of midday. She guided the horse around the corner and up to the white picket fence in front of the small brick house. Daphne's feet hit the ground before the buggy was fully stopped. Cleo secured the reins and then followed her friend.

"What do you want me to get?" she called as she entered the house.

"My jewelry," Daphne replied from the room she used for an office. "It belonged to my mother and I couldn't bear to lose it. It's in the box on my dresser."

Cleo hurried into the bedroom and grabbed the jewelry box. Then she decided to take some dresses from the wardrobe. No use having room in her arms when she could just as easily fill them up. By the time she was out of the room, Daphne was there, lugging a suitcase. From the way she carried it, it was obviously heavy.

"What's in there?"

"Journals and books. Lots of them."

Of all the things Daphne could rescue, a bunch of books didn't seem all that important. What about the silver service and fine china? What about that painting that hung over the sofa, the one Daphne said she'd bought in Italy?

Outside, Cleo dropped the gowns and jewelry box into the back of the buggy, then took the suitcase from Daphne and tossed it on top of the other items. "Anything else?"

"I'd better not take more. Gwen will have things she needs too."

Cleo looked around, undecided if she should encourage Daphne to go back inside one more time. That's when she saw Woody's horse, tied to a fence at the end of the block. In that instant, she realized there was nothing more important than finding him and making certain he wasn't in danger. If the worst happened and the fire reached town, she needed to make certain he got away to safety. He was, after all, still a greenhorn. He would need her . . . and she would need him.

"Daphne, take the buggy back to Morgan's house. Get Gwen, and the two of you head up to New Hope. If she tries to say she can't go because she's the mayor, remind her she has a baby to think about. And for pity's sake, tell the staff to get out of town too. Take them with you to the spa."

She didn't wait for a response. She took off running, down Wallula onto Shenandoah and straight to Jefferson Street, where firemen were spraying rooftops with water. Thank God for the new hoses. They'd been one of the first purchases Gwen had seen to as mayor.

She scanned the area for a glimpse of her father, Morgan, or Woody. Woody's horse was only a block away. He was on foot. He must be nearby.

Seeing the fire chief, she ran toward him. "Mr. Spooner! Have you seen my father or Morgan?" The chief might not know Woody or she would have asked after him as well.

Chief Spooner barely glanced at her. "Over the ridge." Then to one of the men handling a hose, he shouted, "Stay on that, Mason."

Cleo turned and started up the hillside. Hell must be like this, full of soot and smoke and noise and heat and fear. Her lungs ached as if she'd run a mile. Her eyes watered, and her throat felt like raw meat in a grinder.

When she reached the hilltop, she stopped to survey the activity below. It looked as if every man who could walk — at least all those who weren't helping the fire department in town — was down there. Trees were being felled; several teams of horses dragged them away while another team pulled a plow, turning under grass and brush, making a wide swath of land that was barren of fuel for the flames. In the ash and confusion it was impossible to distinguish one man from another.

Part of her wanted to go down and lend a hand. She was strong enough. Couldn't be harder than busting a bronc. Another part of her knew she should go back and look after Gwen and Daphne, as she'd promised Morgan she would. But surely they were preparing to leave for the spa. Wouldn't discovering that Morgan and their dad were okay be another way of helping Gwen?

And Woody. She wanted to know that Woody was okay as well. She *had* to know.

She pressed her neckerchief to her nose and mouth and started down the hillside.

Sherwood gave the heavy chain a yank to make certain it was secure. Then he waved for the man driving the team to drag away the fallen tree. He turned to see where he was needed next and winced as pain shot up his leg into the small of his back. But there was no stopping to rest. Not as long as the fire continued its swift march toward the town.

Through the haze of smoke, he thought he saw Cleo talking to someone at the bottom of the hill that separated the firebreak from the town. But it couldn't be her. She was supposed to be with the other women. He squinted. It *was* Cleo. He would recognize that narrow frame anywhere.

He walked toward her as fast as his leg allowed, pulling down the borrowed kerchief he now wore. "Cleo!"

She turned, saw him, and hurried forward. "Woody. How can I help?"

"You can go back to the McKinley house."

"I'm needed more here. Who's giving orders?"

"Morgan asked you to look after his wife and sister. He told me."

She stood a little taller. "Gwen and Daphne are preparing to go up to the spa right now. They may already be on the road. I've got two good arms and a strong back, and I want to protect this town as much as any man here."

If Sherwood had learned anything since his arrival in Bethlehem Springs, it was that Cleo Arlington didn't care much what traditional wisdom said a woman should do or not do. He might as well relent. Besides, her arms and back were undoubtedly stronger than his. Not to mention her two good legs.

"You can help me. Take over fastening the

266

trees for clearing away while I spell one of the men felling them."

Cleo nodded, but stopped him with a hand on his arm before he could turn away. "I couldn't see Dad or Morgan. Do you know where they are?"

He shook his head. "I believe Morgan sent Griff back into town." He motioned toward the sky. "We were afraid being in the thick of this smoke wouldn't be good for his lungs. Because of the influenza."

Relief flickered across her face.

He wanted to give her even more peace. He wanted to promise her that the fire would be stopped, that the town would be saved, that no one would lose their possessions, that there would be no loss of life. But he couldn't make such a promise. The odds were stacked against them. The fire burned too hot and was coming too fast, creating its own wind on top of that made by the storm. It would take a miracle to save the town — and Sherwood couldn't remember a time when he'd believed in miracles. If ever one existed, it had been blown to smithereens on the battlefield.

He was about to turn away from Cleo when something strange happened. The wind died down. He seemed to feel it in his chest even more than on his skin. And then it began to blow again, but this time it was cool and came from the north. Seconds later, rain stung his cheeks. Not a light rain either. A downpour. He was drenched clear through almost at once. The sounds of chopping and dragging and plowing ceased as others realized what was happening. From the top of the hill that separated them from the town, someone shouted something. Words he couldn't make out.

Cleo grabbed for his hand. "I think he said the fire's stopped."

Impossible.

"Come on." She pulled on his arm. "Let's see for ourselves."

He didn't try to resist. He had to see it to believe it.

The rain-slick climb up the angled hillside was made more difficult by the pain in his bad leg, but he gritted his teeth and some-how managed to keep up with Cleo. When they reached the crest, they stopped and turned in unison.

It was true. Even through the sheets of rain, he saw that the wind had pushed the fire back upon itself. Back to where the fuel had been consumed. Flames that had burned high and hot minutes before were fizzling in the cloudburst.

"It's a miracle," Cleo cried. "God sent us

a miracle!"

A miracle. Sherwood looked up, squinting against the rain. *Did You do this?*

Somebody cheered and others joined in.

"It's okay!" Cleo grabbed hold of both his hands, a huge smile lighting her face, almost as if the sun had broken through the clouds. "The fire's dying! We've won!"

Sherwood didn't know how it happened. One moment he was holding her hands while she grinned and shouted for joy. The next, his arms were around her and he was kissing her, a kiss that stirred something inside of him, something he'd never felt before, something far more intense than physical desire. Something in his heart. Something that felt a great deal like —

Cleo took a small step backward and stared at him, her hair and face dripping with rain, her eyes wide with surprise. But she couldn't be more stunned than Sherwood himself. Perhaps if he kissed her again, the shock of it would go away. Perhaps if he kissed her again, he would understand that foreign sensation in his chest.

"Cleo!" The sound of Griff's voice shattered the invisible bonds that had held them motionless. "Sherwood!" They turned toward the town and saw her father climbing the hillside, along with a number of other citizens. "Is it true? The fire's out?"

"It's true," Cleo answered. "The danger's over."

Sherwood looked at her again.

Was the danger over? Or had it simply changed its form?

TWENTY-ONE

Eyes closed, Cleo sank down in the tub of hot water until it covered all but her nose. Here, in this liquid cocoon, there was silence. Nothing to intrude upon the memory she wanted to savor — the memory of Woody holding her in his arms, the rain pouring down upon them, his lips locked upon hers.

She hadn't expected him to kiss her. Why would she expect it? He'd given her no reason to think he might be fond of her.

Fond? Was that the right word?

No, she might not know much about kissing and wooing and the fine art of flirtation, but if what had happened between them on that hillside today expressed only fondness, she'd eat her hat.

A frisson of pleasure moved through her.

Could this be love?

She sat up and opened her eyes.

Love? No. Loving Woody would be a fool

thing to do, no matter how much she liked kissing him. Yes, he'd come a long ways in the weeks he'd been here. He wasn't snooty, like she'd expected him to be, and he wasn't lazy. But he would never be a cowboy, and she was sure as shootin' that it would take a real cowboy to make her happy.

And yet . . .

She shook her head, driving off whatever thoughts might have followed. Then she reached for the soap and began to scrub away the dirt and soot she'd brought back with her from town — perhaps hoping she could wash away the memory of that kiss. Fifteen minutes later, she left the bathroom, clad in a clean pair of Levi's and a pale-blue cotton shirt.

The front door was open, and through it she saw her father, standing on the porch. She went to join him there.

"Your turn in the tub if you want it." She stopped beside him.

"I want it."

There were smudges of ash on her dad's forehead and cheek. "How do your lungs feel?"

"I'm fine, Cleo." He met her gaze. "What about you?"

Did he mean something more than the effects of the fire? Had he seen Woody kiss her? "I'm okay."

"I sent Randall and Allen into town to help watch overnight for hotspots. Stitch volunteered to go with them."

Cleo glanced toward the bunkhouse.

Her father continued, "I invited Sherwood to join us for dinner. No reason for him to eat alone."

"He wouldn't be alone in the kitchen. Cookie is there." She sounded cold and uncharitable, but she couldn't help it. She wouldn't be able to eat a bite with Woody seated at the same table with her. Every time she looked at him, she knew she would remember that moment on the hillside in the rain. She would remember and want him to do it again.

"All the same," her father said as he turned toward the door, "he's going to eat with us."

Cleo remained on the porch, stepping closer to the railing and wrapping an arm around a post as she stared out at the barnyard. Overhead, the sky continued to weep, and suddenly she felt an overwhelming desire to do the same.

Sherwood sat on the edge of his bunk, his forehead cradled in the palms of his hands, elbows on knees. Regret burned hot inside

273

him. He should never have kissed Cleo. He'd confused her. He'd confused himself.

Why had he done it? Why had he lost his head?

Because in that moment, he'd believed in miracles. Because in that instant, he'd forgotten the fears and the smells and the sights that he'd carried around inside himself for the better part of a year. Because when he'd looked at her, he'd seen a woman who laughed and loved and embraced life with abandon, and he'd wanted to do the same. Because she'd made him feel alive.

Because he cared for her. Perhaps cared too much.

He feared he'd begun to love her.

Once it had been amusing to imagine the duke's reaction if he were to meet Cleo Arlington. It wasn't amusing now. Sherwood's father would be horrified by her manner, by the clothes she wore, by her speech. He might not hold his youngest son in high esteem or even warm regard, but he would never allow him to become entangled with an American nobody. The proud name of Statham must be protected at all times. That was, after all, why Sherwood had been sent to America, so the Statham name wouldn't be sullied by his reckless behavior.

A groan rose from his chest.

Cleo was wonderful. She was an original. And the aristocrats of England, his family, his friends, would cut her to shreds the moment they met her.

Sherwood had to do the honorable thing. He must protect her. He must emotionally distance himself from Cleo even if he couldn't do so physically. He mustn't allow her to know his feelings about her.

Above all, he must not kiss her again. Never again.

There was no doubt in Griff's mind that something had happened between Cleo and Sherwood earlier today — sometime between that first roll of thunder and the moment he'd found them on the hilltop in the pouring rain. He was fairly certain that whatever it was, at least one broken heart and probably two of them would be the final result.

As Cleo's father, he'd wished, hoped, and prayed for her to fall in love, marry, and have a family because he knew it was what she wanted. But he didn't want her to know the same heartache he'd experienced. He'd made the mistake of marrying a woman too different from himself. Elizabeth hadn't wanted the life he could offer her, and after four years of marriage, she'd returned to her parents' home in the East rather than spend another year with him in Idaho.

Three weeks ago, he'd decided that he couldn't protect Cleo from the hard things in life, that he would have to let her make up her own mind, make her own mistakes, love whoever she loved. Now he feared he'd made a poor decision. Sherwood and Cleo came from worlds far more different than even Griff's and Elizabeth's had been. Sherwood had managed to adjust to ranch life without too much difficulty — at least it seemed so — but the young man also knew his time in America was brief. And Cleo would never fit into the kind of life Sherwood led in England. Not in a million years.

God help them.

Cleo was a lot like Griff. When she loved, she loved without reserve. She held nothing back. She was like that with her family. She was like that with her friends. She would be even more so with the man who won her heart.

But neither of those two young people were foolish or stupid. They had to know all the reasons an alliance between them was fated for catastrophe. Which must be why they'd both sat at the dinner table earlier in the evening, silent and miserable.

God help them both.

TWENTY-TWO

Cleo rested her arms on the stall gate and looked at the palomino mare inside. By the look of her, she was set to foal soon. Could be tonight. Might not be until tomorrow morning.

"It's gonna be fine," she said softly. "You wait and see. You'll be nursing your colt real soon now."

This would be the mare's first foal. Since the horse was a bit high strung, Cleo planned to keep a close eye on her to make sure all went well.

"Cleo."

Her heart hiccupped at the sound of Woody's voice.

"Is it her time?"

She turned toward the barn doorway, hungry for the sight of him. She hadn't seen him all day. He must have avoided her on purpose because most days their paths crossed often. Yesterday, after the kiss, she hadn't wanted to see him, to talk to him, or to be near him. Today she hadn't seen him, talked to him, or been near him . . . and she'd been miserable.

Ignoring his question, she said, "You were extra long at the spa today. You missed dinner."

"I went into Bethlehem Springs to mail some letters on my way back from the resort, and I saw Reverend Barker in the post office. He invited me to dine with him at the Gold Mountain." He moved toward her, his limp more pronounced today than it had been in a while. "Everyone in the restaurant was talking about how close the fire came to the town. People are still nervous."

"I can imagine." *I'm feeling kinda nervous myself, only not about the fire.* She turned toward the stall, trying to calm the storm in her belly.

"Cleo." He spoke her name again, softly this time. "I need to apologize for yesterday."

"Apologize?" As if she didn't know what he meant.

"My actions were less than gentlemanly. I shouldn't have . . . I shouldn't have forced myself upon you."

"I wouldn't say you *forced* anything."

278

"But I did, and I am sorry. It will not happen again. You have my word on it."

His words hurt. They shouldn't but they did.

Bravado seemed the best course of action. "It's already forgotten. Don't give it another thought." She cast a smile in his direction. "I know I won't."

The last was a lie. She would think of his kiss again and again and again.

The mare snorted and moved in a tight circle, rustling the straw with her hooves.

Woody placed his forearms on the top rail. "She's restless."

"Yeah. She wasn't interested when I tried to feed her earlier."

"Are you going to stay with her until the foal is born?"

"Reckon so." She felt Woody watching her but stubbornly kept her eyes on the mare.

After a lengthy silence, he said, "I hope the birth goes well."

"Thanks."

"Goodnight, Cleo."

"Night, Woody."

When he left, it seemed to Cleo that the oxygen was sucked from the barn right along with him.

It was too late, she realized as she pressed her forehead against the top of the gate. It was too late to keep from falling in love with him. There was no doubt — she loved him already, and she would continue loving him even after he returned to his home in England. She wouldn't get over this. Her infatuation with Tyler had ended the instant she'd learned of his true character. But what she felt for Woody was greater than infatuation. This was love and it was strong. Even his absence wouldn't diminish it. She knew that was true, deep in her soul.

Straightening, she whispered to the restless mare, "But we'll have until next spring. We'll have at least that much."

Until spring would have to be enough to last her a lifetime.

After turning his saddle horse into the paddock to graze, Sherwood went into the house, entering through the kitchen. The door to Cookie's room was open, and he saw the man sitting in an easy chair near the window, an open book in his lap.

"Good evening, Cookie." He rapped on the doorjamb.

"If you're wantin' dinner," the cook answered without looking up, "you'll have to make do with something cold from the icebox."

"I'm not hungry, thank you. I ate in town."

Now Cookie raised his head, his eyebrows cocked, as if to say, *Why are you bothering me, then?*

"I have some matters to attend to in the office. Enjoy your book."

Cookie made a sound of dismissal in his throat as his gaze returned to the printed page.

In Griff's office, Sherwood set a few pieces of mail on the desk. One letter was for him. Jack Cummings, a former school chum who had served with Sherwood in France, had written. He sat and opened the envelope.

Dear Sherwood,

I received a letter from Haywood this week. I suppose you know that my sister Kate is in his parish, and knowing that you and I were in school together, she asked after you and gave him my address. Haywood wrote that you had recovered enough from your injuries and have gone to America. You always were a lucky bloke. Better there than here.

Last week C Company went in lorries to a country place a few miles behind the firing line. The weather was good, and we enjoyed the ride as we have had a rough time of it, going out at night to dig trenches. We haven't lost any men in ten days but that last battle was fierce and many died that day. Harry got a slight wound from shrapnel but he did not need to go to the doctor.

The rations have been very low lately, and I told Kate not to send any cigs as we get plenty of them. Anything to eat is received with joy. Sardines, biscuits, chicken paste, chocolate are always good. Very different from how we ate at school.

Do write, as letters are always welcome, and you still have friends in the company who want to know how you are faring. Tell us about America and if you think the Yanks will ever join us here in France.

With best regards,
from Jack

Sherwood folded the letter and returned it to the envelope. It was good to know his friend was alive and well. Or at least he had been when he wrote this. Considering how long it took a letter to make it from the front to England, let alone to America, Jack Cummings could be long since dead and buried. But he hoped not. He hoped Jack would make it through the war alive. He would like to see him again, perhaps sit down over a pint and celebrate together that they hadn't died along with so many others.

He looked up, eyes toward the window, but in his mind he remembered the night Jack had saved his life, risking his own in the process. He could still taste the blood on his tongue and feel the smoke searing his nostrils. And the pain. The memory of that unbearable pain never quite left him. It seemed decades since that night, yet at the same time it felt like yesterday.

He released a shuddered breath, forcing his thoughts back to the present.

It was because of men like Jack Cummings that he'd wanted to go back to France, that he'd wanted to fight again, that he'd wanted to kill as many Germans as he possibly could. It had taken him a long time to admit his injuries would prohibit his return to active service. And it was knowing that many more good men like Jack would die before it was over that had made him half crazy in those first months out of the hospital.

May God protect you, Jack.

He'd heard it said that there were no atheists in the trenches. Maybe so. Maybe not. He couldn't say he'd turned to God for comfort or guidance when he was at the front, as he'd seen others do. How different might his experiences have been — in the trenches, in the hospital, and back in England — if he'd been a man of faith? A man like Griff Arlington? Very different, he was sure.

But perhaps it wasn't too late to become that kind of man. Too late for the war but not too late to change the rest of his life. And for that Sherwood could thank his father. Ironic, wasn't it? The duke had sent him here as punishment, and instead of retribution Sherwood had been blessed with a valued friendship. He'd been shown examples of authentic faith that had made him hunger for the same.

Turning his head, he glanced at the clock and was surprised to see how much time had passed. He pushed back from the desk and left the office, too restless to sit and work. It wasn't his intent to return to the barn, and yet that was the direction his feet carried him. Outside, gloaming had arrived, a gray blanket that softened the land, but golden lamplight beckoned from inside the barn.

He heard Cleo's voice before he saw her. "That's it, girl. Here he comes." She was in a corner of the stall, well back from the mare that lay on her side in a bed of fresh hay. "You're doing fine."

Sherwood reached the stall in time to see

the foal slip into the world, seventy-five pounds or so of horse visible beneath the opalescent birth sac. Neither mare nor foal moved for a period of time, both of them needing rest. That was when Cleo moved to the gate and stepped out of the stall.

"Things went well," Sherwood said.

A hint of a smile tugged the corners of her mouth. "Without a hitch."

"What happens next?" He didn't need to ask. He'd been present at foalings before. Still, he wanted her to tell him.

"The mare'll stand and break the umbilical cord and eventually she'll deliver the placenta. In the meantime . . ." Her gaze returned to the mare and foal. "The little guy will struggle to get up, and once he does, he'll give nursing a try. Usually happens within the hour, but it can take longer."

"I have never known any woman like you before."

She stilled, then shrugged, not looking at him. "Gwennie says God broke the mold after He made me."

"I believe she's right. You are one of a kind."

"I don't imagine I'd be me anywhere but here." Now she looked at him.

"Perhaps not." Were there tears swimming in her dark-blue eyes or was the lamplight playing tricks on him? "But have you ever *tried* fitting in anywhere else?"

She was silent a short while before answering, "You saw me up at Morgan's shindig. Did it seem like the place for me? Couldn't you tell I was miserable, all gussied up in that dress Gwen gave me?"

"That was only a few hours. That isn't the same thing as settling someplace new. Look at me. Haven't I adjusted to a life that was strange to me? I've done all right, haven't I?"

"What are you trying to say, Woody?"

Good question. What *was* he trying to say to her?

"I'm a simple gal with simple needs. I like things the way they are."

He took a step toward her. "Do you?"

Yes, those were tears in her eyes — tears that she was trying to keep from falling, trying for all she was worth.

"Cleo?"

She lifted her chin.

"You know what Reverend Barker said to me earlier tonight when we were at dinner? He said all things are possible with God."

She lost her battle with tears. Down they came, leaving damp tracks in their wake.

"Don't cry." He reached out and gently swept them away. "It isn't my wish to make

286

you unhappy."

"That's just it." A tentative smile. "When I'm with you, I'm not unhappy."

He cupped her chin with his right hand. "Could we see what happens?"

"What happens?"

"Between us. No expectations. Just see what develops without being afraid of tomorrow."

"I reckon that could be a terrible mistake," she whispered.

"Or maybe not."

He was about to kiss her again, but neither of them would be surprised this time. Eyes open, she watched his mouth descend toward hers, saw the incline of his head so their noses wouldn't bump. At first the kiss was nothing more than a soft brush of his lips upon hers. But then his arms encircled her and he drew her closer. She closed her eyes and savored the tenderness she found in his embrace and the discovery she found in his kiss.

For this moment, here in the coolness of the barn, silence surrounding them, she refused to worry about what would happen down the road. She would love him now and let the chips fall where they may.

Twenty-Three

A month had passed since the last time Cleo sat in the mayor's office. Only a month since Gwen had said, *"Oh, my. You do like him, don't you?"* and Cleo had vehemently denied it.

There was no denying it today.

"I love him," she told her sister.

Several emotions skittered across Gwen's face, chief among them a look of concern.

"Gwennie, I know you figure I'm gonna get my heart broke, and you're probably right. But I can't help it. I can't stop loving him just because I know there's little to no chance of a future for us."

"Does Dad know how you feel?"

"I'm pretty sure he's got an inkling."

Gwen rose from her chair. "Maybe Morgan should give Lord Sherwood a position at New Hope. Then you wouldn't see him everyday and —"

"You want to take him away from me that

much sooner?" Cleo stood too. "That wouldn't be doing me any kindness."

Gwen rounded the desk and took hold of Cleo's hands. "Does he return your feelings? Does he love you too?"

"Yes." Joy bubbled up inside her chest. "Yes, I reckon he does."

"But he hasn't said so?"

"No. Me neither, except to you just now. How was it he put it last night?" She heard Woody's beloved voice in her head and repeated the words aloud. "We want to see what develops without being afraid of tomorrow."

"I like him, you know. We all like him. But what do the two of you have in common?"

"Not much as far as I can tell." Cleo chuckled, remembering the first time she'd laid eyes on Woody on the railroad station's platform.

"Oh, Cleo. I wish I hadn't teased you about this. I'm so afraid you'll be hurt. After what happened last year . . ."

Her amusement vanished. "It's not the same thing. Besides, I reckon the only way to keep from getting hurt is to quit living, to never take a risk of loving. Sometimes life's just hard, Gwennie. We both know that."

Gwen drew Cleo close and hugged her.

"Be careful."

"I will be. I promise."

"No." Gwen pulled back and looked into Cleo's eyes. "I mean . . . be careful when you're with him. That you . . . that you aren't tempted . . . that you don't . . ." She let the words fade away, her warning unfinished as a flush rose into her cheeks.

Cleo realized what her sister meant and felt a matching blush warm her own face. She'd grown up on a ranch and had a fair understanding of how things were between a man and a woman. "Don't worry. I haven't lost my head." *Just my heart.*

Gwen hooked her left arm through Cleo's right. "It's almost lunch time. Let's eat together. And for dessert, I think my baby is asking for a piece of pie at the South Fork."

"If your baby isn't careful, he's going to make his mama fat." She smiled, grateful for the quick change of subject.

After completing his morning chores, Sherwood paused to admire the new colt in the smaller of the two paddocks. He was the same yellow color as his mother and had a similar white blaze on his forehead. Already he moved about as if he'd been on all fours for years instead of less than twenty-four hours.

Griff joined Sherwood at the fence. "He's a good-looking little guy, isn't he?"

"That he is."

"Cleo bought the dam as a yearling three years ago at a sale down in Boise. I didn't think she looked like anything special, but Cleo saw something I didn't. She's been like that since she was a young girl. Always a good judge of horseflesh. Usually a pretty good judge of people too."

Sherwood nodded.

Griff looked at him. "My daughter's special."

"I agree, sir."

"She's got a heart as deep and wide as this valley. I don't want her hurt."

Sherwood understood that he was about to receive a father's warning. "I won't hurt her if it's in my power to keep from it."

"I believe you mean that, son, but I wonder if it can be helped."

Sherwood wondered the same.

The older man nodded, then walked away, and Sherwood returned his gaze to the paddock and the gawky colt.

He meant what he'd said. He would do all in his power not to hurt Cleo. The man he used to be might have spoken those same words without any intent of honoring them. That's the kind of man he'd been after the war. But no longer.

Sherwood had changed in the time he'd been here in Idaho, in the time he'd known the Arlingtons and the McKinleys. But had he changed enough? Was the change permanent? Or would he revert to his old self when he returned to England?

Change me for good, Lord.

He lifted his eyes and looked — really looked — at the surrounding countryside, the lush green valley and the pine-covered mountains beneath a clear blue sky. Beautiful and peaceful. No wonder God could work on his heart. In this place. With these people.

At the South Fork, townsfolk were still talking about the narrow escape from the fire. One couple stopped by Gwen's table to thank her for the changes she'd made since taking office.

"One ember on a dry roof, and the whole town coulda gone up in smoke," the elderly husband said. "Chief Spooner and the other firemen did a good job of protecting us."

"I'll be sure to tell him you said so, Mr. Smith."

Cleo leaned back in her chair and admired

her sister. Who would have thought Gwen would be so perfect as the mayor? Cleo hadn't doubted her sister could do the work required, but she hadn't known Gwen would take to politics like a duck to water. There was a lot going on inside that pretty head of hers. She had both beauty and brains. Cleo found it hard to believe she and her sister were related, let alone twins.

The couple moved on, and Gwen's gaze returned to Cleo. "Have you decided what you want? It's my treat."

"I thought the meatloaf looked good."

"Mmm. I think I'll have the same. And a piece of apple pie for both of us?"

"Sure. Why not?"

The waitress came and Gwen gave her their order. As she was doing so, Cleo saw Doc Winston come into the restaurant. His suit looked rumpled, and weariness lined his face. It seemed he'd had a difficult morning. Could be someone died. Old Mrs. Cooper had been ailing for quite a spell.

The doctor nodded to Cleo and Gwen as he took a seat at the empty table next to them.

"Good afternoon," Gwen said.

"Afternoon." Even the word seemed to take something out of him.

Cleo and Gwen exchanged a look, but

before either of them could say something more to the physician, the waitress arrived at his table.

"Afternoon, Doc." She set a menu before him. "Care for some coffee?"

"Please."

"You okay?"

"I've just come from a long and difficult delivery. For a time, I didn't think mother or child would survive, but they seem to have rallied. I came back to town to get a few things I need and thought I'd better eat while here. But I'm in a hurry."

"I'll get your coffee. Do you know what you want?"

"How about biscuits and gravy?"

"Good choice. That won't take long. I'll have it out to you in a jiffy." The waitress moved away.

Doc Winston glanced in Gwen and Cleo's direction. "Henrietta King delivered a baby boy." Then beneath his breath, he added, "Poor girl." He rubbed a hand over his face.

Poor girl, indeed, Cleo thought, remembering the day they'd met on the sidewalk outside this restaurant.

"Please give the Kings my congratulations," Gwen said. "And tell Mrs. King that I'll pray for good health for both her and the baby."

Cleo didn't add to her sister's good wishes. She doubted Henrietta would want to hear anything from her. Instead, she raised a silent word of thanks to God for bringing Woody into her life, someone she could love without reserve.

Twenty-Four

At Woody's invitation, Cleo accompanied him to the spa the following afternoon. Riding beside him in the buggy, she felt almost giddy with pleasure. While she and Woody had plenty of opportunities to spend time together at the ranch, this felt different, special, intentional.

When they reached the bridge, Cleo looked at Woody and said, "Tell me about your family."

"What would you like to know?"

Everything. "Why don't you begin with how your parents met?"

"I don't believe anyone has asked me that before."

"Well, I'm asking."

"Very well. A cousin of my mother's introduced my parents at a ball. My mother was seventeen, beautiful, sweet natured, and from a good family. My father was thirty-two and had recently inherited his title. It was his duty to take a wife and provide an heir for Dunacombe. He decided rather quickly that my mother would make a suitable duchess, and they were married a few months later."

Cleo wondered if it had been as cool and calculated as Woody made it sound. Yes, she decided, looking at his bland expression. It probably had been.

"My mother successfully performed her most important duty by giving birth to three sons over the next three years. I was born five years after the last. I believe I came as a surprise to them both."

"A good surprise, I trust."

He returned her smile but his seemed bittersweet. "Perhaps."

She leaned over and kissed his cheek, unable to bear the flicker of sadness she saw in his eyes.

"Now it's your turn. Tell me how Griff met your mother."

"They met in San Francisco. They were guests at a wedding. Dad says it was love at first sight on both their parts. Mother's parents tried to tell her she would not be content living on a cattle ranch, but she wouldn't listen. They were married, and Dad brought her to Idaho. The ranch wasn't much back then, but Dad had big dreams for it." Cleo shrugged. "He just couldn't make them happen fast enough. Mother hated everything about the ranch. So after four years, when Gwen and I were two, she packed up, took Gwen, and moved back with her parents, where she's stayed ever since."

"Was there a divorce?"

She shook her head, her gaze shifting to the river off to the right of the road. "Dad expected her to divorce him, but she never did and he never would."

"When did you last see her? When you were two?"

"No. She came last year for Gwen and Morgan's wedding, and she stayed on for a lot longer than any of us thought she would. I think Dad hoped she would decide to stay for good, that she would see how different things were now and move back in with him, be his wife again. But it didn't happen. She finally went back to New Jersey."

Woody reached over and took her left hand in his right one, squeezing gently. It was only then that she realized tears had formed in her eyes. She blinked them away. After all, she'd made peace with her mother's choice a long time ago, and sure as shootin' she wouldn't have wanted to grow up anywhere but on the ranch. She'd always figured her own kids would grow up there, too, assuming she was blessed with any.

Maybe that explained the tears. If she never married, she would never have children, and she couldn't imagine loving any other man than Woody — and he belonged in England.

He drew in on the reins, stopping the horse. Then he twisted on the buggy seat and gathered her into his arms, kissing her the way she'd longed for him to do all day. When he drew back, he said, "I'm sorry."

"For what?"

"That you were hurt. That you felt rejected."

She was going to deny it, or at least say she was over it. But she realized something: he'd felt the same way. He'd felt rejected too. Perhaps he felt it still.

Tears returned to her eyes as she leaned close to brush her mouth against his. Then she whispered the words she hadn't meant to say this soon, something she'd been told a woman shouldn't say first: "I love you, Woody."

What was it she read in his eyes? She couldn't be sure. Had she made a dreadful mistake? She drew back and forced a smile to her lips. "Don't worry. I didn't say it to try to make you say it too."

"That wasn't what I thought."

Wasn't it?

"I was remembering the promise I made to your father yesterday."

"What promise was that?"

"That I wouldn't hurt you if it was in my power to keep from it."

How could she help but love him when he said something like that? "I thought we weren't going to worry about tomorrow. We wanted to see what developed between us. Now I've said what's developed in me."

"Oh, Cleo." His hands on her cheeks, he stared into her eyes. "You're too trusting, I fear."

"Maybe so, but that's who I am."

Something fierce stirred inside of Sherwood. He loved Cleo without question. He loved her openness. He loved her swift changes of mood. He loved her when she wore trousers and when she wore dresses on Sundays. He loved her strength of will and her daring heart. He loved her trusting nature because it was so much a part of who she was. He'd even grown fond of her short hair. And without question, his father would despise all of these same things about her. He would find her wholly unsuitable as wife to a Statham.

But perhaps, with his mother's help, Sherwood could overcome his father's objections, no matter how numerous they were. He reminded himself once again what the reverend had said: with God, all things were possible. He could only hope that Dagwood Statham, Duke of Dunacombe, was not the exception to that rule.

"You said that when you are with me you cannot be unhappy. Did you mean it, Cleo?"

"Of course I meant it."

"Could you be happy away from the ranch?"

For a long while after he asked the question, she said nothing. Simply stared at him with those beautiful blue eyes of hers — eyes that revealed her fervent search for the true answer in her heart. And he knew the moment she'd found it. He saw the unspoken questions leave her gaze as the smallest of smiles curved her mouth. "I reckon I could learn to be happy anywhere, as long as you were with me."

He almost asked her if that included England, but he stopped himself short. Before he could ask her to marry him, he had to write to his father. Like it or not, without the duke's approval, he would have nothing to offer a bride. No money. No home. No position. Nothing.

"If we don't hurry, I'll be late for my appointment." He kissed her lightly one more time, then turned forward on the seat and slapped the reins against the horse's rump.

While Woody was with his therapist, Cleo went into the lodge to pay a visit to Morgan. But it turned out her brother-in-law wasn't at the resort that afternoon, so she decided to walk about the grounds until it was time for Woody to be finished.

Gardeners had been busy since the opening of the resort. Many varieties of flowers and shrubs were on display, a colorful feast for the eyes. Dozens of rose bushes had been planted along the front of the chapel. Later in the summer, what a sweet fragrance would hang in the air to greet the guests who went there to pray.

Cleo went inside and sat on one of the wooden pews. Light filtered through stained-glass windows, and several lamps, turned low, burned near the altar. The peaceful atmosphere invited her to bow her head.

She began with prayers for the resort, for Morgan, for the people who would find relief there. She prayed for her sister and for the baby she carried, that all might go well in bringing the child into the world.

Then she prayed for Woody, for an even greater healing than he'd experienced already. And finally, she prayed for the two of them.

He hadn't said he loved her. Not yet. He hadn't asked her to marry him. But she believed that was what he'd meant when he'd asked if she could be happy away from the ranch. Of course she didn't *want* to leave. She didn't *want* to be separated from her father or her sister. But could she ever be happy again if she were separated from Woody? She feared not. A life in England with him would be better than a life here without him, wouldn't it? Yes, her heart told her. Yes. Yes. Yes.

"Mrs. Sherwood Statham," she whispered and felt her pulse quicken at the sound of the words.

Was it possible for love to multiply in intensity with each passing day? It seemed so to Cleo. It seemed that she loved Woody twice as much today as she had yesterday, and she was certain she would love him even more tomorrow.

Father, I want to be his wife more than I've ever wanted anything in my life. I don't want him to go back to England and leave me here. Please let it be Your will for us to be together. She drew a deep breath and released it. *I reckon I could even take to wearing dresses and letting my hair grow, if need be.*

She sat in the stillness for a long while after that. Not praying. Not thinking. Simply being quiet. Waiting for an answer. But this was not a day when she heard God speaking in her heart, and so finally she rose and quitted the chapel.

Shadows had lengthened while she was inside. Woody's session must be over by now. If so, he would want to leave. She hurried toward the lodge, and when she rounded the corner of the building, she saw him standing beside the buggy. But he wasn't alone. There was a woman with him. A rather pretty one.

Cleo felt a stab of jealousy. So strong it stole her breath away. *Mercy.* She inhaled while forcing herself to walk more slowly, to appear unconcerned. When she drew near, both Woody and the young woman looked in Cleo's direction. Their reactions were quite different. As her eyes traveled the length of Cleo, the young woman's expression was one of surprise, followed by dismissal.

Woody's expression was one of welcome. "Here you are. I was about to come looking for you."

The warmth of his smile and the tone of

his voice caused Cleo's jealousy to evaporate.

Woody held out a hand and she took it, letting him draw her to his side. "Cleo, may I introduce an acquaintance of mine, Miss Marjorie Lewis. We met when she visited England a number of years ago. Miss Lewis, this is Cleo Arlington. I work with Miss Arlington on her father's cattle ranch."

"You work together? How interesting. I suppose that explains your unusual attire, Lord Sherwood."

"I assure you, my attire is not at all unusual in Idaho." Woody glanced at Cleo. "Miss Lewis was here for the opening of the resort, and now she and her family have returned for a longer stay." To Miss Lewis he said, "Cleo is Morgan McKinley's sister-in-law. As a matter of fact, she and Mrs. McKinley are twins."

"Good heavens. Twins? I would never have known you were related."

"Most folks don't see the family resemblance," Cleo answered.

"You'll have to excuse us," Woody said to Miss Lewis. "Cleo and I must be on our way. I hope you enjoy the remainder of your stay at New Hope." He turned and continued to hold Cleo's hand as she stepped into the buggy.

Cleo didn't need his help, of course, but she liked that he gave it, instinctively knowing it was for Miss Lewis's benefit, that Woody was saying, *I'm with Cleo. She's my girl.*

Hope for the future sparkled in her heart.

Sherwood tried several times to write to his father, but each attempt ended up in the waste bin. It had never been easy to communicate with the duke. Not in person. Not in letters. He was always conscious of his father's quick disapproval of him. In the end, he wrote to his mother.

Dearest Mother,

I hope this letter finds you well. I trust you will be pleased to know that my health is much improved. I am now able to ride for long periods on horseback, and the pain I once suffered is greatly reduced.

It has been three months since I was last at Dunacombe Manor. England seems almost another world, and America is no longer such a strange place as it once seemed to me. I have become accustomed to the different way these Americans speak, and I enjoy new friendships with a number of people in the area.

It is one special friendship that I write to you about today. I have grown fond of a young woman named Cleo Arlington. She is the daughter of my employer, Griff Arlington, and her sister is married to Morgan McKinley.

The truth is that I'm more than fond of her. It is my desire to ask for her hand in marriage. Cleo is an unusual woman, to be sure, but I know that when you meet her you will like her as much as I do.

Mother, Cleo is not a woman of great fortune or one of what Father would consider proper society, but she is the one I want to be at my side for the remainder of my life. I love her, and she will make me happy as I hope to make her happy. Will you help me prepare the way with Father? I know it is a great deal to ask, but with so much distance between us, I don't know how else to do this.

Give my regards to my brothers. I will write again soon.

> With deep affection, your son,
> Sherwood

It was cowardly of him to send such a letter, to leave it to his mother to tell the duke about Cleo. Like a schoolboy instead of a man. He might as well be back at Dunacombe, walking that hallway to the library, expecting another dressing down.

He was tempted to wad the letter into a ball and toss it in the trash along with the previous attempts. Instead, he folded it and placed it into an envelope. Better not to delay. Better to make at least this small effort. He knew his mother would do as he requested, that she would speak to the duke on Sherwood's behalf. And perhaps, given a few more months, his father would resign himself to an American daughter-in-law.

TWENTY-FIVE

Every woman should fall in love in the month of June Cleo decided. The weather was warm without being miserably hot. Most days were sunny with crystal blue skies and the occasional cotton ball clouds. The mountains and grasslands sported wildflowers in an array of colors — royal purples and cobalt blues, sunshine yellows and passionate pinks. Colts and fillies and young calves cavorted in the fields. Puppies ran and tumbled in the barnyard, and kittens meowed in the hayloft. It was a time of new life and happy spirits. A glorious time of year to be in love.

Such were Cleo's thoughts as she lay on a blanket on a hillside, staring up through the tree limbs at the sky. Beside her, Sherwood reclined on his side, bracing himself with his left elbow while he read to her from a book of poetry.

" 'It is not Beauty I demand, A crystal

brow, the moon's despair, Nor the snow's daughter, a white hand, Nor mermaid's yellow pride of hair . . .' "

Cleo smiled to herself as a wave of contentment washed over her. Woody still hadn't said he loved her. Not in so many words. But it didn't worry her. He told her with his actions, even with his choice of poems, and that was enough for now.

" 'Tell me not of your starry eyes, Your lips that seem on roses fed, Your breasts where Cupid trembling lies, Nor sleeps for kissing of his bed . . .' "

She closed her eyes, warmth rising in her cheeks. She longed for the day when they might marry, and Woody would take her to his bed.

What sort of wedding would they have? A simple affair here in Bethlehem Springs? Or would the son of a duke be required to marry in England? England. A place so far from home. But home would be wherever her husband was. Cleo wasn't like her mother. She wouldn't run away. She would adapt. She would put down roots in a foreign soil. She would be happy as long as she was with Woody.

Once they were living in England, he wouldn't wear the blue jeans, plaid cotton shirt, and boots that he wore now. He would once again wear the attire of an English gentleman, a lord of the realm. And she would have to wear fashionable dresses and shoes that weren't as comfortable as her boots. Would she be called Lady Cleo? Gracious. She wouldn't care for that. Not at all. Only for Woody would she consider it.

" 'Give me, instead of beauty's bust, A tender heart, a loyal mind, Which with temptation I could trust, Yet never linked with error find. One in whose gentle bosom I Could pour my secret heart of woes. Like the care-burdened honey-fly That hides his murmurs in the rose . . .' "

He could pour his secret heart of woes into her. She would take them and hold them and pray about them. She would —

"I say. Have you been listening?"

She opened her eyes to find him watching her over the top of his book. "Yes." It was only a small lie. She might have missed a few stanzas while her thoughts wandered.

He closed the book. "I believe I shall leave off there. You'll have to wonder how Mr. Darley ended his poem."

"I love to listen to you read. You make every word sound elegant. 'Course, maybe all poetry sounds elegant, even without a British accent. I can't say I've read much of it myself."

311

"You're too busy breaking horses." He smiled as he leaned in to kiss her.

Cleo doubted there was much call for wranglers in England, especially not a female wrangler. What would she do with her days? As he hadn't proposed, she couldn't very well ask him that, and so she asked him something else. "What will you do when you return to England?"

"Do you mean as a profession?"

"Yes. Will you become a lawyer?"

"I think not."

"Why's that? It's what you've trained for. Right?"

"I fear I would make a very poor one. I am not a great orator, nor am I particularly persuasive when trying to influence others."

Some men of the upper classes, Cleo understood, did little with their time. Would Woody be one of those? Would he be satisfied to be idle, day after day? She could be wrong, but she didn't see him that way. He'd worked too hard, done too much around the ranch, for her to think him a wastrel by nature. As for herself, doing nothing would drive her crazy.

"Thankfully I don't have to make a decision yet. There is still time to consider my options. But for the next nine months, I am content to be a ranch hand." He lay on his back beside her and stared up at the heavens as she had done a short while before. "And a very lazy one at this moment."

"We all deserve a brief respite now and then. Even you." Her hand slipped into his as natural as you please.

He turned his head, his face close to her own. "Isn't it fortunate that you deserved a respite, too, Miss Arlington?"

"I reckon it is, Mr. Statham."

His kiss this time was slow, long, sweet. It made her want to write poetry of her own, sonnets of love that would go on for pages and pages, words that would make other hearts soar as high as her own. Cleo wished they could remain right there forever, perfectly happy on that glorious summer day.

Sherwood wanted to take Cleo into his arms and drink more deeply of her love for him. But they had already strayed into dangerous waters. She might be too innocent to recognize the hazard, but he was not. Wisdom required that he end the kiss and put some distance between them.

He withdrew and rose as quickly as his right leg would allow. "Perhaps we should start back."

"So soon?" She sat up, disappointment

visible in her gaze.

"We have been gone several hours."

"There's still some food left."

He patted his stomach. "I couldn't eat another morsel."

She sighed as she stood. "I suppose you're right." She leaned down and picked up the blanket.

There was a rare and beautiful innocence about Cleo, he thought as he watched her fold the blanket. An innocence that made him all the more determined to remain on his guard. When the day arrived that they married, she would come to him sweet and pure. He couldn't claim the same. What a hedonist he'd been. It was a wonder his own mother loved him, let alone that Cleo did.

God was indeed merciful. It was enough to make him thankful for the injuries he'd suffered in the war. Without them, he wouldn't have sought oblivion in drinking, gambling, and women, and as a result, he wouldn't have been sent to America. Without them, he never would have known Cleo, might have continued to turn a blind eye toward heaven, might never have come to the moment of wanting to change, of wanting to be a better man.

"Cleo."

She turned from putting the blanket into

the saddlebag.

"I love you."

The smile came slowly to her lips. "I know. I reckon I knew it before you did."

He wanted to say more, but he couldn't. Not yet. At present, he was a man without prospects. He needed the blessing of his father before he could marry. Otherwise, he would have no income, no way to support a wife and family. Here in America things might be done differently, but in England, among the nobility . . . No, he had no choice but to wait awhile longer.

But waiting to marry Cleo Arlington could be the most difficult thing he'd ever had to do.

TWENTY-SIX

It rained again for the first few days in July, but the Fourth dawned with clear skies, promising a perfect day for the Bethlehem Springs Independence Day celebration. There would be a band playing in the band shell, dancing on a wooden floor made for the occasion, lots of games in the park, and all kinds of food to eat. There would even be fireworks after darkness fell, although those would be kept to a small area, far away from the forest and underbrush. No one wanted to risk another fire.

Cleo loved the Fourth of July. It was the sort of holiday where everyone seemed in perfect spirits, ready to smile and to laugh. And this year, she would attend with Woody and people would see they were a couple. Being with him was almost enough to cause her to put on a dress. Almost. But how did a woman run a three-legged race in such feminine trappings? Maybe some could, but she couldn't. She would end up tumbling to the ground with her skirts up over her head. Now wouldn't that be a fine kettle of fish? No, she would save her dresses for Sunday services.

But that didn't mean she wasn't going to look nice for the festivities — and for Woody. She wore a new pair of denim jeans with a blue-and-white shirt and her best pair of boots, nicely polished. And she donned a white Stetson that had been a gift from Gwen on their last birthday.

The Arlingtons, their ranch hands, and Cookie left for town in the early afternoon. Cleo's dad and Cookie rode in the wagon, the bed holding several blankets, jars of lemonade, and boxes holding two cakes and three pies. Cleo and the rest of the cowboys rode on horseback. The merry mood of the company made the journey into town pass quickly.

Not long before they reached Bethlehem Springs, Stitch looked over at Woody and said, "Is it legal for you to join us today, you being English and all? You do know that what we're celebratin' is our freedom from British rule."

"I believe I have heard that somewhere before." Woody's tone was droll.

"Well, just didn't want you gettin' into

trouble once you're back in England. Could be viewed as consortin' with the enemy."

"Cleo tells me there will be games at these festivities. Perhaps the Brit will whip a Yankee or two in one of them."

Stitch protested that such a thing would never happen while everyone else laughed.

"This oughta be good." Cleo grinned at Woody.

He leaned sideways in the saddle and said in a low voice, "Perhaps I shall even beat you."

"Ha!"

He straightened. "We shall see."

"You bet we will." She might love him to pieces, but she would never enter a game that she didn't want to win.

The town park, located on Shenandoah Street between the boarding house and the Methodist church, bustled with people. Tables had been made from sawhorses supporting planks of wood, and onto those tables folks were placing their contributions to the celebration — fried chicken, biscuits, salads, fruits and vegetables, cakes, pies, cookies, donuts, and plenty more besides.

While Cookie and Allen carried the food they'd brought with them to the tables, Cleo and Woody looked for Morgan, Gwen, and Daphne and soon found them in the shade of some poplars.

"Looks like everybody's going to be here." Cleo spread a blanket on the ground next to her sister. "Are any of the guests from New Hope coming down?"

"Yes, quite a number of them. They'll be here in time to eat. Not long now."

"When do you give your speech?"

"It isn't a speech," Gwen answered. "Just a quick welcome from the mayor."

The musicians began warming up in the band shell, drawing the sisters' gazes in that direction.

Cleo leaned close to Gwen. "I hope Hank Mason's fiddle playing is better than Mooney O'Rourke's was last year."

"Cleo, be nice."

"Maybe you were too excited about winning the election to remember how bad it was."

Gwen laughed softly. "No. I remember. It was dreadful."

Cleo turned toward Woody. "Reckon we ought to have a look at things?"

He nodded.

To Gwen, Cleo said, "We'll be back after a while." Then she and Woody walked toward the band shell. "That's Hank Mason on the fiddle and Doc Winston on the drums. Doc's niece, Rose, is playing the flute. I'm not sure who that is on the bass fiddle."

They stopped for a short while to listen as the band played "Yankee Doodle Boy." Cleo sang along with them and did just fine until she realized Woody was watching her instead of looking at the band shell. Self-conscious, she stopped.

"I like to hear you sing," he said with a smile.

"Gwen's the musical one in the family, but I guess I can carry a tune all right."

"I think you're perfect."

She felt the blush warm her cheeks. "Hardly."

But she loved him for saying so.

As the musicians struck up a new tune — the fiddle player announced its title as "In the Good Old Summertime" — Sherwood and Cleo moved on from the band shell and headed for the tables bearing food.

"Just to see what we'll have to choose from." Cleo's expression was impish; he found her adorable. She spoke to almost everyone they met, greeting them by name and then adding, "I don't know if you've met Lord Sherwood Statham from England. He's working for my dad."

Strangely enough, he wished she wouldn't

use the formal introduction. He'd grown fonder of the nickname she'd given him at the same time he'd grown fonder of Cleo. His father would hate it should Cleo ever call him that in the duke's presence. In fact, his father would forbid her to do so.

He frowned at the thought. When they married — *if* they were able to marry — Cleo would be expected to change many things about herself. She wouldn't be able to dress as she was now. She wouldn't be able to spend her days working with horses or birthing foals. She would be expected to learn and observe all the rules of British society. It would be like caging a wild animal: completely unfair.

Some of the fun of the day was lost for him upon that realization.

They moved on from the tables to some booths set up near the Methodist church. There was one where children could fish for prizes. There was a dunking booth, and one for tossing darts at balloons. All of them were busy, people buying tickets to take their chances on winning a prize.

They were circling back to join the rest of their party when Sherwood heard Cleo suck in a small gasp. She stopped still, her eyes turned across the street toward the school. Sherwood followed her gaze. A man and woman stood in the shade of a tree, the fellow's hands resting against the bark on either side of the young woman's head as he leaned his body close to hers.

"That snake," Cleo whispered.

"What is it?"

"That's Tyler King. I don't know who the girl is, but it sure as shootin' isn't his wife." She looked at Sherwood. "You'd think he'd try to be a little discreet. His wife just gave birth to his son a week ago."

"If it would make you feel better, Cleo, I'll go over there and tell him he belongs at home with his wife and child."

Surprise widened her eyes and then brought a smile to her lips. "I believe you mean that."

"I do." He returned her smile. "Although I imagine I might come away a little worse for wear should he not take kindly to my words of advice. I'm not as nimble on my feet as I once was."

"But you're right. I shouldn't simply take offense. I should speak up. I don't imagine he'd take a swing at me." She stepped away from him. "Wait here. I'll be right back."

"Cleo!"

She didn't stop or look back.

He followed her but she outdistanced him, marching right up to the couple who stood in the shade of the old oak tree. He couldn't hear the first words of the dressing down she gave Tyler King, but he arrived in time to hear her finish with a few words for the young woman who stood beside him — a girl of about seventeen, Sherwood guessed.

"And if you aren't careful, miss, you'll be the next gal to bear a child for Mr. King, but he won't be able to marry you 'cause he's already got himself a wife. I was fooled by his charm once, but God had mercy on me and kept me from making any worse mistake than just taking a fancy to him."

The girl burst into tears and ran away, disappearing around the back of the school-house.

Cleo turned her attention back to Tyler. "Go home to Henrietta. Look after your wife and baby. You owe it to them."

"What I do isn't any of your business, Cleo." The cowboy's face was dark with anger.

Sherwood moved a few steps closer.

"When a married man trifles with a young gal," Cleo answered, "I make it my business."

Tyler called her a foul name.

Sherwood didn't think about what he was going to do. Three strides carried him past Cleo, and in the next instant his fist collided with Tyler's jaw, knocking the lout to the ground.

"Woody!"

Sherwood rubbed his stinging knuckles with his other hand as he glared at Tyler. "No one speaks to Miss Arlington that way in my presence. No one."

Tyler got slowly to his feet, and Sherwood braced himself. But Tyler didn't take a swing. Sherwood wished he would. He'd love a chance to knock the fellow flat a second time.

"Woody." Cleo spoke his name softly as her hand alighted on his arm. "Let's go."

He turned toward her, gave her a tight smile, then put his hand in the small of her back and guided her back toward the town park.

"You didn't have to do that," she said after a few moments.

"Perhaps not. But sometimes you must allow me to be chivalrous."

"Chivalrous?" She stopped and turned toward him. "In case you've failed to notice, Sherwood Statham, I'm not exactly the kind of girl who needs to be rescued by a white knight."

"I've noticed, my darling Cleo, but I'm not much of a white knight either. I'm simply the man who loves you and wants to do the best he can to take care of you. Will you not allow me to do so? At least on a few occasions?"

Griff watched Cleo and Sherwood from a place in the park not too far away. The couple seemed oblivious to others around them. They didn't seem to be arguing, and yet . . .

"Stop worrying, Dad." Gwen slipped her arm through his.

"I can't help it."

"They love each other."

He looked at her. "But love isn't always enough to make two people happy."

"Happy? I don't believe I've ever seen Cleo happier than she's been since she realized what she feels for Lord Sherwood."

"True." Griff drew in a deep breath and released it. "All the same . . ."

"Let's get our food before it's all gone." Gwen tugged on his arm, drawing him with her toward the tables. "I'm famished."

Griff went with Gwen while silently sending up another plea to God to protect Cleo from too much heartache.

"But sometimes you must allow me to be chivalrous."

Cleo sat cross legged on the blanket,

watching the fireworks display. Woody lay beside her, braced on his elbows, the most comfortable position for him because of his bum leg. Her family and the boys from the ranch surrounded them.

"I'm simply the man who loves you and wants to do the best he can to take care of you."

She didn't need anyone to take care of her. She could take care of herself. *Been doing so since I was a teenager.* Sure, she lived in her dad's home, but she carried her weight around the ranch. Did she *look* helpless? Of course not. She worked as hard as anybody and harder than some.

She glanced at Woody. He was watching her, and when their gazes met, he smiled. Land o' Goshen! What that man's smiles did to her. Made her go all soft and squishy on the insides. She supposed it was kind of sweet of him to say he wanted to take care of her. Might not be so bad, lettin' a man do so every now and again.

He sat up and leaned over to whisper in her ear, "Marry me, Cleo."

If his smile made her go soft inside, his proposal made her go soft in the head. She couldn't seem to think straight, couldn't seem to speak, could hardly breathe.

He looked into her eyes. "Will you be my wife?"

She managed to nod.

And right there in front of anybody who might be watching them instead of the fireworks, he kissed her — soft, long, and sweet.

Land o' Goshen!

Dear Father and Mother,

I write to you with happy but surprising news. I have asked Cleo Arlington to be my wife, and she has given me great joy by assenting to do so. Although this proposal might seem rather soon to you, I promise you it is not. My affection for Miss Arlington has been growing for many weeks now.

While I know it is tradition for Stathams to be married at Dunacombe Manor, our desire is to have the ceremony here in Bethlehem Springs. We do not wish to wait until my return to England in the spring, and naturally my intended wishes to take her vows with her family and lifelong friends in attendance.

I feel it is time that I begin working in a profession. Something you, Father, have encouraged me to do for quite some time. Now, with a wife to support, I realize it cannot be delayed much longer. Needless to say, a career in the military is not possible, and I have shared how disagreeable I find the law. Outside of the aforementioned occupations, as well as the church, I have no idea what professions you would consider acceptable. To be perfectly frank, I believe I would be well suited to overseeing management of one or more of the family estates. Working with Griff and Cleo Arlington on their ranch has shown me how much I enjoy such work. But I do not imagine you would approve of that. Perhaps the church is the only place left for me. I have found a deepening faith in God, but He alone knows if that is where He would have me serve Him.

Miss Arlington and I plan to be married on the 26th of August. It would please us both if you would journey to America to be present for our nuptials. You would be guests at Morgan McKinley's resort throughout your stay. I believe you would find the accommodations more than adequate.

I look forward to hearing from you.

With affection, your son,

Sherwood

The duke would not be pleased when he read the letter. He wouldn't rejoice with Sherwood because, as his youngest son knew well, his permission should have been received before Sherwood asked this unknown, unproven girl for her hand in marriage. It was possible Sherwood would now be cut off from both the family and his father's fortune.

But it was done. Sherwood had proposed and Cleo had accepted. All of the bride-to-be's family and friends had given their blessings and expressed their wishes for much happiness. If it was up to him, they would have married at once, but he understood it couldn't be so. Cleo's mother must come from the East, and even the simplest of ceremonies took some time to plan.

And so, he would have to wait, and hope Cleo never came to regret loving him.

TWENTY-SEVEN

Her stomach churning, Cleo stood on the railroad platform with Woody, her sister, and Morgan. How had she let Gwen talk her into this trip? The two of them were on their way to Boise to shop for clothing appropriate for the daughter-in-law of a duke. Gwen had invited Morgan's sister to join them, but Daphne had declined. Cleo wished she'd done the same. Not that she hadn't tried.

"I'm not even married yet," she'd argued when the trip was first mentioned. "New clothes can wait until the time is closer for us to leave for England."

Gwen had answered back, "Every bride deserves a trousseau. This will be Morgan's and my gift to you." She'd wagged a finger at Cleo. "And don't even try to tell me that you have too much work to do. Dad can get along without you for a few days."

Cleo moistened her lips as she looked

down the tracks. Maybe she would feel better if her sister hadn't convinced her to wear a skirt and blouse for the trip to Boise. On the other hand, she would have to get used to dressing like this. She had almost nine months before she and Woody would leave Idaho, but she suspected that the time would rush by all too quickly to suit her.

She glanced at Woody, and he offered an encouraging smile. "You'll have a grand time. Stop fretting."

"I wish you were coming too."

"My dear, I believe I would be in the way on such a trip."

"I don't reckon that's true. I'd wager you've got some idea how English women dress."

"Quite the same as American women, I assure you. Your sister will be able to advise you."

He was right. Gwen would be able to advise her. Not simply about current styles but about much more besides. Her sister knew how a lady should act, walk, and speak. But would eight or nine months be long enough for her to change Cleo from a sow's ear into a silk purse? Doubtful.

Sounds of the approaching train reached her ears a moment before it chugged into view and came to a hissing stop beside the platform. Passengers disembarked, some coming home to Bethlehem Springs, others who were visitors bound for New Hope. And in very short order it was time for those departing to get onboard.

"Enjoy yourself," Woody said as he took her hand and kissed the back of it. "I'll miss you and will look forward to your return on Friday."

"Keep an eye on Dad. Don't let him overdo. You know how he is."

"I'll look out for him. I promise."

Cleo took her travel bag from Woody's hand and turned to see Gwen and Morgan exchange a quick kiss of farewell. Then she followed her sister into the passenger car.

The last time Cleo had visited the capital city, she and her father had gone by wagon and had camped under the stars at night. It was difficult to believe the trip took only a matter of a few hours by rail. Bethlehem Springs had Morgan's resort and political connections to thank for this convenience in transportation.

The train didn't linger at the station. Before long, it began to move. Gwen and Cleo waved good-bye to their men until a curve in the tracks blocked their view. Then they settled into their seats and watched as the train followed the river south out of the mountains.

Sherwood was silent on the drive back to the ranch in Morgan's automobile, and Morgan seemed content to leave him to his own thoughts. A good thing. He had much to think about.

Cleo — a bundle of nerves as she went off to buy a new wardrobe, dresses and shoes and hats that she would never truly like. He loved her even more because he knew she was doing it out of love for him.

The duke — who couldn't have received Sherwood's letter yet but who would be livid once he did.

A future profession — how could he support Cleo, especially if his father cut him off once and for all? Where would God have him work? Could he be a vicar? He'd never thought so before. Would he make a decent lawyer, even though it didn't appeal to him? Probably not. Would his father consider allowing him to manage the Dunacombe estates? He doubted it.

When they arrived at the ranch, Griff invited Morgan to stay and eat dinner with them, but Morgan declined. "I have a considerable amount of work waiting for me at the resort. But I'll come for you and Sherwood on Friday so we can meet the train together." With a cheery wave, Morgan drove away, leaving a cloud of dust in his wake.

"I guess Gwen and Cleo got away all right," Griff said as the two men climbed the steps onto the veranda.

"Yes, but Cleo wasn't happy about going."

"Gwen will make sure she enjoys her visit to Boise."

"I hope so."

"It'll be quiet around here for the next few days."

Sherwood nodded. He'd discovered he felt like a piece of him was missing whenever Cleo was away, even for just an hour or two. Perhaps that empty feeling was how he'd realized he loved her. He'd known many women over the years, and there wasn't a one of them he hadn't been content to leave when the evening was done or the fox hunt over.

"There's Stitch." Griff's words intruded on Sherwood's thoughts. "I'd best get my gloves and help him unload the wagon."

Remembering Cleo's request, Sherwood said, "I'll help him, Griff. Why don't you put your feet up and rest for a while."

"Don't tell me you're going to start treating me like an invalid too."

Sherwood grinned. "I believe you have

found me out. But I was acting under orders."

"And I know whose orders. How about you let me look after myself? When Cleo gets back, you can tell her I was well behaved."

"As you wish, sir, but if it's all the same, I'll still help Stitch unload the wagon."

"Fine with me. Three of us will make the work go that much faster." Griff went inside, and when he returned, he wore his leather gloves.

Minutes later, Sherwood had a heavy sack of grain tossed over his shoulder and was carrying it into the barn. He remembered how difficult this kind of task was for him to accomplish not so very long ago. In fact, he wouldn't have tried anything like it before coming to the ranch. He listened to his footsteps and took pleasure in the sound. While not a perfectly even pace, there was no audible slide, no drag.

Thank You, God.

One day, he hoped he would be able to tell his father how many ways he'd been blessed by his time in America, that the punishment had produced an unexpected fruit. He hoped he would be able to show the duke how changed he was, not just physically but in character as well.

■ ■ ■ ■

Grass didn't grow under Gwen's feet, that was for sure.

Cleo looked at her reflection in the long mirror while two seamstresses pinned and measured a dress made from midnight-blue fabric.

"You're so thin, *mademoiselle,*" the youngest of the two said.

Cleo didn't believe for a minute that the girl was French. She'd wager the accent was fake, feigned to make customers feel their money was well spent.

"You have so little curves, yes?"

"Yes." The word came out on a sigh.

"Cleo," Gwen said from the settee against the opposite wall, "you're stunning. I would look awful in that dress."

That was a bald-faced lie. Her sister could wear a gunnysack and look gorgeous. Cleo, on the other hand, could make the finest gown in the world look like a gunnysack. She released another sigh.

Gwen stood. "Miss Rabelais, I believe we've been here long enough for today. We shall return tomorrow morning. Would ten o'clock be convenient?"

"*Oui, madame.*"

"We'll want to see some suggestions for my sister's wedding gown, as well."

"Oui, madame."

Cleo was assisted out of the dark-blue gown and back into the simple blouse and skirt she'd worn on the train. If only the skirt could have been trousers instead.

Gwen drew her out of the dress shop and down the sidewalk toward their hotel. Main Street was busy, automobiles parked at the curbs and driving to and fro. Many more motorcars than Cleo had expected, although there were plenty of saddle horses and horse-drawn wagons too. And lots of dust and noise to go along with them. It made her head hurt. When she remembered that Boise was no San Francisco or New York . . . or . . . London . . .

Mercy! She hadn't even been in the capital city a day, and already she longed for the quiet of the ranch at twilight.

"I thought we might go to the theater tonight," Gwen said, "but on second thought, perhaps we should make an early evening of it. The baby and I are feeling tired."

Cleo couldn't have been happier to concur.

TWENTY-EIGHT

As it turned out, Cleo didn't hate and despise *all* dresses. After several days of trying on countless frocks for daywear and glittering gowns for formal evening affairs, she had finally found something she liked. The high-waisted, ankle-length bridal gown of white satin and lace, along with the veil of tulle, made her feel soft and feminine. Almost pretty. Of course, she needed to wear gloves to keep her work-roughened skin from snagging the delicate fabric.

"This is the one," Gwen said, meeting Cleo's gaze in the mirror.

"Yes, this is the one."

"I can hardly wait to see you in it on your wedding day." Gwen squeezed Cleo's shoulders. "Even more, I can hardly wait to see Sherwood's expression when *he* sees you in it."

Lord Sherwood. "I reckon I need to start thinking of him that way."

"Sorry?"

"I'll have to get used to referring to him as Lord Sherwood."

"Well, not in private. No one could object to you calling him Sherwood or Woody when the two of you are alone."

Cleo turned to face her sister. "What if his parents hate me?"

"Impossible."

"No." She shook her head. "It isn't impossible. He's a duke and she's a duchess. And I'm not much of a lady. I'll never pass myself off as refined or genteel. There isn't much about me to make them want me as a daughter-in-law."

"If they don't love you at first, they will learn to love you. You have many sterling qualities, Cleo, honesty and a goodness of heart chief among them."

"Woody's not close to his father the way I am to Dad. I can tell he's nervous about what his folks will say when they learn we're getting married."

"He invited them to the wedding, didn't he?"

"Yes." She drew a deep breath and exhaled. "But I'm hoping they won't come. I think he is too."

"That might be best. You'll have enough to deal with when Mother arrives. Can you imagine her with a duke."

Cleo laughed, although it wasn't a happy sound. "Mercy."

Gwen took hold of her hands. "Did you know that I almost broke my engagement to Morgan last summer? I was so nervous, so afraid that I couldn't be the kind of wife he wanted me to be. When I think how close I came to throwing away my own happiness . . ." She pinned Cleo with a stern look. "Don't you dare let doubts rise up to steal your joy, Cleopatra Arlington. You love Sherwood and he loves you. That will be enough to see you through whatever problems arise, including our mother and his parents."

I hope she's right. Cleo turned to look at her reflection in the mirror again. *Please, God. Let our love be enough.*

The first mowing of hay happened on the late side that year, but the harvest was plentiful, thanks to the new sections of land that had been put to the plow. And with the influx of funds the early sale of cattle had brought, the Arlington accounts were in fine shape once again.

Sherwood closed the ledger and put it into its proper place. A quick glance at the desk told him there was nothing left for him to accomplish in the office, so he rose and went outside.

The barnyard was quiet, the temperature hot. Bear and one of the other cattle dogs slept in the shade of the bunkhouse, flat on their sides, looking more dead than alive. Horses stood in the corrals and paddocks, tails swishing at pesky flies. Occasionally, one of them stomped a hoof in irritation. Overhead, the sun blazed in a pale-blue sky.

Sherwood missed Cleo. He missed everything about her. He missed her laugh, and he missed seeing her walk across the barnyard in that long, loping stride of hers. He missed watching her tend the horses and hearing the calm, even tone she used when addressing the animals. Most of all, he missed hearing her call him "Woody." The ranch was much too dull without her. Life seemed grayer in her absence. Tomorrow couldn't get there fast enough to suit him.

He stepped off the porch and walked to the barn, where he fed and watered the animals in the stalls. With nothing else demanding his attention and the other ranch hands and Griff scattered in various directions, Sherwood decided to saddle his gelding and go for a ride. The last time he'd gone to the resort for therapy — a twice-per-week affair now — he'd ridden up with

Griff in the buggy, which meant his horse needed the exercise.

A short while later, he led the bay out of the barn, mounted him, and rode away from the ranch house, first at a walk, then a jog, and finally an easy lope. When he reached the bridge over the river, he almost turned around but instead kept going, riding on into Bethlehem Springs.

Now what? he wondered. The town looked almost as sleepy as the barnyard had appeared at the ranch.

With his wife out of town, Morgan had stayed at the resort this week, so Sherwood couldn't drop in on him. There was nothing he needed from the mercantile, and if he stopped at the South Fork for pie, he would spoil his appetite for whatever Cookie prepared for dinner.

He rode down Main Street, past the *Daily Herald,* the South Fork, the millenary shop, and the High Horse Men's Club. Once he turned onto Bear Run Road, he rode by the firehouse and the opera house. That was the moment when he decided to stop at the church. He reined in and dismounted, then tied his horse to a hitching post. Inside, the church was as quiet as a tomb and several degrees cooler than it was outdoors.

"Reverend Barker," he called as he

stopped in the narthex.

"Yes." The reply came from the sanctuary.

Sherwood moved into the doorway. Kenneth stood near the altar, an open Bible in his left hand. "Am I intruding?"

"Not at all. Come in, Sherwood. How are you?"

"I'm well, thank you."

The reverend walked toward him. "And Cleo? Has she returned from her shopping expedition?"

"No. Not until tomorrow."

"I assume you're feeling at loose ends without her." The reverend motioned toward one of the pews. "Let's sit down, shall we?"

After they'd done so, Sherwood broached the subject that had been much on his mind. "I've been thinking a lot about how different life will be for Cleo once we are in England. Am I —" He stared down at his hands, clenched between his knees. "Have I been selfish, asking her to leave everything she knows? I worry that she'll be unhappy there."

"Are you contemplating withdrawing your offer of marriage?"

Sherwood's gut twisted as he looked up. "Do you think I should?"

"No," Kenneth answered, his voice low,

his gaze gentle. "That isn't my place to say. But I would advise you to discuss your concerns with Cleo. She's the one who must decide, although I expect I know what she will tell you."

He wasn't sure he wanted to know, but he asked anyway. "What is that?"

" 'Entreat me not to leave thee, or to return from following after thee: for whither thou goest, I will go; and where thou lodgest, I will lodge: thy people shall be my people, and thy God my God.' "

Sherwood knew those words came from the Scripture, and they brought some comfort with them. And yet Cleo's feelings weren't his only concern. "There is also the matter of how I shall support a wife. I have few options that would be acceptable to my father."

"What do you feel God calling you to do, Sherwood?"

"I . . . I don't know."

The reverend was silent for a spell, his gaze steady upon Sherwood's face. Had it been anyone besides Kenneth Barker, he might have squirmed, but he was comfortable here, with this man of God, in this house of God.

At long last Kenneth cleared his throat. "My friend, only you can know what God is speaking into your heart. But I can tell you this: God makes each one of us for the time into which we are born. He creates us for a purpose. Our job is to know Him well, discover what He created us to do, and then do it for all we're worth for the rest of our lives. Ask God to show you your purpose. He will answer."

Sherwood mulled the words over in his head. Find God's purpose and then do it for all he was worth.

"Would you like to pray about it?" the reverend asked.

"Yes, I believe I would."

On the sisters' last night in Boise, they attended the theater, seeing a production of Shakespeare's *As You Like It.* But as much as Cleo wanted to love the play — and in some parts did — she found it difficult to keep up with what the actors meant. *"What wilt thou do?" "Herein I see thou lov'st me not." "How now, daughter and cousin, are you crept hither to see the wrastling?"* Simple enough if heard one line at a time, but too often the words came rapid fire, one upon another, and while she was making sense of them in her head, the play moved on without her.

Gwen had no such difficulties. She

laughed and applauded and smiled right along with the rest of the audience.

Cleo decided Mr. Shakespeare was not her playwright of choice. She'd adored the two Oscar Wilde productions that had come to the Bethlehem Springs opera house a few years back — *An Ideal Husband* and *The Importance of Being Earnest* — and she was always up for an amusing vaudeville act. Even an Italian opera, where she couldn't understand a single word they sang, was more enjoyable to her than an evening with William Shakespeare.

She wondered if Woody was fond of the Bard's plays. For that matter, was that something she should already know about the man she planned to marry? Would he seem an entirely different person once they were in England?

The curtain came down and the audience rose to the sound of applause. Cleo stood with them, clapping her hands and exchanging a smile with her sister. Hopefully Gwen wouldn't guess that the real reason for her smile was because the play was over.

"What a fine company," Gwen said over her shoulder as they moved out of their row of seats.

"Have you seen this play before?"

"A number of times. Once on Broadway.

That was thrilling. You cannot imagine what the theater district in New York looks like at night unless you've seen it for yourself. It truly is the Great White Way with all those marquees and billboards lit up."

Gwen hooked arms with Cleo as they stepped out of the lobby of the theater and onto Jefferson Street. Some theatergoers hailed cabs or waited for their drivers to arrive with their automobiles, but most left on foot. The sisters were part of the crowd that moved along the sidewalks.

When they were only a couple of blocks from their hotel, Gwen asked, "Did you enjoy yourself while we've been here as much as I hoped you would?"

"Want to know my favorite part of this trip?" Cleo smiled. "The best part was being with you, day and night. We haven't spent this much time together since I campaigned for you last year."

It was, Cleo thought, an artful dodge of the real question. While she was delighted to have found a wedding gown and to have her sister's help in selecting a new wardrobe, clothes shopping was not her favorite thing to do. And the play tonight? Well, she'd already decided she and Shakespeare weren't good companions.

"But you'll be glad to get home," Gwen

said softly.

"I can't deny it. I miss Woody and Dad and everybody I'm used to seeing." She looked up at the stars sprinkling the inky sky overhead. "I reckon I need to store up as many memories of them and you as I can. It won't be all that long before there's an ocean between us." Her chest grew tight as she spoke those words. Leaving the ranch, leaving Idaho, was something she tried not to think about too much. And since she would rather go to England than not be Woody's wife, than not be with him for the rest of her life, she would have to let the sad thoughts take care of themselves.

TWENTY-NINE

Elizabeth Arlington arrived at the end of July and installed herself in one of the guest bedrooms at the McKinley home. But she found plenty of reasons to visit the ranch, and she took almost as many meals with her estranged husband, future son-in-law, and Cleo as she did with Gwen and Morgan. To say she was pleased by Cleo's engagement to an English lord would be a gross understatement.

On this particular afternoon on the first day of August, she stood in Cleo's bedroom, once again admiring the wedding gown. "Gwen has exquisite taste in clothes," she told Cleo, "but I despair of you ever learning to walk down the aisle like a lady." She turned around. "You really should put on those satin shoes and practice some more."

"I'll do it later. There's no hurry. I've got time."

"Believe me, Cleopatra. Your wedding day

will be here before you know it. You don't want to make a fool of yourself by stumbling over your own feet at your wedding. Think of the embarrassment that would cause Lord Sherwood."

"I reckon you're more worried about that than I am."

As if Cleo hadn't spoken, her mother continued, "And whatever shall we do with your hair? It's too short to pull up. And those curls. They're so unruly. The veil will cover it for the ceremony, but later —"

"Sorry. I've gotta see to my chores." Cleo rushed out of the bedroom before her mother could try to stop her, and she didn't slow down until she was in the shadowed safety of the barn. To her relief, Woody was there too. She threw herself into his arms and burst into tears.

"I say. What's made you unhappy?" He drew back enough to look into her eyes.

"Nothing. Everything."

"Your mother?"

"Yes." She pressed her face against his shirt a second time. "She's afraid I'll ruin my own wedding."

"How could you ruin it?"

"By being me."

He chuckled, and she felt the rumble in his chest.

"Sure. I reckon you can afford to laugh."
She looked up a second time. "Mother thinks you're perfect."

"And I think you're perfect."

The frustration and hurt began to drain from Cleo. Later, she was sure, it would boil up again, but for right now, her world had righted itself. "Let's take the horses for a ride. Maybe you could read me some more of that fancy poetry."

Before Woody could answer, the sounds of an approaching automobile drifted into the barn. Cleo hoped it was Gwen, come to take their mother back to town.

"Sounds like company." She moved toward the door, Woody right behind her.

It looked like the motorcar used by the Washington Hotel. The driver had a couple of passengers, a man and a woman, in the car with him. Cleo narrowed her eyes, trying to see who it was. She couldn't quite —

"Good heavens!" Woody said softly.

She glanced at him and was taken aback by the ashen color of his skin.

He met her gaze. "Prepare yourself, Cleo. You are about to meet my parents."

"Your parents?" She watched as the automobile rolled to a stop at the front of the house. Woody moved forward, but Cleo stayed put, preferring to watch the reunion from a distance. *His parents.*

The duke was an imposing man. Taller and broader in the shoulders than his youngest son, he had a full head of hair and a beard, all of it steel gray in color. From where she stood, Cleo thought his eyes cool and his mouth hard, but maybe she was inclined to think so because of what Woody had told her about his father.

The duchess was petite with a generous figure. A large hat and netting covered her hair and face, but something about the way she held out a hand toward Woody made Cleo think she must be smiling with joy. Mother and son embraced, and he kissed her cheek through the netting. Then Woody turned to his father and offered his hand. The duke waited several heartbeats before shaking it.

"I didn't know you were coming," Woody said, "or I would have been at the station to meet your train."

"There was no time to alert you to our travel plans. We left Dunacombe as soon as we could after receiving your letter. What is this about you wanting to propose to some American girl?"

Woody glanced over his shoulder at Cleo before facing his father again. "I must assume then that you didn't receive my second letter. It is no longer my intent to propose. I have asked Miss Arlington to marry me. She has agreed, and the wedding is set for later this month."

"The devil you say! Have you lost your senses, boy? I didn't send you to America to let some female ensnare you. Who is she? Who is her family?"

With a sinking heart, Cleo moved across the barnyard until she arrived at Woody's side. The duke gave her only a cursory glance, no doubt irritated that a stranger would intrude upon his conversation with his son.

"Sir. Mother." Woody put his arm behind Cleo, his hand in the small of her back. "I'd like you to meet Cleo Arlington, the woman I'm going to marry. My dear, may I introduce my parents, the Duke and Duchess of Dunacombe."

The duke uttered an oath as he stared at her, disbelief in his eyes.

Cleo swallowed hard. "It's a pleasure to meet you." She nodded to Woody's mother. "Your grace." Then to his father. "Your grace." At least she'd remembered how they were to be addressed. "Welcome to the Arlington Ranch. Won't you come inside? My father isn't here right now but . . . but my mother is." She realized it must sound as if this was her parents' home, but she didn't know how to correct that impression.

"Excuse me." The driver of the automobile raised himself up to look over the glass. "Will you folks be needing a ride back to the hotel anytime soon?"

Woody answered him. "You needn't wait. I will see my parents back to town when they're ready to leave."

The duke looked none too thrilled to have his son speaking for him.

Cleo turned to Woody's mother. "Please come inside, your grace. You must be thirsty. It's a dusty drive from town."

"Thank you, Miss Arlington. I would appreciate something to drink." The duchess fell in beside Cleo as they walked to the house, climbing the steps onto the veranda, and then going inside.

"Are you mad?" the duke said the instant the women were out of sight. "You cannot possibly go through with this."

"I am in love with Cleo, sir, and we will marry at the end of August. All the arrangements have been made."

"Great Scot, Sherwood! You can't bring that . . . that woman back to England as your wife."

"I don't intend to leave my wife in

America when I return home, and she *will* be my wife."

"How do you intend to keep a household, to support a wife? You'll find no help from me."

"I'm not sure, sir. I am praying about it, but God hasn't revealed the answer to me as yet."

"Praying about it?" His father's words dripped with sarcasm.

"Yes, sir. Praying about it. I'm trusting that God will guide me in this as in all future decisions."

Sherwood couldn't remember the last time he'd stood up to his father. Had he ever? He'd always found it easier to avoid the duke rather than endure confrontations with him. And when confrontation hadn't been avoidable, it had been easier to acquiesce and take the path of least resistance. But he wasn't the same person who'd left England four months earlier. He had much in his past to atone for — including his own part in the difficult relationship he had with his father — but from now on he meant to be true to himself, true to the man he'd become, true to the man Cleo saw when she looked at him, and true to the God who had made him a new creation.

"Let's go inside, sir." He motioned toward

the front door. "Mother and Cleo must be wondering what is keeping us."

He didn't wait to see if the duke followed. He walked as he'd learned to walk, with only a minimal limp, back straight, head held high in confidence rather than cockiness. He walked like a man who had learned to lean into God for whatever strength he needed.

Inside, he saw that the women, including his future mother-in-law, Elizabeth Arlington, had taken seats in the parlor. He moved to stand beside Cleo's chair and placed a hand on her shoulder, giving it a slight squeeze.

"Lord Sherwood," Elizabeth said, "I was just telling your mother what a wonderful surprise this is. You told us you didn't expect your parents to come for the wedding, but here they are, several weeks beforehand. We shall be hard pressed to find enough ways to entertain them. Bethlehem Springs is so wanting in refined society."

Softly, Cleo said, "Mother, I believe Morgan offered a suite at the resort for the duke and duchess."

"Well, of course. That would be much better than for them to continue to stay in town at the Washington Hotel." Elizabeth turned toward Sherwood's mother again. "I believe my son-in-law Morgan is the reason Lord Sherwood came to Idaho in the first place. Isn't that right?"

His mother didn't answer. Her gaze had remained on Sherwood from the moment he entered the parlor. Now a small smile played upon her lips. "You look well, Sherwood."

"I am well."

"You look stronger."

"I am stronger." He glanced briefly at Cleo. "In many ways."

"When you walked into the room just now —" His mother broke off as tears filled her eyes, and several moments passed before she could speak again. "Your leg is much improved."

"Yes."

His mother finally turned her gaze upon Cleo. "And I believe I must have you to thank for the wonderful changes I see in my son."

Cleo shook her head. "No, ma'am. Woody's gotten there by his own hard work."

Sherwood saw his mother's eyes widen at the nickname, but the return of her smile told him she was amused rather than offended by it.

"Cleo's being modest. She and her family

deserve all the credit."

Before his mother could reply, the duke entered the house and stopped in the parlor doorway. His expression was dour, his discomfort in his surroundings obvious.

"Sherwood," he said, "you told our driver that you would see us back to our lodgings. I believe now is the time to do so."

Elizabeth exclaimed, "Oh, but surely not! You have only just arrived."

The duke looked at Cleo's mother as if she were a bothersome insect. With his eyes, he demanded to know how she dared to address him in such a fashion.

Hoping to avoid any additional unpleasantness even as he dreaded the trip into Bethlehem Springs, Sherwood said, "I will hitch the horse to the buggy now, sir. It won't take me long."

"No." Cleo grabbed his hand before he could move away. "I'll do it. You stay with your parents." She was gone from the room in an instant.

If only she'd been wearing a dress for this first meeting. If only she'd followed her mother's advice to practice walking in those miserable satin shoes. If only she'd been upstairs. If only . . .

Well, there was no use crying over spilt

milk. They'd seen her the same way Woody had seen her the first time, the way she really was. They might as well know the worst. Maybe then they would be pleased with whatever progress she made by the time she got to England in the spring.

THIRTY

The Duke and Duchess of Dunacombe moved from the Washington Hotel to the New Hope Health Spa the next day, and two days later, Cleo, Woody, and her father drove the buggy up to the resort to dine with them, joined by Cleo's mother, sister, and Morgan. Unlike her first meeting with Woody's parents, Cleo wore one of the new dresses from her trousseau.

"Relax." Woody patted her knee.

"I can't."

"It will be all right."

Cleo found that hard to believe but hoped he told the truth. He had paid visits to his parents twice since their move to New Hope, and he'd told her they were growing used to the idea of having an American daughter-in-law. But there was much he hadn't said to her. She could tell it in his manner and read it in his eyes.

The nervous feeling in her stomach worsened when the lodge came into view. Silently, she prayed that she wouldn't make too many horrid gaffes before the evening was over.

Woody stopped the buggy, got down, then offered Cleo his hand. She couldn't remember how many times she'd ignored his proffered assistance. She wouldn't do so tonight. She welcomed his steady grip more than he could know.

"Stop worrying." Woody slipped Cleo's hand into the crook of his arm. "You look beautiful."

They walked toward the lodge, her father following right behind them. Inside, they found their party awaiting them in the sitting area. Like Woody and her father, the duke and Morgan wore black suits. The women, however, were dressed in an array of colors — Gwen in her signature pink, their mother in soft lavender, and the duchess in a gown of gold.

"Sir," Woody said to his father, "may I introduce Cleo's father, Griff Arlington. Griff, this is my father and mother, the Duke and Duchess of Dunacombe."

Her father gave a slight bow toward Jane Statham and, after doing the same toward Dagwood Statham, he offered his hand to the duke. "It's a pleasure to meet you both."

The duke shook her father's hand and responded with a "Likewise" that sounded anything but.

"And," Woody continued, "I'm sure you remember Miss Arlington."

There went those nerves in her belly again.

"My dear," the duchess said, "you look lovely. What a charming gown."

"Thank you, your grace."

Morgan stepped forward and suggested they go in to dinner. With Gwen on his arm, he led the way to a private dining room. Cleo was thankful for that. If she embarrassed herself, at least it wouldn't be in front of every guest in the lodge, only a duke and duchess.

Heaven help me.

The table in the private dining room was the perfect size for a party of eight, one chair at the head and the foot, three chairs on either side. The white tablecloth had been set with fine china trimmed in gold that reflected the light from the chandelier overhead. This was the kind of setting where a duke's son would always feel at home, and where Cleo, she feared, would never feel at home.

They settled into their places — Woody and Cleo opposite each other in the middle side chairs — and several waiters arrived to fill their glasses and serve two platters of hors d'oeuvres. Cleo shook her head when the appetizers were offered to her. She doubted she would be able to swallow just yet.

"I'm sorry I wasn't at the ranch to greet you the other day," Cleo's father said to the duke. "I hope you'll return soon and allow me to show you around. We've got over thirty thousand acres of prime grazing land with about four thousand head of cattle on it right now. Your son has been a huge help to us, and we've increased our hay production thanks to suggestions he made in the spring."

The duke looked down the table at Woody but said nothing.

Her father continued, "When I was down with the influenza, Sherwood took over managing things for me and did such a fine job, I've left that responsibility to him. I'm not sure what I'll do without him when he and Cleo leave."

Her heart ached at the thought.

The duchess turned toward her. "My son tells me that you help your father with the horses."

"Yes, your grace. I've been the ranch wrangler since I was sixteen. Working with horses is my favorite thing."

Woody said, "Cleo has a gift with all animals but especially with horses. You should see her ride a wild mustang. It's unforgettable." The last words were spoken in a low, intimate tone as he leaned closer to her.

Cleo blushed with pleasure, feeling good for the first time this evening.

"Young lady," the duke said, "I trust you know there are no wild mustangs to be ridden in England."

The good feeling departed. "Yes, your grace. I know."

"And do you think if you two wed that you'll make my son a proper wife?"

His use of the word "if" did not go unnoticed, but Cleo chose to ignore it. "A proper wife? No, I don't reckon I'll make him a proper wife. But I love Woo—" She stopped herself, squared her shoulders, and then started again. "I love Lord Sherwood, your grace, and I'll do everything I can to make him happy."

Sherwood admired Cleo more in that moment than ever before. He knew she was nervous and unsure of herself and that she felt outside of her element. Yet she had answered his father with her usual directness and honesty.

It was fortunate Elizabeth Arlington was unaware of her daughter's discomfort or the duke's attempt to bully her. The woman was quick to fill the ensuing silence with her own voice. "Oh, your grace, you can be assured that I will do all in my power to prepare Cleo for her role in English society. I'm sure my wonderful son-in-law —" She smiled at Morgan. "— will help us. He has traveled extensively and knows many of your customs. You will help us, won't you, dear boy?"

Morgan answered, "I believe Lord Sherwood, as her husband and an Englishman, will be of more help than I could be."

"But of course." Elizabeth colored. "How silly of me. Lord Sherwood will instruct my daughter. But even so, she'll need all the help she can get. I have often despaired for her."

Sherwood looked across the table at his fiancée and saw an emotion in her eyes that he could not read. If he were sitting beside her he could take her hand in his beneath the table and squeeze it.

Thankfully, Gwen turned the subject from Cleo to the play the sisters had seen when in Boise. From there, with a skill and finesse the likes of which Sherwood had seldom seen, she guided the conversation from one

365

topic to another, none of them about Cleo, Sherwood, or the upcoming wedding.

After a restless night, Cleo arose early on Saturday, washed, and donned her work clothes, eager to be busy with something. Busy with anything that would take her mind off of the previous night.

The evening at the resort had been excruciating. Between her mother and the duke, she'd wondered why on earth Woody wanted to marry her. If she were in his shoes, she wouldn't. A time or two during the wee hours of the morning, she'd even wondered if it would be best for all concerned if she called off the wedding, if she told Woody — Lord Sherwood — that she couldn't marry him, that she couldn't be his wife. But the thought was unbearable. Imagining her future without him was physically painful. She would rather walk through fire than give him up. Making herself over as a proper wife, as the duke had put it, must surely be better than walking through fire.

As she left the house to take care of her morning chores, she remembered a conversation about men and marriage that she'd had with her sister over a year ago. *"I reckon if God had wanted me to change, I would have done it by now. I sure won't change to hide the real me any more than you would."*

But how could she have known that she would fall in love with an Englishman, with a nobleman? How could she have pictured herself living anywhere else but Idaho, let alone moving half a world away from it?

Search me, O God, and know my heart: try me, and know my thoughts. Change me in good ways. Make me into the kind of person I'll need to be when I get to my husband's homeland.

She'd told Gwen that she wanted a man whose heart would leap for her just the way she was. That was true of Woody. He loved her right now — unruly short hair, dusty Levi's, battered hat, worn boots, and all. Knowing Woody loved her as she was gave her courage enough to face the rest.

"Sherwood," she reminded herself. "I must start calling him Sherwood."

In the barn, she entered the stall of a two-year-old colt that had tangled with some barbed wire a few days before. It wasn't too serious, but she preferred to keep a close eye on him, make sure the wounds didn't become infected. After brushing him, she put ointment on the wounds on his chest and legs, then led him into the paddock so he could run off some of his stored energy.

Her father and the hands would be up

soon. Cookie was probably about ready to start breakfast. She should go back to the house and wash up. Instead, she decided to go for a ride. She wanted the wind on her face. Hopefully it would blow away her troubled thoughts.

It didn't take her long to saddle and bridle Domino, and when she was done, she swung onto his back and rode away from the barn as fast as the pinto could carry her.

Griff saw his daughter gallop her horse through the pasture, scattering cows that grazed near the ranch complex. His heart ached for her. He felt helpless. What words of advice could he give her now? He believed God had brought these young people together. He believed Cleo and Sherwood were truly in love. He no longer feared that they would wind up like him and Elizabeth. But the path Cleo would walk in the future wouldn't be an easy one for her. He'd never had a moment's worry about Gwen fitting into Morgan's way of life. But Cleo? She might as well be moving to another planet. She was strong willed, but she had an equally tender heart.

Did I do wrong, Lord? Did I allow her to grow up too wild and free? Perhaps Elizabeth was right. Perhaps I should have sent her to stay in the East and be raised like her sister. But I couldn't part with them both. I was too selfish.

In marriage, he would have to part with Cleo. She would belong with her husband. She would belong to Sherwood's world.

Sherwood spent several anxious hours that morning, waiting for Cleo to return from her ride. He hoped they could talk before his parents arrived. He hoped that he could find some way to reassure her that all would be well. At least, he *thought* all would be well. He'd certainly prayed for it to be so.

Cleo rode into the barnyard only moments before the approaching automobile was heard. Eyes wide, she said, "It's your parents. I must change."

Stitch was nearby. "I'll take care of Domino. You git on with yourself."

"Thanks, Stitch. I'll hurry, Sherwood. I promise."

He barely had a chance to realize she'd called him "Sherwood" instead of "Woody" before she dashed toward the house. She disappeared inside seconds before the motorcar, chauffeured by an employee of the resort, rolled to a halt near the house. Sherwood went to greet his parents.

"Good morning, Mother. Sir."

"Good morning, Sherwood." His mother turned her head and tilted it to one side to accommodate his kiss on the cheek.

"It was good of you to accept Griff's invitation," he said, looking at his father.

The duke gave an abbreviated nod of his head. "I hope that you and I shall have time to talk privately. There are matters we must discuss."

"Of course." He doubted that would be an enjoyable conversation, but it was one he couldn't avoid. "We can use Griff's office. But perhaps it can wait until after we dine and you've had a chance to see more of the ranch."

His father agreed with a curt nod.

"Come inside." Sherwood offered his arm to his mother. "Cleo will join us shortly." He escorted his parents inside where they sat on the sofa, side by side. "Excuse me while I let Mr. Arlington know you've arrived." He left the parlor and went into the kitchen.

"He went down to the creek to pray," Cookie answered when Sherwood asked after Griff. "He must have lost track of time. Are your parents here?"

"Yes, they're here."

"Well, you go on back to them, and I'll send one of the boys to fetch the boss."

"Thank you, Cookie."

He left the kitchen but stopped in the dining room when he heard Cleo's voice. She was in the parlor, talking to his parents. Her words were polite, but she didn't sound like herself. She was trying hard to be something she wasn't, making herself over into a suitable daughter-in-law for a duke and duchess.

Making herself into a proper wife.

In all of his life, he had never known such sacrificial love as he'd witnessed in Cleo. She was prepared to turn her back on everything and everyone she loved — this ranch, Bethlehem Springs, her father and sister — all for him. She would try to make herself over into that proper wife the duke demanded for his son.

But I don't want a proper wife. I want a real one. I don't want to be a lawyer or a vicar in England. I want to help manage a cattle ranch with Cleo at my side.

And with that, his prayers were answered. He saw everything with a clarity that hadn't been there before. He'd found God's purpose.

Why should Cleo have to change? To please his father? She would never be able to change enough to please the duke. And what about himself? Who would he be in

371

England? The old Lord Sherwood or the man he'd become here on this ranch — the man Cleo loved, Woody Statham?

"Darling." He stepped into the doorway of the parlor. "I'm a fool."

She rose from the chair, looking pretty in a pale-yellow blouse and brown skirt. But she didn't look like his Cleo.

His father muttered, "Isn't that what I've told him? That he's been a fool."

Sherwood ignored the duke. "You don't want to go to England, Cleo. You don't want to leave this ranch and your family and friends."

"What are you saying?" Her voice quivered and her face grew pale.

"Why *should* you leave? Why should *I* leave?" He moved toward her.

"Sherwood!" The duke stood. "I will speak to you in private."

He didn't take his eyes off of Cleo. "Not now, Father. Right now I have something to say to my bride."

"By heavens, it will be now! I've listened to enough of your nonsense over the past five days, and I will listen no more."

Sherwood released a silent sigh as he faced his father. "Then say whatever you wish to say here and now. I'm listening." He waved his hand around the room. "We're all listening."

The duke, his face flushed, sputtered in anger.

From the corner of his eye, Sherwood saw Griff enter the front door, then hesitate when he heard the duke begin to shout.

"I forbid you to marry this woman, and that is final. Sending you to America was supposed to bring you to your senses. It was supposed to separate you from those reprobates you called friends and those females who wanted nothing but my money. It was supposed to make you responsible. I will not allow our family's good name to be harmed by an unwise union."

Sherwood's right hand curled into a fist. How he would like to —

"Don't, son." Griff gripped Sherwood's left shoulder, drawing his gaze. The older man shook his head before moving two steps into the parlor. "Statham, I'd like to stop you before you say anything more you'll regret."

"This is none of your concern, Mr. Arlington."

"Well, now, that's where you're wrong. This is my concern. It concerns my daughter and the young man who's going to be my son-in-law. You're in my house, and I believe that gives me a right to decide what goes on here." Griff motioned toward the sofa. "Now why don't you sit down."

"I will not!"

"Suit yourself." Griff looked over his shoulder at Sherwood. "Woody, would you take a seat over there with Cleo?"

"Of course." He strode across the room and took hold of Cleo's hand as the two of them sat down, Cleo in the chair, Sherwood on the arm of the chair. The silence in the room was deafening, but it didn't last long.

Griff took another step closer to the duke, looking him in the eye with an unflinching gaze. The kind few had the courage to use on Dagwood Statham. "It's my understanding that your son was living hard, drinking too much, gambling too much, womanizing too much. That's why you sent him to America. Is that right?"

The duke grunted.

"Well, let me tell you about the young man I've come to know. He's worked hard from the day he got here. Now I realize at first it was because he had nowhere else to go and nothing else to do. He was stuck on this ranch because he had no money, no friends, no mode of transportation, no way of escape. He didn't much care for living in our bunkhouse or taking orders from Cleo."

He glanced at Sherwood, then back at the duke. "But he did his best. You wanted him to change. Well, he changed. He's a young man I feel privileged to know. One I'm proud to think of as a son. One I'm glad to welcome to my family."

Raw emotions burned in Sherwood's throat as he rose to his feet. "Thanks, Griff." The words came out in a hoarse whisper, and he felt Cleo squeeze his hand. He looked at her, smiled, then let go and moved several steps closer to his parents. "Mr. Arlington is right, Father. I've changed. Maybe not in the ways you wanted me to, but in the ways that matter. I don't belong in your world any longer. I don't want to belong in it. I'm going to stay here and marry the woman I love and try to become an even better man than I am today because of her. You can stay for the wedding or you can go back to England. It's up to you."

The flush returned to his father's face. "Jane," he said to his wife, "come with me. We're leaving." Without another word he strode out of the house.

Sherwood's mother rose from the sofa. A sad smile flitted across her lips as she moved to stand before him. "I'll talk to your father. Give him time." She placed the palm of one hand against the side of his face. "I'm proud of you, Sherwood, and I shall miss you terribly." With a tearful wave toward Cleo, she hurried after her husband.

Sherwood swallowed the lump in his throat as he turned around.

Cleo stood. Tears streaked her cheeks. "Are you sure?" she whispered.

"I've never been more sure of anything in my life. We belong here, the both of us." He drew her into his arms, ignoring Griff. "If I'm not mistaken, you didn't fall in love with Lord Sherwood and probably never could have. Why should you have to love him now?"

More tears glittered in her eyes, but she smiled through them.

He leaned close, his mouth hovering near hers. "Say it," he whispered.

"Say what?"

"Say you love me."

"I love you."

"More."

"More?"

"I . . . love . . . you . . ." He raised his voice in question.

Understanding filled her eyes. "I love you . . . Woody."

He kissed her, feeling almost as if it were for the first time, and silently thanked God for every circumstance, every failure that had brought him to America, to this ranch, to this woman, and to this moment.

FROM THE AUTHOR

Who says a woman can't be a wrangler?

Dear Friends:

I had so much fun writing Cleo and Woody's story. I hope you had just as much fun reading it.

Cleo, of course, was always slated to be the heroine of the second book in the Sisters of Bethlehem Springs series, but I had no idea who would be the hero. Just like Cleo, I expected he would be a cowboy. So imagine my surprise when Lord Sherwood introduced himself to me. How on earth would these two ever find love? Talk about oil and water! And what fun to see them come together in the end.

And what about this wrangler/cowgirl business? The early American West was a great training ground. Girls and women worked right alongside the men in their families to carve out new lives in an oftentimes harsh land. In fact ranches and farms were where many future rodeo cowgirls (among the first professional female athletes in the United States) learned their riding and roping skills. Between 1890 and 1943, more than 450 women worked as professional cowgirls. In addition to rodeos, many worked at Wild West shows, exhibitions, and eventually in motion pictures.

As I write this note to my readers, I have just begun writing Daphne's story (*Who says a woman can't write dime novels?*). Look for *A Word to the Wise* in the spring of 2010.

I hope you'll visit my Web site (*www.robin leehatcher.com*) and my Write Thinking blog (robinlee.typepad.com) for the latest information about me and my books.

Until the next time, "May the LORD keep watch between you and me when we are away from each other" (Genesis 31:49 TNIV).

In the grip of His grace,
Robin Lee Hatcher

ACKNOWLEDGMENTS

Many thanks to Tammy, who came up with exactly the right title for this book, and to my editor, Sue, who had such great suggestions on how to make the story even better.

ABOUT THE AUTHOR

Robin Lee Hatcher (www.robinleehatcher
.com) is the author of sixty novels, including *A Vote of Confidence, When Love Blooms, Wagered Heart, Return to Me,* and *Catching Katie,* named one of the Best Books of 2004 by *Library Journal.* Winner of the Christy Award for Excellence in Christian Fiction, two RITA Awards for Best Inspirational Romance, and the RWA Lifetime Achievement Award, Robin lives in Idaho.

The employees of Thorndike Press hope you have enjoyed this Large Print book. All our Thorndike, Wheeler, and Kennebec Large Print titles are designed for easy reading, and all our books are made to last. Other Thorndike Press Large Print books are available at your library, through selected bookstores, or directly from us.

For information about titles, please call:
  (800) 223-1244

or visit our Web site at:
  http://gale.cengage.com/thorndike

To share your comments, please write:
  Publisher
  Thorndike Press
  295 Kennedy Memorial Drive
  Waterville, ME 04901